17

ıR

ABOUT A
GIRL

ALSO BY

SARAH McCARRY

ALL OUR PRETTY SONGS
DIRTY WINGS

ST. MARTIN'S GRIFFIN ☙ NEW YORK

ABOUT A
GIRL

SARAH McCARRY

ABOUT A GIRL. Copyright © 2015 by Sarah McCarry. All rights reserved. Printed in the United States of America. For information, address St. Martin's Press, 175 Fifth Avenue, New York, N.Y. 10010.

www.stmartins.com

Designed by Anna Gorovoy

The Library of Congress Cataloging-in-Publication Data is available upon request.

ISBN 978-1-250-06862-0 (hardcover)
ISBN 978-1-250-02713-9 (e-book)

St. Martin's Griffin books may be purchased for educational, business, or promotional use. For information on bulk purchases, please contact the Macmillan Corporate and Premium Sales Department at 1-800-221-7945, extension 5442, or write to specialmarkets@macmillan.com.

First Edition: July 2015

10 9 8 7 6 5 4 3 2 1

for my parents, who kept faith in the outcome despite a number of doubts about the process

What are the dead, anyway, but waves and energy? Light shining from a dead star?

—DONNA TARTT

So Love the destroyer
blazed in a coil round her heart.

—APOLLONIOS RHODIOS

At sea there are no atheists.

—MAURICIO OBREGÓN

ABOUT A
GIRL

They are sitting at the kitchen table in the apartment where she grew up. Morning light slanting in and patterning across the floorboards; smell of bread baking and coffee brewing in the stovetop percolator; patchwork curtains shifting in a wash of summer breeze. Mint blooms in the windowsill, leaves more than green. Outside, the whole world waiting—*Let's go,* she says, *where have you been*. Across the scarred old table (spilt candlewax, a smear of oil paint at one corner where she used to work before she was banished from painting in the kitchen, fraying runner dusted with bread crumbs), the girl takes out a cigarette. Silver click of her lighter, smoke curling from her mouth. So many years—*she is dreaming, she must be*—but here they are, and if her hands are older, marked with a network of fine lines, paint stained and smelling faintly, always, of turpentine—if her hands are older, the girl across from her is unchanged and luminous. Close-cropped dark hair and white sleeveless shirt, her collarbone sharp as the edge of a mirror. The cigarette burns, already forgotten, between the knuckles of her first and second fingers.

I can't stay, she says. *Babycakes, you know that.*

Come home. You can't be happy there. So much she wants to ask, so much to say; but there isn't enough time for any of it—clouds move across the sun outside; a shadow falls. The air gone dim and cool—*blink* and she is in the bone forest, bare white branches clacking in a fetid, noiseless wind—*blink* and they are in the park by the canal, soft guitar, sun on their shoulders—*blink* and the dog howls, once, twice, three times, the black river surging, thick and viscous as oil, past her bare, bloody feet.

No, the girl says, *but I wasn't happy here, either. I brought you something.*

What kind of something—don't go—

But it is too late: She is standing, stubbing out her cigarette on the table. A black mark spreads across the wood. *You know how much I love you.*

Not enough to stay.

The girl reaches forward and touches her mouth with two

fingers, gentle as a kiss. *It was never about that. You know that. It's good to see you; you look so happy. But I have to go.* She turns, walks away, the way she did the first time. Not looking back. In her wake, the smell of burning: the scorch of her absence, searing itself into the world over and over again.

When she wakes it takes her a while to come back to herself. Where she is now: her room in her apartment in the city. Through the window she can see the trees, winter-stripped of their foliage, branches stark against a murky grey sky. The dream hums electric under her skin. She stumbles out of bed, pulls on a sweatshirt and wool socks to stave off the chill of the floor, wanders into the living room. Raoul is perched on the couch, a mug of coffee in his hand and one on the table waiting for her.

"I heard something," he says. "At the front door."

"No one rang the buzzer."

"No," he says.

"You didn't look?"

He shakes his head.

"I dreamed about her," she says.

"So did I."

She sighs, walks to the front door, opens it, looks around. Nothing. The hall is still and cool, their neighbors' doors shut tightly. No ghosts, no long-gone girls. And then she hears a rustle at her feet and looks down at the doorstep, and there it is, straight out of the Old Testament. A baby, its eyes closed tight, wrapped in a grey blanket, fast asleep on the *Aliens*-themed welcome mat Raoul had bought her when they moved in.

"Oh for fuck's sake," she says resignedly.

Raoul comes up behind her, puts his chin on her shoulder, starts to laugh. "Good thing we rented a three-bedroom," he says.

THE

BLACK

SEA

Tonight is my eighteenth birthday party and the beginning of the rest of my life, which I have already ruined; but before I describe how I arrived at calamity I will have to explain to you something of my personal history, which is, as you might expect, complicated—

If you will excuse me for a moment, someone has just come into the bookstore—No, we do not carry the latest craze in diet cookbooks—and thus she has departed again, leaving me in peace upon my stool at the cash register, where I shall detail the particulars that have led me to this moment of crisis.

In 1969, the Caltech physicist Murray Gell-Mann—theorist and christener of the quark, bird-watcher, and famed perfectionist—was awarded the Nobel Prize for his contributions to the field of particle physics. In his acceptance speech, he referenced the ostensibly more modest remark by Isaac Newton that if he had seen farther than others it was because he stood on the shoulders of giants, commenting that if he, Murray Gell-Mann, was better able to view the horizon, it was because he was surrounded by dwarfs. (Newton himself was referring rather unkindly to his detested rival Robert Hooke, who was a person of uncommonly small stature, so it's possible Gell-Mann was making an elaborate joke.) While I am more inclined to a certain degree of humility in public, I find myself not unsympathetic to his position. I am considered precocious, for good reason. Some people might say insufferable, but I do not truck with fools. ("What you're doing is good," Murray Gell-Mann told his colleague Sheldon Glashow, "but people will be very stupid about it." Glashow went on to win the Nobel Prize himself.)

—What? Well, of course we have *Lolita,* although I don't think that's the sort of book high-school teachers are equipped to teach—No, it's not that it's dirty exactly, it's just—Yes, I did see the movie—Sixteen-eleven, thanks—Cards, sure. Okay, goodbye, enjoy your summer; there is nothing that makes me so glad to have escaped high school as teenagers—

My name is Atalanta, and I am going to be an astronomer, if one's inclination is toward the romantic and nonspecific. My own inclination is neither, as I am a scientist. I am interested in dark energy, but less so in theoretical physics; it is time at the telescope that calls to me most strongly—we have telescopes, now, that can see all the way to the earliest hours of the universe, when the cloud of plasma after the Big Bang cooled enough to let light stream out, and it is difficult to imagine anything more thrilling than studying the birth of everything we know to be real. Assuming it *is* real, but that, of course, is an abstract question, and somewhat tangential to my main points at present. And though much of astronomy is, and has always been, the management of data—the recognition of patterns in vast tables of observations, the ability to pick the secrets of the universe out of spreadsheets thousands of pages long—there are also the lovely sleepless nights in the observatory, the kinship of people driven and obsessed enough to stay up fourteen hours at a stretch in the freezing dark tracking the slow dance of distant stars across the sky; those are the people whose number I should like one day to count myself among.

I am aware that I am only one day shy of eighteen and that I will have time to decide more carefully in what I will specialize as I obtain my doctorate and subsequent research fellowships, and I will be obliged as well to consider the highly competitive nature of the field—which is not, of course, to say that I am unequipped to address its rigors, only that I prefer to do work that has not been done already, the better to make my mark upon the cosmos. At any rate I like telescopes and I like beginnings and I like unanswered questions, and the universe has got plenty of those yet.

I live in an apartment in a neighborhood of Brooklyn that has only recently become relatively wealthy, with my Aunt

Beast, who is not my aunt, but my biological mother's childhood best friend; my uncle Raoul, who is not my uncle, but my aunt's childhood best friend; Henri, who presumably was once someone's best friend, but is now more notably my uncle's husband; and Dorian Gray, who is technically Raoul's cat but I am privately certain likes me best. Atalanta is a ridiculous name, which is why most people call me Tally, including Aunt Beast, who picked it. My situation would be confusing to the average person, but this is New York, where unorthodox familial arrangements are par for the course. In my graduating class there was a girl who was the literal bastard child of a literal Luxembourgian duke; a boy whose father was a movie director so famous the entire family traveled with a bodyguard; a lesser Culkin; and a girl whose mother had made her fortune as a cocaine dealer before successfully transitioning to a career as a full-time socialite and home decorator, and I didn't even go to private school. My household of two gay not-dads and a sometimes-gay not-mom doesn't even rate a raised eyebrow.

My biological mother, Aurora, ran off right after I was born, which is unfortunate, but I've had seventeen years and three hundred and sixty-four days to accustom myself to her untimely departure. More accurately, she ran off before I was born, ran back briefly to deliver me to the household I now inhabit, and then ran off again, but as I was too small for these technicalities to have any effect on me at the time, for all intents and purposes it is easiest to say simply that she ran away. I have gathered she was something of a flibbertigibbet and a woman of ill repute, although Aunt Beast is not so unkind as to say so outright. I can only imagine she was dreadfully irresponsible on top of her flightiness, as

I think it extremely poor form to cast off the fruit of one's womb as though it is little more than a bundle of dirty laundry. No doubt this abandonment has left me with lingering psychological issues, but I prefer to dwell in the realm of the empirical. Aurora left me on Raoul and Aunt Beast's doorstep, which is a good origin story, if not very original. (That was a pun, in case you were not clever enough to catch it.) Aunt Beast is not a beast at all, but she did read me *A Wrinkle in Time* at an impressionable age, and I have since refused to call her anything else, even though I am very nearly an adult and a fine scientist and high-school graduate who has secured a full scholarship to an excellent university you have certainly heard of in order to absorb the finer points of astrophysics before I go on to alter the course of history in whichever way I see fit.

Other pertinent points: Aunt Beast is a painter, Raoul is a poet, and Henri used to be a dancer but isn't any longer. Raoul teaches English to young hooligans, and Henri, who was once a principal in one of the best ballet companies in New York, retired over a decade ago, his body shot and his knees ground to dust, and became a massage therapist. As you know already, I work in a bookstore. I do not technically need my job; my grandfather, who died long before I was born, was both a tremendously famous musician and tremendously rich. (I am no particular aficionado of rock music, but Shane—*oh*, Shane, more about *him* in a moment—who is, has informed me that my grandfather's band was seminal, if derivative. I prefer Bach, personally.) Had I wanted to, I could have gotten into his considerable estate, which slumbers quietly in a trust, increasing itself exponentially every year. But Aunt Beast is adamant about not touching any of his money, and we live instead off the now-tidy sums she makes selling her paintings to museums and ancient, embittered Upper East Siders fossilized in their own wealth. New York does not teach one to think highly of the rich, a class of persons so inept they are incapable of even the most basic of tasks, including cleaning their own homes, laundering their own garments, cooking their own food, raising their own offspring, and riding the subway. Money cannot buy much of anything that interests me other than a fine education, which I have already managed to obtain for myself, and an orbiting telescope of my own; but even my grandfather's legacy is not quite enough to fund the construction of a personal satellite or particle accelerator, and so I see no use for it.

I am told Aurora was a great beauty. The only evidence I have of this fact is an old Polaroid of her and Aunt Beast when they were teenagers, taken in the garden of my grandmother's old house in the city where they grew up, which has hung over our couch in a battered wooden frame for as long as I can remember. It's summer; you can tell because of the backdrop of lapis sky and jumbled wildflowers. Aurora is laughing, her chin tilted up; her sharp cheekbones cut the light and send clear-edged panes of shadow across her face. Her skin is a few shades darker than mine and her hair, straight as my own, is bleached white where mine falls down my back in a waterfall of coal. She is indeed beautiful by any objective measure, not that it has done either of us any good. Aunt Beast is in her shadow, dressed in the same black clothes she still wears, her habitual sullenness battling a reluctant smile. You can't quite make out the color of Aurora's eyes but Aunt Beast says they were brown, in contrast to the blue of my own, which I have apparently inherited from my grandfather. My father is a mystery, not in the sense that he is mysterious, but in the sense that I have no idea who he is at all. From what I have heard of Aurora, it is not unlikely that she had no idea, either. Oh bother, excuse me—

Dear lord, you shouldn't get that; I think books about children with cancer are invariably maudlin and that one is a wholly abysmal example of the genre—Yes, I know it's popular, but why don't you get a book with actual literary value—Yes, certainly, I'd be happy to recommend something, you might try *Titus Groan*. No, it's not that long, and anyway it's good, so that doesn't matter—Oh, fine, as you like. Fifteen ninety-nine. It's your funeral, ha ha ha ha. Yes, thank you, goodbye—

At any rate, I myself am not a great beauty, so it is lucky I am preternaturally clever, else I would have no assets whatsoever to recommend me. My person is overly bony; I have the ungainly locomotion of a giraffe; and while my face is not unattractive, it is certainly not the sort of symmetrical countenance that causes strangers to remark upon its loveliness. My nose is somewhat beaklike. My skin, at least, is quite smooth and a pleasing shade of brown, but not even a white person ever got cast as the lead of a romantic comedy because they had nice skin. Additionally, white people are not subject to the regular and exhausting lines of enquiry my skin and vaguely *ethnic* features occasion ("What are you? No, I mean where are you from? No, I mean where are you *really* from? No, I mean where are your *parents* from?"). These interviews have nothing to do, obviously, with my attractiveness, and everything to do with the troglodytic nature of my interrogators, but I find them inconvenient nonetheless. My eyes are striking, but they are not enough to distinguish me.

The apparatus of popular culture would have one believe that one's success with the opposite sex is irreparably hampered by a disinterest in, and lack of, conventional attractiveness, but I can attest from experiential evidence that this is not always the case. I have thrice engaged in penetrative intercourse. The first instance was at the age of fifteen, at science camp, with one of the graduate-student counselors. It was not a memorable experience. The second was after some dreadful dance my junior year, with a paramour Aunt Beast had dug up for me somewhere (double date with Shane; awkward, beery-breathed post-dance groping on the couch of Shane's date's absent parents; actual moment of entry so hasty and uninspired I was uncertain for several moments as to whether I was having sex at all; the next day, my temporary beau sent me *flowers* at *school,* which I threw away immediately), and whom I elected not to contact subsequent to the occasion. I had thought, in the spirit of scientific enquiry, that I would repeat the experiment, in order to ascertain whether my own results would more closely match the ecstatic testimony of romantic poets and cinematic heroines upon a second trial, but I am sorry to report they did not. But the third time—the third—oh, *god.*

Which leads me to Shane. I don't know if there is any point in telling you about him, since I don't know if I will ever—oh, I am being melodramatic, and also getting ahead of myself. I have known Shane for so long that his name is as much a part of me as my own. As a small child, I'd opened the door to our apartment, alarmed by the thumping and cursing of a small army of movers carting furniture and various boxes down the hall, and caught a brief, tantalizing glimpse of a pigtailed urchin of about my age being towed along behind a set of parents in the movers' wake.

"They have a girl in there," I announced to Henri, "help me get her," and so Henri baked cookies and sent me out to bear them to our new neighbors. Shane answered the door and we ate all the cookies on the spot, and Shane and I have been best friends ever since. I stood next to him when he told his mom he was a boy ("Well," she wept, clutching him in a moist embrace while he gazed stoically at a point over her shoulder, "it's not like you ever wore dresses anyway, and you know your father and I will always love you, but can't you at least still come to *church* with us?"); I was there when Shane grew boobs, and assisted him in assessing the most efficient and low-cost mechanism for concealing them (both of us cursing the cruelty of genetics, which had bestowed upon me the spindly and uniformly flat physique of a teenage boy whilst endowing him with lush feminine curves I, vain though I am not, would happily have sported in his stead); in unison we suffered the depredations of middle-school socials; as an ensemble we pilfered Shane's parents' liquor cabinet for the first time, supplementing the significantly depleted bottles with water from the tap so that his parents would not notice our theft (I was sick afterward for *days,* and have not touched spirits since; Shane, on the other hand, immediately embraced a path of dissolution with a singular enthusiasm)—in short, every first step into the adult world has been one we have taken as a united front (him stoned, me bossy and admittedly overly loquacious). I was there the first day of our freshman year, when Aaron Liechty, senior, hulking sociopath, prom king, and national fencing star (this is New York; only the automotive high school, last refuge of miscreants, has a football team), cornered him in the hallway and sneered, "I don't know what to call you, a little faggot or a little bitch," and Shane said, cool as you please, "You can call me sir," and punched Aaron Liechty square in his freckle-smattered nose. Blood geysered forth, redder even than the flaming crown of Aaron Liechty's hair, Aaron reeled away moaning, and from that point onward, Shane was a legend and folk hero amongst our peers. Only I knew the truth: that Shane had never hit anyone before in his life, that breaking Aaron Liechty's nose was a stroke of sheer luck, and that afterward he had dragged me into the girls' bathroom, where we'd locked ourselves in a stall and he'd cried into my shirt for ten minutes. Hold on a moment—

Yes, it's cool in here, thank you—Yes, awfully hot for this time of year—No, I only read the first one and thought it was sort of badly done—Yes, children seem excited about them—No, I don't have a problem with *wizards,* I just prefer *science* fiction, and I think the rules of magic in her world-building are so arbitrary, it's clear she's just making things up as she goes along—why is it always a *boy* wizard, anyway, it's clear the girl wizard is significantly more intelligent; it's always the case, don't you think, that less-talented young men take credit for all the work done by women who are much cleverer than they—Fine then, go find a Barnes & Noble in Manhattan, I'm sure no one will argue with you there—

As I was saying, Shane and I did not excel in high school so much as endure it; he, like me, is a genius, but his gifts lean in the direction of being able to play guitar riffs back perfectly after hearing them only once, unknotting the tangle of chords and distortion and tying the resultant bits back together again in flawless replicas of whatever he just listened to. And, of course, he writes his own songs, a skill that seems as elusive and astonishing to me as the ability to, say, walk cross-country on stilts. I have always been considerably more intelligent than people around me are comfortable with, and unskilled at concealing it, and I had in addition an unfortunate habit of reading science-fiction novels in public long after such a deeply isolating quirk was forgivable. Other students were disinterested in the finer points of celestial mechanics, and I, once I thought about it at any length, was disinterested in other students. I was not lonely (how could anyone be lonely, with the heavens overhead? All the motion of the stars, and the planets turning, and beyond our own humble solar system the majesty of the cosmos), but I was grateful to have my family, who were boundless in their affection for me, and of course I was grateful beyond measure for Shane. Only he—and thank god I had him, boon companion, coconspirator, confidant, and literally my only friend—would let me ramble on ad nauseam about Messier objects and telescope apertures. Only he never made me feel odd or untoward for my outsize and grandiose ambitions, my unwavering passion for Robert Silverberg, and my penchant for quoting particle physicists in moments of great strife or transcendent happiness. I had the sense sometimes that even my teachers were frightened of me, or at the least had no idea what to do with me. It was only Shane's friendship that insulated me from any greater miseries than being the person no one wanted to sit next to in AP calculus. People were afraid of me, but they all liked

Shane, and I suppose they imagined that even such an easily ostracized specimen of humanity as myself must have had some redeeming qualities if he was willing to put up with my company. Shane, a stoner Caramon to my bitchy and superior Raistlin, acted as a generous and often oblivious buffer between me and the outside world. People gave me a wide berth, but they left me alone.

I do not blame Aunt Beast or Raoul for failing to educate me in the delicate task of disguising myself enough to make other people understand how to talk to me. Aunt Beast barely graduated high school herself, and although I have never asked Raoul about it I do not imagine growing up a poet and gentleman homosexual is a thrilling experience for teens of any era or clime. I am an only child—so far as I know, anyway—and never had friends my own age, save Shane. Even as a small child, I spent my evenings in the company of Aunt Beast, Raoul, and Henri's witty, funny, brilliant friends, who treated me as though I were a person in my own right with opinions of interest—which, obviously, I was. Aunt Beast and Raoul raised me to have a kind of fearless self-possession that is not considered seemly in a girl, and I cannot help being smarter than the vast majority of the persons who surround me. The prospect of college was the only thing aside from Shane that got me through the sheer unending drudgery of adolescence.

Shane has no plans to go to college, preferring to eschew the hallowed halls of higher education for the chance to make a career as a rock musician, and if anyone I know is capable of this feat it is indeed he. He is forever trying to get me to listen to better music. He was, anyway, before—

oh, *god*. I am not accustomed to this sort of—anyway. I *have* ruined everything—but I can't—oh, *god*. He has an insatiable and catholic palate, his tastes ranging from obscure Nigerian jazz to obsessively collected seven-inches from long-forgotten eighties punk bands. He likes a lot of the same old stuff—goths weeping into synthesizers—that Aunt Beast and Raoul listen to; he likes hip-hop; he likes, although he would never admit to it in public, hair metal, a clandestine affection he shares with Raoul, to the extent that they sometimes swap records with as much furtiveness and stealth as if they were dealing narcotics. His record collection takes up an entire wall of his room and is sorted alphabetically and by genre, and if you let him he will discourse extensively about stereo equipment with the obsessive focus of—well, of an astronomer citing observational data. I am prone to frequent bouts of insomnia, and sometimes I will call him late at night and ask him about different kinds of speakers, and drift off to sleep at last with the murmur of his voice in my ear.

I used to do that, anyway. I have not for—well.

The problem, of course, is feelings. Of all the banal and pedestrian impediments! The florid indignity! Shane and I had marched along for years, platonically intertwined, inseparable as glass-jarred conjoined twins bobbing in a formaldehyde bath, until one day without warning I looked over at Shane as he played video games with the fixed intensity of the very stoned, and felt a sudden and astonishing ache in my loins. I was quite sure I had gotten a cramp, and went home and took several ibuprofen—and then I thought of the delicate beadwork of sweat along his upper lip, the burnished glow of his skin under his nearly worn-through white undershirt, his perfect mouth slightly opened in concentration—and the ache blazed forth into a fire, and I understood (belatedly, to be sure, but the landscape of the heart is a country I have with determination left untrespassed) that something awful had befallen me, and our friendship—our blissful, majestic, symbiotic bond—was under the most dreadful threat it had ever faced.

Matters only worsened from there. Where last summer I would have thought nothing of lounging about in my underwear, dozing in his bed in the hazy June heat and watching him play Super Mario Brothers on his old Nintendo, or practice the guitar, brows knitted together in concentration, thick dark hair falling over his high forehead, now the elegant line of his neck and the soft slope of his shoulders, his rounded back (his mother is forever trying to get him to sit up straight), summoned forth in me an all-pervasive nervousness that sent me pacing around his room until he snapped that I should calm down or leave. I could no longer look at the curve of his mouth without imagining it on my own, no longer punch him on the shoulder without wishing he would retaliate in turn by pinning me to the ground and ravishing me, no longer grab carelessly at his hand without willing the electricity I now felt at his touch to spark an answering flare of light.

All of this might have been bearable had my passions been gentle, but they were most emphatically no such thing; the dissatisfaction of my prior forays into the field notwithstanding, sex with my best friend now seemed the only possible resolution to the terrible forces that raged within me, and I was unable to think about anything else—

electrons, stars, planetary orbits, the grocery list—in his presence. Watching the dirty parts of movies with him was an extended study in misery; I could be unexpectedly rendered speechless if the two of us wandered past a couple making out in the park; when he hugged me goodbye, careless and oblivious, I had to will myself not to lick his skin. His long, lovely hands, bitten-nailed, working the Nintendo controller or moving up and down the neck of the guitar, would come to my mind unbidden later, in the humming air-conditioned dark of my own room. I would think of those hands actively engaged in doing deeply un-chaste things to my person, and bring myself nightly to new heights of lust before becoming overcome with terror that he could somehow see through walls and blankets and the thick pane of my skull to observe the pornographic specta-cle of my thoughts—or, worse still, my own hand as it moved beneath the sheets—and then I would desperately attempt to turn my imagination to other, less salacious imagery.

I told myself at first that I was coming down with some-thing, that I had been watching too much television and my formidable mind was going soft as a result, or that I had been reading too much Shakespeare and too little Wheeler (al-though Wheeler himself is prone to unscientifically poetic fits of exegesis), but finally even I had to admit that my feel-ings for my best friend in all the world had abruptly leapt the track from the blissfully platonic to the mundanely carnal. Oh, for god's sake—

Can I help you find anything? The red book that was on the third shelf down? Or the fourth one? No, I don't know what book that would—Well, how long ago? A *month*? I couldn't possibly tell you—Oh, you mean that stupid fake economist who writes for the *Times*—Well, you can't argue that his data is questionable—Yes, it's over there. Seventeen fifty-seven. Do you need a bag? No? Okay, have a nice day—

Shane had girlfriends in high school—not many, and none serious, and none remotely threatening to the umbilical bond that united us. I'd never been jealous because none of them ever registered: a short lineup of pretty, bland-faced girls with shiny hair whom Shane occasionally perambulated around school dances or took out for dim sum but who were nowhere near as smart as I was, did not know every word Shane would utter before it left his mouth, and were not invited to the womblike environs of our respective apartments, where we regularly holed up on his or my couch watching eighties slasher movies and eating microwave popcorn by the bagful, Shane occasionally and unsuccessfully trying to beguile me into smoking marijuana out of a soda can with a hole punched in its side.

Every morning this summer, since we graduated (me, naturally, with a 4.0, Shane by the skin of his teeth) and launched ourselves into the last months before the rest of our lives began, I told myself upon waking, firmly and with conviction, that I would spare myself the torture and stay home, go in to work on my days off and dust the bookshelves, insist Raoul accompany me to a museum, take up oil painting under the tutelage of Aunt Beast—anything but open the door of my apartment and walk, with bated breath, down the hall to his. Every afternoon I abandoned my resolve and capered, aquiver with anticipation, to his door, imagining that day would be the day he would at last fling it open, take me in his arms, and kiss me until our knees buckled; every day, instead, I curled up in a state of frenzied anguish in his bed while he, oblivious, lit another joint. As June wore on I stayed over later and later, hoping against hope that my patient, enduring presence in his house would evoke in him the same disgusting and inconvenient emotions that had taken hold of me—that he would be seized, as I was, by the overwhelming urge to bring our friendship out of the phenomenological world and into the sublime. But the forceful (and admittedly silent) messages I beamed at him continuously went entirely unheeded—and some part of me, the last bit of my brain still operating under the auspices of reason, was relieved.

When not distracted by lust, I existed in a more or less constant state of seething rage—I was furious with him for making me feel something that was outside of my control and even more furious with him for not, at the very least, reciprocating it; I was furious with myself for having feelings; and I was furious with biology in general, for wiring me so faultily—adolescence had been bad enough, without its sending a wrecking ball careening through the perfectly satisfying equilibrium I had enjoyed up until the moment oxytocin went riotous in my brain and turned me into a dithering idiot, ruining the last summer I would have with my favorite person in all the world.

This dreadful torment continued until a fateful afternoon a week ago. "I got something you have to hear," he said— me, freshly showered, hair brushed, even a dab of Aunt Beast's vanilla oil at my wrists and throat, as close to pretty as I could make myself; him, stoned and oblivious ("Something smells like cookies," he'd said, confused, when he hugged me hello)—both of us sprawled on his floor, gazing vacantly at the ceiling (his stupor drug-induced, mine a paralysis of lust). He sat up and fiddled with a pile of cassettes next to his record player. (*Turntable,* he always corrected me.) "Unbelievable," he said, "this album is unbelievable. I finally tracked it down. Hold on." He selected the cassette he'd been looking for, extracted it reverently from its plastic case, and inserted it gently into the tape deck. The soft click of the play button, a rustling hiss of static, and then, low and sweet, a honeyed drift of chords on an acoustic guitar, and a man began to sing. The sound was furry and muted, but the voice that came out of Shane's speakers was like something out of another world, deep and pain soaked and full of loss. We listened to the entire tape without speaking: one bittersweet, yearning song fading into another, weaving together a rich and gorgeous and strange tapestry that carried me out of my body and its perilous wants into some other, more transcendent place of sorrow and hope and waiting. At last the final, aching chord faded and I sat in stunned silence, slowly coming back to my body, the messy familiarity of Shane's room, the feel of cool air moving across my human skin. My heart was pounding as hard as if I'd just gone running with Aunt Beast. "Holy shit," I said.

"Jack Blake," Shane said reverently. "He was the real deal. Total mystery: never did interviews, never made music videos, never did any press. Just released one album—it doesn't even have a title—and then he disappeared. Nobody knows what happened to him or if he's still alive. There's, like, books about him, and all of them say the same thing. Nobody even knows how old he is or where he was born or anything."

"Like a myth," I said, intrigued.

"There are all kinds of crazy stories about him. People

who were at his shows would say they had these ecstatic visions. Supposedly he played one show at the Coliseum in LA, and when he finished the crowd was surrounded by all these animals—wolves, bears, cougars, animals that don't even *live* in that part of California. Like they had come to see him play. People would try to record his shows, and their cameras would break."

"Huh," I said; we had ventured into wildly speculative—and, I thought, although I did not wish to burst Shane's excited bubble, highly dubious—territory. "I've never heard of anything like that."

"Nobody has. They don't say stuff like that about, like, Keith Richards. Just that he did a ton of drugs and banged a lot of chicks." *Banged chicks,* I thought. *Bang this chick, son.* "But this guy—there's practically a cult devoted to him, all these people who saw him back in the day and still get together to talk about it. He played a few shows up and down the west coast, and then he vanished. Never played a live show again that anybody saw. You can't get his records now, no one can, they're worth thousands of dollars. I finally got the guy at Bleecker Bob's to tape this one for me but it took me, like, years of harassment."

"I didn't know they still made cassette tapes. Even *Raoul* doesn't listen to cassette tapes."

"*Obviously* they still *make* them," Shane said, in a tone that I often used myself to emphasize the inferior intelligence of the querying party.

I ignored his temerity, which I would not have done pre–Great Lust. "I should ask Aunt Beast about him," I said. "I think she saw every band that existed back then."

"Oh man," Shane said, excited, "you *have* to. That would

be amazing. I've never met anyone who was at one of his shows. He was supposed to be the most incredible live musician in, like, the history of ever."

"He must have been," I said drily, "if wolves came to see him."

"Right?" he said. "I mean, even if it's not true—"

"It seems pretty likely that it's not true."

"Who would make up something that weird? We're talking lots of people saying things like that happened, not just one or two loonies."

"Come on," I said, "*wolves*? I don't even think there's a wolf in the entire state of California. Wolves are quite endangered."

"What do you know about California? You've never been to the west coast."

"Neither have you."

"That doesn't have anything to do with it," he said. "The point is, this guy is a total legend, and you would have to have had a telescope up your ass for your entire life to never have heard of him."

"I've heard of him now, and I like his music."

"You should," he said, mollified. "My mom made sushi last night, you want some leftovers?"

"Do I ever." His parents were neither of them ambitious or enthusiastic cooks, but once in a while his mom would go on a tear and spend all day constructing an immense platter of variegated sushis, with which we supplemented our more habitual fare of bologna-and-Velveeta sandwiches on Wonder Bread.

I spent the whole day at Shane's house. "Sleep over," he said when the unholy June sun had gone down at last, lessening slightly the unseasonable heat. "You never do any-more." He undressed in front of me, careless as we'd always been, and I had to look away. The T-shirt he gave me to sleep in was a faded New Order shirt, so ancient its band logo was nearly illegible, which I thought might once have been Raoul's or Aunt Beast's. I turned my back on him to put it on. "What's gotten into you?" he asked, finally noticing. "You're, like, the least modest person in the world."

"I finally hit puberty," I said faintly.

"You look the same to me." *Therein lies the rub,* I thought. The shirt smelled like him; it was all I could do to keep from burying my nose in my own armpit. I could hardly tell Shane that the reason I never slept over anymore was because it had become a project freighted with peril to lie next to him in his narrow bed, acutely conscious of every accidental touch of his body, the soft curve of his hips, the dirty-sweet smell of his unwashed hair.

Oblivious to my suffering, he put on Jack's tape again before he crawled into bed. The rough, low voice was so rich, so near, that I could almost imagine the singer was in the room with us, the quiet sorrowful chords of his guitar bringing a veil of starlight through the window and casting a spell over us so heady I nearly forgot I was a fraction of an inch away from the person I most wanted, and was least able, to touch. The song went on around us, all the sadness and hope and longing in the world constellated into that single voice, that single guitar, and I thought, *This is the moment when it all changes.*

You were the bullet in my gun, Jack sang,
the needle in my vein

however far we've come
you were ever the only one

and when the song came to an end at last I let out a deep, shuddering breath, and Shane wriggled around and worked one arm around me. I froze in terror and then let myself pillow my head on his shoulder.

"I don't want to grow up," I said thickly.

"We don't have to."

"Everybody has to."

"Not us." He kissed the top of my head. His shirt had ridden up, and my hand somehow found its way to his bare belly, and I moved my chin, just barely, and he tilted his head on the pillow and then his mouth found my mouth, or my mouth found his mouth—whose mouth found whose, I don't know, it didn't matter, we were kissing, kissing like we had neither of us kissed anyone before in our lives, kissing like the world would end in the morning, kissing like we had invented it, his chapped lips tasting of Blistex and pot, his hands tangling in my hair, cupping my cheeks, tracing a line down the ecstatic length of my spine and up over my hip again to find its way between my legs, gentle at first and then more insistent as I arched my body up to meet him. My breath catching in the dark, the feel of him even more tantalizing, more deliciously new, than I had hoped for; his musky boy-smell heady as wine, his sweat-salted skin under my tongue, his mouth at my throat, between my breasts, moving down the curve of my belly to meet and match the work of his hand—*oh dear god,* I thought, *I believe* this *is why people have sex*—the tape had flipped over, Jack's rough low voice filling the room as I buried my face in Shane's pillow lest his parents overhear my wails of ecstasy—all that Nintendo had done tremendous things for his manual dexterity, it was a wonder any of the girlfriends had let him go—and it flipped over again more than once before we fell asleep at last in a tangle of sticky limbs, just a few hours before the hot sun rose into the merciless furnace of a new day—

No, sorry, we don't have a public bathroom, try the Starbucks—

—but in the morning nothing was different. I woke up alone in Shane's bed, my eyes crusted over with sleep, his shirt bunched in my armpits and soaked with my sweat. I blinked at the watery light, disoriented, unable to place for several moments where I was or why I was looking at a poster of Iggy Pop and not my own pale walls, before the memory of what had transpired in the night flooded in and I gasped aloud, trying to assess what kind of damage I'd done. Or not done. The close, hot, boy-reeking air of his room was overlaid with an unfamiliar, animal scent that I realized—belatedly, and with horror—was the heady aroma of sex. *Oh god,* I thought, *oh god oh god oh god.* I considered climbing out Shane's window and fleeing into the anonymous morning, but we lived on the fourth floor. At last I kicked away the covers, pulled on my shorts, and stumbled into the kitchen, where his mom had made us coffee and where he sat, staring sleepy eyed into a bowl of cereal. He did not look up when I came into the kitchen.

"Tally," his mom chirped, "I haven't seen you in ages, look how tall you are, my goodness." I looked over at Shane, who would not meet my eyes, and felt a hot flush start on my cheeks. Yuki Weiss was not the most perceptive person in the world, but even she would notice if I had a panic attack in her kitchen. *Oh god oh god oh god oh god.* Shane hated me, I hated me, he would never forgive me, I would never forgive myself—*I am a* scientist, I thought to myself in fury, *I am* rational, *I am* empirical, *I am not set to ruination by* brain chemicals, *for god's sake,* but it was no use. "Look at Tally," Shane's mother said to him briskly, "so pretty, such a good daughter, so obedient, why can't you be more like her? You spend all your time in your room, with your terrible haircut—"

"Mom," Shane said.

"My daughter," she said to me, "I don't know what to do with him, I tell you, not even going to college—"

"*Mom,*" Shane said. "Come *on*. Leave me *alone.*"

She gave an exaggerated sigh and rolled her eyes dramatically. "So unappreciated, your mother, after everything I do for you, your father works his fingers to the bone, we save for years and years to give our only child a better life than the one we had and this is how you thank us. Tally, why don't you sit down and have some cereal and coffee, no reason we can't be civilized in this family. . . ."

"I should probably go, Yuki," I interrupted, edging toward the door. "Thanks for the offer, but I have to—help Raoul. With his—poetry." Raoul had never needed help with his poetry a day in his life. "I'll see you later," I whispered, and fled, not waiting to hear if Shane responded, not wanting to see whatever it was that would happen if he finally chose to look at me. The door closed on the sound of his mother's voice. If I had known that was the last time I would speak to him, would I have stayed? I don't know, gentle reader, I'm only just at the end of seventeen.

I went into my room and lay down on my bed and put

my face in my hands, pressing against my eyelids until I saw green sparks (this effect, interestingly, due to manual stimulation of the photoreceptor cells, a fact that was little use to me in my present state). Dorian Gray wandered into my room, leapt onto the bed, and clambered heavily onto my back, where he put the tips of his claws into my flesh and purred happily. "Ouch," I said, and propped myself up on my elbows to dislodge him. He thumped to the floor, shooting me a dirty look before sauntering away with his tail waving jauntily. I rolled over onto my back and looked at the ceiling, dotted with yellowing blobs where, years ago, Henri had helped me painstakingly re-create the wintertime Northern Hemisphere night sky in glow-in-the-dark paint. I heard Raoul call my name. "In here," I said miserably.

"Oh dear," he said when he saw my face. "Do you want to talk about it?"

"Ask me in a couple hundred years," I said.

"I'll make a note in my calendar. Can I come in?"

"Sure," I said.

"Can I do anything?"

"Distract me," I said. "Tell me about the poets." Raoul had a book coming out with a collective poetry press based in Brooklyn; the poets, according to his reports, were an astonishing and erratic group of entities, prone to sending late-night drunken emails, giving away all their books in fits of sporadic generosity, publishing enraged philippics on highly specialized points of semiotic doctrine in competing literary journals, and sleeping with their interns. He did not seem as alarmed as I would have been to have his manuscript entrusted to the poets' care, but he was happy to recount their various—and, to my mind, increasingly bizarre—exploits for my amusement. He had once taken me to one of their parties, where there were a lot of white people with beards and thick-rimmed spectacles and leather patches at the elbows of their coats, and where the poets' chieftain, a slim, ageless sprite with pale blue eyes, had got very tipsy and for some reason gone round with a fez perched askew on his head, talking to people animatedly about conceptualisms.

"They've been fairly tame lately."

"I still don't know what a conceptualism is."

"I'm not sure anyone does, to tell you the truth, but it's a subject about which a very small number of people are extremely passionate," he said. "Do you want me to make you some lemonade? Bring you Dorian Gray? Put on a movie?"

"Dorian Gray already abused me under the pretext of consolation," I said, "but a movie and lemonade sounds pretty good." I struggled mightily to my feet and followed Raoul out into the living room; he went into the kitchen to fetch the lemonade. I put on *Aliens,* which my entire family, save Henri, regarded as gospel. I had been raised on its central tenets—loyalty, bravery, self-reliance, resourcefulness, being better than boys at everything—the way other children grew up with catechism and Sunday school. Raoul and I settled in with our lemonades, the living-room fan turned on and directed at our faces.

Henri came in just as Hicks was demonstrating the use of the grenade launcher to Ripley. "Oh," he said, with equal parts bemusement and dismay, "you're not doing this *again,* are you? It's the middle of the afternoon. It's beautiful out."

"Shhhh," Raoul and I said in unison, not looking at him.

"It is not beautiful," I added under my breath. "It's ninety-six degrees."

"I can handle myself," Ripley said on-screen.

"I noticed," Hicks, Raoul, and I chorused.

"You both know this movie by *heart*."

"*Shhhhhhhh*," I said. Henri rolled his eyes and sat on the couch next to Raoul, who took his hand without looking away from the screen—

Sorry, what? You heard an interview with the author on NPR? When was that? Two months ago? No, I have no idea—No, "a woman" isn't helpful in narrowing it down—Yes, I understand it was a science book, but there are quite a few women who write about science, shockingly enough, we're many of us considerably more clever than we—Goodbye, then—

Raoul met Henri when I was young enough not to re-member the time before him, and he is so much a part of my life now that I cannot imagine any sort of world that did not have him in it. His parents are from Senegal, and he was born in France, and so, though he has lived in New York since before I was born, he speaks English with a sweet and lovely melody behind it that makes me think of sun on the water. The longest Raoul and Henri have ever been apart was a few years ago, when Raoul took me to Arizona for a month to see my grandmother, Maia, and Aunt Beast's mother, Cass, and to meet his own family, who still live on the Navajo Nation, where Raoul grew up. Cass and Maia had left the distant wilderness of the Pacific Northwest, where both Aunt Beast and Aurora spent their formative years, for the dubious rewards of a hippie commune out-side Tucson, where clothing was (to my utter horror) op-tional and where the aged denizens, who had constructed their various domiciles out of old tractor tires and bales of hay smothered in dried mud, spent their days in some mysterious quasi-agricultural pastime Cass referred to as "permaculture." It was not the sort of life I would have ever voluntarily chosen for myself, but Cass and Maia seemed happy enough. "For these noble purposes was this desert watered with the blood of my ancestors and stolen from my family," Raoul said drily, as we watched a field of naked and wrinkly hippies toiling under the white-hot noonday sun.

My grandmother Maia was spacey and feeble, from so many years of doing so many drugs. I could see in her face some of the lines of my own: the arch of her brows; the sharp chin; the way she wrinkled the corners of her eyes when she laughed, which was only once. I did not like to recognize myself in her and was glad to quit her company.

Cass was ropy with muscle, though she must have been in her sixties, and tanned a seamy dark brown that almost worked as a camouflage in the dust-cracked earth around her. She worked every day in the commune's greenhouse and went hiking in the red hills and seemed as much a part of the desert as if she had sprung forth from it fully formed. She asked if I wanted my chart done, and I said no thank you, I did not believe the orderly movements of the stars contained in them anything other than the natural results of the laws of physics, and to my surprise, she laughed. "There are more things in heaven and earth, Horatio, than are dreamt of in your philosophy."

"I've read Shakespeare," I said, nettled. "He doesn't make a convincing argument for astrology."

"Only witches and ghosts," she said. "Anyway, it's good to see you're doing well. Tell my daughter to call more often."

After the hippies, I thought Raoul's family would be a

relief. They were not. He abandoned me immediately to the scant mercy of his aunts, who observed me in cool silence as we all drank coffee from a pot they had made by throwing grounds into boiling water. They spat coffee grounds in my general direction and each time an aunt spat, I winced. "You should have introduced yourself," Raoul said afterward, "they're your elders, it's respectful," and I said, "You didn't *tell* me that," and he smiled, and said, "The aunts are a test of your mettle, sweet pea." His uncles derived enormous amusement from startling me with a butchered goat's head and insisting I eat sheep's intestine sopped up with frybread, after which an ebullient uncle shouted jovially, "Look who's Indian now!" and slapped me repeatedly on the back. "Don't get any ideas," Raoul said, laughing. Later he told me that his oldest aunt, who was originally picked by her own elders to be a medicine woman, had gone instead to the off-reservation boarding school, where the teachers had cut off her long braids and burned them in front of her, the same way they had beaten his father for speaking Navajo (Raoul, quoting Gloria Anzaldúa: "Who is to say that robbing a people of its language is less violent than war?"). He told me this as dispassionately as if he had been reporting the average annual rainfall in the desert, and I wondered, for the first time, what it had cost him to leave his family, and what it cost him again to return.

His family was obviously and enormously proud of him. His mother had at least ten copies of every one of his books, arranged neatly on a special shelf next to a series of photographs of Raoul from infancy onward; his father referred to him a number of times as "My son, the poet"; and his numerous cousins congratulated him effusively on his successes and his life in the big city; but as someone who had grown up in a family made up out of choice and love, not circumstance and biology, I saw for the first time that there were perils I had not imagined to having a place that you came from that both was and was not your home. Raoul's Mexican grandmother and I fell in love with each other at first sight. She was a full foot shorter than me and spoke almost no English, and I, to my embarrassment, spoke even less Spanish. "Too skinny, too skinny," she murmured, in the universal language of grandmothers other than mine, patting me on the hand and towing me behind her into her kitchen, where she spent the afternoon trying to teach me to make tamales. She did not laugh at me when my hapless attempts fell to bits in the steamer, instead nodding encouragingly and beaming at me until at last, after much labor, scattering masa everywhere, and somehow managing to get pork on her ceiling, I succeeded in assembling something that looked almost edible. Her tamales, in contrast, were uniform packets, lovely to look upon, and magnificently delicious.

Raoul was uncharacteristically quiet for days after we came back to New York, and more than once I wandered into the kitchen late at night for a drink of water or some comestible and found him at the kitchen table with Henri's arms around him, Henri speaking softly in his ear. I had always been envious of Raoul, who spoke Navajo, Spanish, French, and English with equal facility; who knew the names of generations of his ancestors and the history of the land where he was born by heart; and who made out of the places he had been and the place to which he had come poems that even I, Philistine though I was in matters of verse, could recognize were each like tiny, flawless, self-contained worlds; but it had never occurred to me that trading one life for another might be a passage paid for in loss. But after I went to Arizona with Raoul he told me stories about his family, a subject he had never in all my memories of him broached previously, and despite my blazing failure in the aunts' arena he seemed happy I had come with him.

"You're my daughter," he said. "They're your family now, too." I was not so sure that the aunts would concur on that point, but it made me happy to think of anyway—

No, we *don't* have a public restroom, maybe you'd like to buy a *book*, since you're in a *bookstore*, not a *latrine*—

When the movie ended—Ripley, Newt, and Hicks tucked safely in their pods, blissfully unaware of the series of travesties David Fincher would shortly wreak upon their hard-won happiness (Raoul and Aunt Beast and I did not ever discuss the third movie, and preferred to behave as though the fourth installment did not exist at all)—Raoul turned to me. "Are you sure there's nothing you want to talk about?"

"Did something happen?" Henri looked over at me.

"I did something terrible," I said. "To Shane. Last night. But I don't think I want to talk about it."

"*To* Shane?" Henri echoed, alarmed.

"*With* Shane," I said, kicking at the floor, where one of our tattered old rag rugs was slowly decaying into bits across the wooden floorboards. One of us should have thrown it out ages ago. There was a silence.

"Ah," Raoul said. "I see." Henri caught on a second later.

"*Oh*," he said. "You know we're here for you if you—if you need anything."

"I know," I said. "I'll muddle through it. But thanks."

But I was not accustomed to muddling through; I had never met a problem I could not solve with brisk efficiency and diligent application of my tremendous intellect. The possibility that the calculus of the heart might differ from the formulae with which I had successfully plotted forces and velocities was not one I elected to allow. That night after dinner I helped Henri with the dishes. "Let's set up a hypothetical," I said conversationally to the soapy water.

"Tally, you know I don't know the first thing about astronomy. Ask Raoul."

"I'm aware of your shortcomings," I said. "I don't mean a scientific hypothetical. I mean a—um, let's say a personal one. About people." I avoided looking at Henri's expression. "Let's say there are two platonic friends who have known each other for a long time, and one of them, hypothetically speaking, did—um." I coughed. "Did a—did something not very platonic. Hypothetically." Dorian Gray twined sumptuously about my ankles, purring. "I'm going to trip on you," I said to him, "and you're going to be sorry." He yawned and sat on my foot. Dorian was a loving and elegant cat, but not an especially intelligent one.

Henri, who knew me very well, had the courtesy to pretend he had no idea what I was talking about. "Are you asking my advice about boys? I don't know if that's a good idea. Raoul is the expert."

"I heard that!" Raoul shouted from the other room. "I will not have my virtue impugned!"

"What virtue you have left," Aunt Beast said, laughing.

"Oh, *you're* one to talk," Raoul groused. They squabbled affectionately in lowered voices; I couldn't see them from the kitchen, but I could picture them as clearly as if I were in the room with them: curled up on opposite ends of the couch, Aunt Beast with a glass of whisky and a cigarette (Raoul making faces at her for smoking in the apartment, her grimacing back and opening the window wider in an exaggerated manner) and the crossword, Raoul underlining his favorite bits in whatever poetry book he happened to be reading. They were even more like an old married couple than Raoul and Henri were. I felt a dopey, jolting surge of affection: my ridiculous, precious family, patchworked together out of love.

"I'm not asking your advice," I said. "I'm just proposing a scenario."

Henri handed me a plate to dry. "I don't know, dear heart. Whoever it is, he wouldn't be much of a friend if he ran off just because your feelings got complicated."

"We're not talking about me."

"This hypothetical friend, then."

"What if he did, though? I mean, what one of the friends, the one who did—you know, the one who—anyway, what if that person wanted to continue being friends, and the other one didn't? And after the thing happened that person didn't call the other person? I mean the person who didn't do the thing."

Raoul wandered into the kitchen, a pen behind his ear. He came up behind Henri and wrapped his arms around Henri's waist, resting his chin on Henri's shoulder. I never tired of admiring the gorgeous harmony of their faces—Raoul's deep brown skin and shaved head, the unfair perfection of his beautifully symmetrical features; Henri's own skin a velvety black that caught and held light so that he seemed almost to glow, his dense hair twisted up into short corkscrewed locks, his dark eyes glinting with laughter. I thought, as I always did, that they were the two handsomest people I knew. If only one of *them* had been my father, I should have fared much better in the attractiveness department.

"I would say, hypothetically in this hypothetical situation," Raoul said, "that a day would be pretty soon to start worrying about things like the demise of a hypothetical friendship that had weathered a decade already."

"This whole thing is making me feel insane," I said.

"The more you like a person, the more difficult it is to conduct yourself with dignity," Henri said.

"Is that supposed to be helpful?" I asked crossly.

"I think it's early to start worrying, too," Henri said. "And it's normal for this stuff to make a person loopy. Even adults. I mean, I had known Raoul for months before I worked up the nerve to ask him out on a date, but look at us now."

"I asked *you* out on a date," Raoul said.

"You did not."

"I did." They gazed lovingly at each other until I made a vomiting noise. "Anyway," Raoul said, releasing Henri and hugging me in his stead, "the point is, the course of true love never does run smooth, or what have you."

"It ran smoothly for you," I said. They looked at each other and laughed.

"Not so smoothly as it might seem now," Henri said. "There were some . . ."

"Hiccups," Raoul said. "Maybe we'll tell you when you're older. Anyway, I'm sure things will get better. Just give it time. I know that's a stupid thing adults are always saying, but it does usually turn out to be true."

"Press part, six letters, ends with an N," Aunt Beast said from the living room.

"Platen," Raoul said.

Aunt Beast came into the kitchen, chewing the end of her pencil and carrying the crossword. "I can't get half this fucking thing," she said.

"Sunday is always a chore," Henri said, "let us see." She handed the paper to Henri and Raoul, and they looked it over.

"I just don't know anything about sports, I think that's the trouble," Raoul said. I left the three of them to their own devices and escaped to the safety of my room—

What? A good book? There are a lot of good books, it's a bookstore, we sort of specialize in that—No, I'm being serious—I mean, I just read this one—Not that one, okay, people seem pretty excited about this—Not that one, okay—Look, I thought you said *any* good book—Here, try *Middlemarch*, if you don't like it you can hold the door open with it—

—but things have not gotten better. At first it seemed best to leave Shane to his own devices—I wasn't sure if I owed him an apology, or if he owed me one, and I wanted very desperately to know that things between us could be restored to some semblance of normality, but I had no idea how to go about setting them to rights. I briefly considered watching a romantic comedy or reading teen fiction; I knew, though not from personal experience, that these genres frequently dealt with the situation in which I found myself, usually with a happy resolution for all parties, but I did not think I could bear it if the correct course of action turned out to be something like an honest discussion of my feelings, or weeping. Or, god help me, marriage. I waited patiently all week for Shane to call, so that both of us could pretend nothing happened and I might continue nursing my unrequited passion until it finally burned itself out.

But he didn't. He didn't show up on my doorstep, disheveled and stoned, and demand I come over; he didn't push notes under my door; he didn't, as far as I could tell, even leave his own apartment. If it had been bad seeing Shane all summer, it was even worse without him. Aunt Beast, Raoul, and Henri, perhaps cautioned by my bloodshot eyes and sullen, monosyllabic responses to the most innocent of enquiries, did not question me on his abrupt departure from the insular orbit of our family, as if he were some malfunctioning satellite that went rocketing off abruptly into the far reaches of deep space. They took turns coming in to say goodnight to me in the evenings, something they hadn't done since I was a small child; I had suspicions that they got together and worked out a schedule behind my back, but I was secretly grateful for their company. Aunt Beast in particular, who is ordinarily reserved and even aloof, took to spending less time in her studio and more around the house, her presence inconspicuous but constant. I did not thank them for their increased attentions, but as a grieving adolescent it was my prerogative to be ungrateful and obstreperous.

All week we ate dinner together every night, something else we hadn't done regularly in years: the four of us gathered around the rickety-legged oak table that Raoul and Aunt Beast dragged in off the street when I was barely old enough to walk, and the three of them taking turns cooking (as the bereaved party, I was apparently off the hook for domestic labor for a while, which suited me just fine). Raoul made rich, lovely curries, so spicy they set us all weeping into our plates; Henri, yassa and salatu niebe; and Aunt Beast—who, for all her ongoing disparagement of hippies, sure eats like one—tofu stir-fry over brown rice, and an enormous salad full of tomatoes and peppers and greens from the farmer's market, studded with nasturtiums and snapdragons.

For the most part I was too listless and despondent to eat, pushing my food around on my plate like the melodramatically anorexic girls from high school I regarded at the time with disdain—Rowan Apple Paine-Lowell, for example, wanton progeny of the black sheep of a venerated New York line and a minor rock star. Cool and colorless as old dishwater, prone to malnourished fainting in the halls, and with the affected melancholy of a nineteenth-century consumptive, she had had a brief cameo on a popular television show about wealthy teenagers on the Upper East Side (as herself), and had, our senior year, fallen unrequitedly in love with the scion of a noted pharmaceutical family and cut his initials into her creamy thigh with an X-Acto blade during art class; where previously I had held her and her ilk in contempt, I was discovering a certain degree of unlikely sympathy. The hunger strike is, after all, a timeless strategy with which to highlight one's grievances. And the less I ate the less I felt like eating, or breathing, or sitting up, or getting out of bed, or doing anything whatsoever with myself other than sinking into a self-created pit of my own increasing filth, encased in Shane's dirty New Order shirt, which I only bothered to change when obliged to come to work, and staring at the walls of my room, willing myself to sleep. I did not leave my apartment all week except to come to the bookstore, which brings me here, to my birthday, and my stool. Every year since I was quite small I have had a chocolate cake, made by Henri and decorated by Aunt Beast (Jupiter and all its major satellites; a pair of happy astronauts laid out in black licorice candies on a vanilla-frosting moon; Voyager 2 painstakingly done in colored icing; that sort of thing); Raoul writes a silly rhyming sonnet; and Shane and his parents come over with sushi. I could not imagine a birthday in which Shane was not a crucial part— but I could not have imagined a week in which we did not speak to one another, and then it happened.

At last it was four o'clock, and the bookstore's co-owner, Molly, came in to relieve me. I often thought that Molly and her business partner, Jenn, had opened the store solely to further their own somewhat obsessive book-collecting habits; the store did a fine business, but probably a quarter of its profits came out of the pockets of the three of us. "God, if it's this hot in June I hate to think of what July will be like," Molly said, pushing her long brown hair out of her face and looking pointedly at the pile of books on the to-be-shelved cart, which I had not touched. I flushed.

"I can put those away before I go," I mumbled.

"It's your birthday," she said, "you shouldn't even *be* here. But don't think my generosity will last all week."

"Sorry. And thanks."

"I'm getting soft in my old age." She smiled at me. "Now get out of here. Save me some cake."

"Deal," I said, and went out into the searing heat of the afternoon.

On my way home I stopped in to see Mr. M, an elderly

gentleman who lives alone in a sumptuous apartment around the corner from our building. I have known him nearly all my life, although I can never remember exactly how I first met him. He is something of a secret—I have never told Raoul or Henri or Aunt Beast about him, for no real reason; only Shane, from whom I have—had—ugh—no secrets, knows of his existence. Although that makes him sound sinister, he is just a lonely and sweet-natured grandfatherly old man who likes to discuss the sciences. As far as I can tell I am his only friend, and I have never known him to leave his apartment, although presumably he must occasionally egress himself. If he ever goes anywhere, he does not tell me, although he went all sorts of exciting places in earlier years, and has interesting stories about traveling around the world. He was once some sort of record executive, and knew a lot of famous people; more of interest to me, he is tremendously well educated and knows even more than I do about physics and astronomy. When I was smaller, he helped me with my math and physics homework—Raoul, Henri, and Aunt Beast, though all of them are very intelligent, possess temperaments more artistic than scientific, and none of them were much use to me after I got through prealgebra. Mr. M gave me books about astronomy and cosmology and mythology, and encouraged me in my projects, and helped me memorize the constellations, and would sit for hours and talk with me about the ramifications of the anthropic principle and the elegance of Kepler's laws of planetary motion, and whether I should focus my future research on gathering observational data or developing theoretical approaches to unsolved problems.

He seemed pleased as ever to see me, sweaty as I was,

perched on his threshold like a lost kitten. He is very tall—taller by far than me, and I am not a small person—and thin; no matter the weather, he is always dressed in elegant and well-cut black clothes, neat black trousers and black shirts whose silky sleeves end in crisp cuffs at his wrists and sometimes a long black coat that moves about him like it has shadowy intentions of its own. Today he had a red silk scarf knotted at his throat like an ascot and a pair of pince-nez that on any other person would look idiotic but on him looked both scholarly and distinguished.

"Tally," he said, putting away the pince-nez, "come in, come in," and I followed him into the blessed cool of his apartment, which has a strange trick of seeming much larger from the inside than it does from the outside. I have been visiting him for years and have never seen all of it. He left me in the big library—heavy, rich red velvet drapes at the windows to keep out the light, floor-to-ceiling shelves on all four walls, bloodred-leather-and-mahogany sofa, heavy oak side tables—and disappeared down the hall for a moment, and I crooked my head sideways to look at his books for the hundredth time. No matter how often I perused his shelves there were always more treasures I'd never before noticed: Aristarchus's *On the Sizes and Distances of the Sun and Moon* in the original Greek, a massive leather-bound volume so old it looked as though its covers would fall off if you made cross-eyes at it, butted up against swaths of Shakespeare (some of them crumbling old folios that looked alarmingly like originals, though I could not imagine anyone in possession of such miraculous items would be so careless as to leave them on a *bookshelf*); Augustine's *Confessions* tucked coyly next to the collected stories of Angela Carter; all of James Baldwin neighboring a first edition of *The Secret History*, its acetate jacket crisp and coolly glittering in the warm dull light of his lamps. He had a copy of Maria Cunitz's *Urania propitia*, which was so tremendously rare that I was afraid to touch it and could not even have begun to imagine how much it had cost—he'd let me look through it, once, and I turned through page after page of her calculations of planetary positions with a kind of shaky awe. After he had unearthed my great affection for old science fiction and fantasy I had stumbled across a whole shelf of first editions: Philip K. Dick, Samuel Delany, Elizabeth Hand, Ursula K. Le Guin, Octavia Butler—even the dopey, shameful, misogynist stuff, although once I had explained to Mr. M how stupid Heinlein was about everything, especially women, his books had disappeared from Mr. M's shelves. I had never asked him for a book he didn't have, though sometimes it took him a while to find it for me.

He came into the library with a silver tray bearing a silver pitcher and a plate of sandwiches that he certainly had not had time to make. "Sit, sit," he said, but a new stack of paperbacks on a side table had caught my eye and I was busy looking through them. "Plooy et what?" I said, holding one up.

"*Pluie et vent sur Télumée Miracle*," he said. "My French is getting rusty, I thought I'd practice. It's quite good. Lemonade?"

"Yes, please," I said, and he poured me a glass and set out a round coaster. I folded myself up onto the sofa, meditatively gumming one of the sandwiches (cucumber and cream cheese) and sipping idly at the lemonade, which was flavored with something that I thought might be lavender. "This is delicious," I said, "did you make it?"

"I thought you might like it. I got it from—" He made an odd face. "From far away." He settled himself in a leather armchair. "You are unhappy," he said.

"I've been having some romantic troubles. Or nonromantic troubles. The trouble being that the romance is sort of one sided."

"I have on occasion had some doings with the romantic affairs of teenagers," he said, "although I'm not sure you would want my advice."

"Do you *know* many teenagers?"

"Over the years," he said. I wondered if he meant musicians. Or if he'd had children. He was such a singular person, and so inscrutable, that I had never felt adventuresome enough to ask him about any aspect of his life he had not brought up himself, and I knew nothing at all about his personal life, or any personal life he might have once had. It was hard to imagine Mr. M parenting adolescents. He cocked his head at me slightly. "'I would there were no age between sixteen and three-and-twenty, or that youth would sleep out the rest; for there is nothing in the between but getting wenches with child, wronging the ancientry, stealing, fighting,'" he said.

"It's sort of irritating that everyone in my life keeps quoting Shakespeare at me when I have difficulties."

"'We know what we are, but not what we may be.'"

"*Stop* it," I said.

He laughed. "Sorry," he said. "I get carried away. Being human is not any more complicated than it used to be, I don't think, but you have the weight of all these repeated plots pushing up against you. I think modernity is something of a burden."

"You think it's harder because people have been doing the same things forever?"

"Don't you? It must be limiting, to know for certain that every path you walk is a closed loop."

"I don't think that's true," I said. "People are always making new discoveries. Think about astronomy, about how far we've come—we're approaching the solutions to problems that people didn't even know existed fifty years ago."

"It is only ever the story of a quest," he said, "all this shuffling along the mortal coil, until you shuffle right off it. I am afraid none of you are so original as you might wish—"

"None of *you*? You mean astronomers? Or people in love?"

"I just think it must be difficult, to have everything one does be so ultimately futile. Fall in love, chase after golden fleeces, pull swords out of stones, sail around to all the islands of the far seas. I used to think it was exciting, all that stink of flesh and death, running around in the dark places under the earth setting traps for the unsuspecting, but I am old and tired now, and I would rather read books and sit by the fire in the winter and practice my French. But you are still young and full of energy, and perhaps to you the world seems as though it might be a different place than it has been to every young person since time began."

I stared at him. "You are being dreary today," I said finally.

He shook his head and laughed. "I am sorry, my dear," he said, "when you get to be as old as I am there is no hope for you to be anything other than a pessimist, but you are young still, and should pay no heed to my tedious ranting.

Tell me what you have been doing lately, other than having troubles; it's been a while since I last saw you."

I had not been doing much of anything at all, other than sulking, but that was not interesting. I thought of the music Shane had played for me. I knew that I was only talking about it because I wanted to keep talking about Shane, even if Mr. M didn't know that was what I was still talking about, and I was annoyed with myself for doing it, but I couldn't stop, either. "My—friend played this tape for me. An old musician who I guess was really famous. Jack Blake. Did you know him?"

A strange shudder went through him, as though he had gone into a cold room, and though I was not admittedly the most perceptive person I saw that he was making a great effort not to look at me. "Jack," he said. "That is a name I have not heard in a long time. I did know him, once upon a time. We can listen to the record, if you like."

"You have the record?"

"Of course." *Shane would kill to hear this,* I thought, and my smugness distracted me from whatever had come over Mr. M. He crossed the room to flip through his shelves of records and select one, carrying it over to the turntable and sliding it out of its sleeve as carefully as if it were made of glass.

We listened to the whole record in silence, disturbed only when the first side ended and he got up to turn it over. The record was like hearing the music new again: the sound clearer and even more piercing, the heartbreak in that rich, rough voice filling the whole room until I thought it must spill over into the world outside. We sat for a long time without talking when it was finished. "I had almost forgotten," he said at last, "how extraordinary he was."

"How did you know him?"

He waved one hand dismissively and looked at me; he was weighing something, I thought, although I had no idea what it was; some arcane decision, known only to him. "I have a picture of him somewhere, if you would like to see it," he said at last. He got up and went into another room and came back after a while with a framed picture—not a print, something blurrier and faded, maybe cut out of a newspaper—of a group of people, well dressed and sleek, at a party (glasses in hands, laughter, behind them an expanse of what looked like a window—an ocean, maybe?). But my eye was drawn immediately to a sharp-featured dark-skinned man, his dreadlocked hair coiling about him, looking straight into the camera with a cool, challenging gaze; he had one arm around a skinny girl who tilted up to him a rapturous face surrounded by a cloud of white hair. They were magnetic, the two of them; next to them the other people, groomed and lovely as they were, faded into the background like shadows. He was not exactly handsome, but there was something so remarkable, so intense, about his face that you could not look away from him, and the girl was, even in the blurry, faded newsprint photo, so beautiful that it made me want to straighten my clothes and brush my hair, ineffectual though these gestures would have been. And then the shot of recognition, sharp as starlight in my veins: I knew who that girl was, the girl Jack was holding. I had seen her picture on my own wall every day of my life.

"Oh my god," I said. "That's Aurora."

"Your mother?" Mr. M said. He did not sound surprised.

"I don't have a mother," I said shortly, and he raised one eyebrow but did not say anything. "'About a Girl.' His song. 'You were ever the only one'—it's about somebody who left him. Do you think it's about her?"

"I don't know," he said. "I never asked him."

"He knew her."

"It seems that way."

In a flash I understood at once the significance—the picture, the song, Aurora, this man. The way she was looking at him in the photograph: complex, radiant, so electric it came off the paper and charged the air around it. "Look at them in this picture. She's totally in love with him. It's all over her face. He could be my *father*. And then she left—" My mind was a whirlpool. "And then she left. She left me, she left him—that song. He wrote that song for her—do you think he even knows I exist? He can't possibly know I exist."

There was a long silence. "I can find him," Mr. M said. "If you like."

"You know where he is?" I asked, astounded.

He shrugged his one-shouldered shrug. "There is no one on this earth who can hide from me if I wish to seek him out," he said.

"But I don't—I mean, what would I even say to him? If he is my father, he must have no idea." If he was my father and he knew—but I refused to think about that. I could not—chose not to—imagine the misfortune of being cursed with two biological parents totally indifferent to my upbringing and well-being. I had once seen an episode of that silly old TV show *The X-Files*—about which Raoul and Aunt Beast were fanatical—where the agents found themselves in a vast, sinister warehouse filled with row upon row of endless file cabinets; I thought that the inside of my own mind must resemble such a storehouse, with all the unruly sorrows I might have otherwise let rampage about within me filed neatly away under *M* for *Mother*; *A* for *Abandonment*; *F* for *Who the Fuck Knows Who He Is, Or Cares*. I did not much like the idea of starting up a new folder. *J for Jack, I Think*. But it would be nice, all the same, to tidy away that loose end before I started up the rest of my life; like a room put in order, upon which I could shut the door for good.

"You could ask him about her," Mr. M said.

"About Aurora? Why would I want to do that?"

He looked at me, and I saw that for once I had surprised him. "Aren't you curious about her?"

"What is there to know about her? She was an idiot, and she left me. If she cared at all about me she would have come and found me by now, or written, or called, or—I don't know, anything. If she didn't love me, I don't see why I should care about her." I looked at the picture again. "But if he's my father, and he doesn't know—I mean, that's different, isn't it? I don't know anything about him. Henri and Raoul are better dads than anybody could ever ask for. But I guess it would be nice to know my biological father. Know who he is, at least."

"What would you say to him?"

"I don't know. Find out what he likes. Doesn't like. See if we get along. I could write him a letter." I stared at the picture, thinking. "Or, I mean—if you know where he is, I could just *go* there. I could find him. He would have to talk to me, if I showed up on his doorstep. My parents would never let me go, though. Not by myself."

"You don't have to ask them," he said calmly. I looked up from the picture.

"Of course I would have to ask them," I said.

"None of the great quests ever came out of obedience. It's epic, don't you think? The lost father. The grand journey." I couldn't tell if he was being serious; his expression was inscrutable, his tone neutral. Had he really known Aurora? I did not know what exactly it was that had led to her and Aunt Beast going their separate ways before I was born—Aunt Beast refused to talk about it, no matter how I pestered her over the years, and Raoul pled ignorance, though I suspected he knew more than he let on.

"It's old, bad blood, sweet pea, whatever happened between them," he'd said to me once. "It hurts your aunt more than you can imagine, even now, and it's nothing to do with you. What matters is that you're here with us now." I knew that Aurora had left the Northwest before I was born, gone somewhere—Los Angeles, maybe; Aunt Beast had never been clear. And that whatever it was that had broken them apart, they'd never spoken again—not even when Aurora had reappeared momentarily, a cosmic flash like a supernova flaring and vanishing again, to leave me at Raoul and Aunt Beast's door. Sometimes I thought about how hard it must have been for Aunt Beast, to lose her best friend forever, have me dumped on her doorstep with nary an if-you-please, and it made me hate Aurora even more. Aunt Beast and Raoul had never so much as hinted that they were anything other than delighted to raise me, but I doubted either of them would have had children if left to their own devices.

"When is this picture from?" I asked. "Where did you get it?"

"Oh, I couldn't possibly remember," he said, his face still blank, and I thought, *There is something you aren't telling me.* But he was as stubborn as I was, in his odd way, and I wouldn't get it out of him until he was ready.

"What was he like?" I asked. "Jack, I mean."

"He was one of the greatest musicians in the world," he said. "He was transcendent. People who saw him play never forgot it as long as they lived. Even me, and I have lived for a long time."

"This can't have been that long ago," I said. "It must have been taken right before I was born, don't you think?"

"Time is complicated," he said. "You of all people should know that. But Jack was something special. It was too much for him, I think. He was not strong enough to bear the price that came with his gifts."

"But he's still alive?"

"Certainly."

"How do you know?"

"I know," he said. His black eyes bored into me, and for half a second I thought I saw something eerie flicker in their depths—the walls of the room shifting, a flash of black wings, tall glass windows looking out over a heaving sea, a girl sitting in a chair; my age, close-cropped black hair, huge, haunted eyes; *I miss you,* she whispered—and then I shook myself and the moment passed. The heat was getting to me; next I'd be hallucinating in the middle of the street.

"Come see me again," he said. "In a few days. I will find him for you, and you will go."

The fuzziness at the corners of my vision—what was

wrong with me? My brain was slowing down, thickening—*This is a terrible idea,* piped up a feeble voice at the back of my skull, but the way he was looking at me, the force of his black stare—

"I could go," I said slowly. "If you found him—you're right. I could go."

"You *will* go," he said again, and the faint voice in my head subsided without further protest. "You won't tell anyone, and that way they can't stop you. I will send you to find him, and to—" He stopped short and looked away from me, staring at his bookshelves without seeming to see them. There was something wrong with the air; I couldn't breathe—and then he blinked and the strange charge ran out of the room and he was just an ordinary old man in his library again, a little sad and a lot lonely, and I—what had we been talking about? About a trip. We'd been talking about a trip. To find my father. I shook my head furiously, trying to knock some sense back into myself. "Would you like some more lemonade?" he asked.

I walked home in a daze, stupid with heat. There was something I couldn't remember, something I had to do—and then I walked in through my apartment door, and Raoul and Henri and Aunt Beast were assembled in the living room and beaming. *It's my birthday,* I thought. *My birthday party.* "You're late," Raoul said. "We thought you must have stopped at Shane's. . . ." He was looking behind me, for Shane, and when he saw I was alone he trailed off.

"Where is he?" I asked.

"I'm sure he'll be over," Henri said. "Why don't you call him, just in case."

There was something wrong with me—I felt high, idiotic;

I felt like I was moving forward through a bowl of gelatin. Their expectant faces, their transparent human need. "No," I said. Their smiles faltered.

"We could just order a pizza," Aunt Beast said.

"I'm not hungry."

"But there's cake."

"I don't want cake." The words were coming out with difficulty, as if from someone else's mouth, and now they were just staring at me, shocked.

"It's your *birthday,*" Raoul said.

"I don't care about my fucking birthday," I said, and I walked past them, into my room, and shut the door and sat on my bed and waited to feel like a normal person again.

I waited for a long time. The light shifted and dimmed, the shadows on my floor lengthened and blurred into dark; still I sat, staring at nothing, until someone knocked on my door softly and opened it without waiting for my acknowledgment. Aunt Beast came in and sat down next to me.

"We're still waiting for you to cut the cake, but we got hungry. We were going to order takeout. You get to pick, for your birthday,"

"I don't want cake," I said again. Aunt Beast said nothing. "I miss him," I said.

"I know, sweetheart. I wish there was something I could do. Are you—okay? I mean, obviously you're not okay. But are you *okay*?"

"I'm not going to go drown myself in the Gowanus, if that's what you're worried about."

"You wouldn't drown. You'd dissolve."

"Even more reason not to."

"Raoul told me once that everybody needs to be loved through their first broken heart."

"My heart's not broken." I registered what she'd said. "Wait, when did you get your heart broken?"

"A long time ago."

"Will you ever tell me about it? Was Aurora there?"

She was quiet for a while. "She was there," she said finally. "I was your age."

"What happened?"

"It was years and years ago. Not worth dragging up all that old history."

"Tell me more about what she was like."

"She was beautiful," she said slowly, "and complicated. We used to get in a lot of trouble together." This I knew about already.

"In bars," I said. "You went to rock shows in bars."

"That we did," she said. "My mother was not the most conventional parent, and your grandmother—well, you know. She did a lot of damage. But in retrospect, things must have been hard for her, too."

"Did she love—Jason?" I could never manage to say my grandfather's name without feeling a little silly.

"Maia? I don't know, honestly. I was so young when he died. Aurora told me once that Maia had wanted to be a concert pianist, which is hard to imagine, but I don't know anything about what she was like before she started doing drugs."

"But who broke your heart?"

She went stiff for a second, and I thought I'd pushed my luck too far, but she relented. "Musician," she said. "He just showed up in town and that was it. I met him at one of Aurora's parties."

"She knew him, too?"

"Yes," Aunt Beast said, in a tone that suggested that if I knew what was good for me I would alter my line of questioning, but I deliberately misread her tenor.

"So what happened?"

"He loved music more than he loved me," she said. "I was just a kid, I thought love was enough to conquer all, tear down the walls—"

"*I'm* just a kid," I said, "and *I* know that's not true."

"You've always been pragmatic. I don't know where you get it from. Certainly not Aurora."

"Maybe my father," I said, shooting a look at her, but if she knew anything she was doing a good job of hiding it. "Do you think she loved me?" I had no idea where this question came from, as unexpected as if someone had come up behind me in the street and punched me in the back of the head, and I nearly put my own hand over my mouth to prevent the further escape of anything so needy and untoward.

"Yes," Aunt Beast said immediately. "I do."

"She left me."

"I know, sweetheart. She left me, too, before you were born. I thought I would never forgive her for it. And it took a long time. But she did love me, of that I have no doubt. And I have no doubt that she loved you. You know," she said, "I dreamed about her. The night we found you. It felt like more than a dream—it felt like she was here. Or that I was there. Where we were, in the kitchen in the house I grew up in. Raoul dreamed about her, too."

"That's a funny coincidence."

"It didn't feel like a coincidence, Tally, that's what I'm telling you. It felt real."

I rolled an inner eye. Aunt Beast was nowhere near as batty as Cass, who, I knew, fancied herself something of a witch, but she had a ludicrous faith in omens and portents, read her horoscope religiously, and still kept a tatty old pack of tarot cards, left over from her youth, on her dresser with an assortment of leaves, rocks, candles, crystals, and small statuary that she referred to as her "altar."

"Dreams are just the garbage disposal of your subconscious," I said sententiously. Aunt Beast laughed.

"Where do you *get* this stuff? Serves us right, we few proud New Age freaks, that we should end up with such a determined rationalist for a kid."

"If you knew more about the universe, you wouldn't need to believe all that weird stuff," I said. "You don't need the supernatural when you understand how beautiful real things are."

She smiled at me and pulled me to her side in a one-armed hug. "You know," she said, "I loved Aurora with all my heart. But you, hands down, are the greatest thing that's ever happened to me." I put my head on her shoulder and she kissed the top of my skull.

"You didn't even want kids," I said into her shirt.

"I wanted *you*," she said. "I just didn't know it until I met you. Anybody else, I would have sent back. Tally, you know I love you. More than anything. I'm sorry Shane is being— well, to be honest, he's being seventeen. I know it's hard. Please come have some cake?" I let her tug me to my feet and propel me into the kitchen, where Raoul and Henri sat anxiously at the table, and Dorian Gray pranced about howling, and my cake waited for me: the Very Large Array, rendered in white frosting with black piping for the outlines.

"Dim sum," I said, "I want dim sum," and Raoul's and Henri's faces lit up, and I saw how easy it was to make them happy, how much they loved me, how much there was still here for me, even as it felt as though the whole world was moving away from me at a nightmarish, terrifying speed, dark energy pushing the universe out into the waiting void until there was nothing left but ice and silence, nothing left of us at all. At the edge of my vision I saw the girl again, the girl I'd seen in Mr. M's apartment: short dark hair, white shirt, huge eyes—I turned, squinting, and she was only a trick of the light, the kitchen curtains moving. *But there isn't any breeze,* I thought, and then Henri and Raoul were hugging me, Aunt Beast calling in our takeout order and demanding I cut my cake. "We'll have dessert first," she said, "it's your birthday," and I willed myself to stop thinking about what I was missing and be at peace instead with what I had.

But that night, back in my room, I thought of the picture Mr. M had shown me, Jack's voice aching in the dark, all the sorrows of the world echoing through each shimmering note, and I thought about coming home and telling Shane that the greatest musician in the world was my father.

"I'm going," I said out loud into the still, warm air. When I fell asleep I dreamed awful and discomforting dreams.

I went back to see Mr. M a few days later. "Come in," he said, "let me get you some water," and I followed him into his library and fidgeted in a chair while he disappeared and came back what felt like hours later with a pitcher of ice water and a plate of cookies shaped like pinwheels. I ate four cookies and drank my water and wriggled about in a frenzy.

"I did find him," he said, and I stopped my impatient dance at once. "I'm afraid I took a bit of a liberty."

"You talked to him," I said.

"I didn't. But I bought you a plane ticket. It's fine if you'd prefer not to go."

"Of course I'm going to go. Where is he?"

"Outside Seattle. You'll have to take a ferry, and then a bus—it's a small town, out on a peninsula. Very out of the way." I thought about this. I'd never been to the city where Aurora had grown up, never even thought of that corner of the world as a real place. It seemed like something out of a John Wayne movie. Like people would ride horses in the streets and carry derringers and run in and out of saloons between their gun battles. I imagined a chorus line of floozies, prodigious bosoms bursting from their tight-bodiced velvet dresses. Did people even have electricity out there? Before Shane had played Jack's tape for me, I'd had no idea he even existed. And now here I was with a plane ticket and the more-than-suspicion that this random, near-mythical stranger was my father. The only way to find out was to go.

"Thank you," I said.

"Don't thank me until you talk to him."

"Right," I said, unsettled. I would worry about that part later. "I can pay you back for the ticket."

"Don't be silly."

"You've already done so much."

"I told you," he said, "don't thank me. I have done very little for you."

"How will I find him, though?"

"I'll give you his address."

"But I mean—I should just show up? At his door? Isn't that kind of weird?"

"It will all work out as it should," he said. "The fates' web will catch you."

"You know I don't believe in that stuff."

"And yet they continue to weave, despite you," he said, and smiled. I stood there looking at him stupidly. "Go," he said gently. "Go, now, into the world. Tell no one. Good luck on your quest."

"Okay," I said, and I went.

Aunt Beast left that afternoon for an artists' residency upstate, one of those places where there's no telephone and everyone works in lofty seclusion in the middle of the woods, communing with their muses, lunch left stealthily in a basket on their doorstep so as not to interfere with their Process. I could tell she didn't want to leave me in my current state, so I did my best to appear functional and chipper, chattering away while she finished packing—Aunt Beast was not much of an advance planner—until she cut me off.

"Tally, the pep club routine is not fooling me," she said. "I don't have to go away if you need me here."

"You're only going for a month, and I have Raoul and Henri. And I would feel like a total shit if you stayed here for me." *And I'm leaving, too,* I thought, *and I have a better chance of getting away with it if you're not around.* Anyway, Aunt Beast's entire sex life in the last couple of years had consisted of steamy, short-lived affairs at artists' residencies— the last one had been some musician who made whole albums out of looped recordings from the Apollo space missions, which I'd appreciated—and I didn't need to curse the whole household with celibacy just because I was batting zero in the romance department. Raoul and I sometimes discussed Aunt Beast's disturbing lack of a personal life when she was out of the house, but she seemed essentially content on her own, wrapped up in her work, sitting for hours in the MoMA or the Met staring at a single painting, running endless laps of the park. Aunt Beast is the most wholly self-sufficient person I have ever met; I have no doubt she loves us, but if an apocalyptic plague wiped us from the map, she'd be the one to calmly hole up in the apartment with a shotgun and a pit bull, occasionally emerging to perhaps eat one of the downstairs neighbors or make a run to the art supply store, happy as Dorian Gray in front of a newly opened tin of wet food.

She hefted her bag experimentally and winced. "I should have just shipped this crap," she said. "Are you sure you'll be okay?"

"You already called the car service. Henri will make me eat, Raoul will nurture my minimal emotional needs; if I totally freak out we'll call the residency phone and they can go fetch you in your cabin."

"That's frowned upon."

"It's fine," I said. "Nothing's going to happen. I'll just go to the bookstore—" *Shit,* I thought, *what am I going to tell Jenn and Molly*—"and put on a brave face, and—and—I don't know, maybe he'll call me and grovel and everything will be normal next week."

"You could call him."

"He stood me up on my *birthday.* I'll call him when hell freezes over."

She looked at me with frank amusement. "The stubbornness, I'm afraid, you got from me." There was a honk outside the window. "That's the car—are you sure, Tally?"

"Yes," I said. She gave me a kiss on the cheek and a brief hug that knocked the air out of my lungs, and dragged her bag out of the room. I watched out her window until she reappeared in the street below, then waved to her, but she didn't look up. *One down,* I thought.

That night Henri had a client, and so I ate dinner alone in the kitchen with Raoul, Dorian Gray meowing pitifully at our feet until I shoved him brusquely with my toe. He gave me an offended look and stalked away with his tail lashing. Raoul frowned at his plate, but I ignored him. Raoul is largely unwilling to acknowledge Dorian Gray's multitudinous faults; I do not agree that loving Dorian Gray means overlooking his inadequacies as a pet.

"Shane played me this tape," I said. Mr. M hadn't said not to mention Jack. "This musician, Jack—I think he knew Aurora?"

Raoul looked up from his soba noodles, his expression unreadable. "He did, yes."

"Did you know him too?"

"Not well."

"Did he know Aunt Beast?"

"We were all—we all knew each other, then," he said slowly. "You'll have to ask her if you want to know anything about Jack."

"Was he Aurora's boyfriend?"

"I don't know. He—" He paused. "He left town the same time she did," he said, but I thought it wasn't what he had meant to say originally. "You have to ask your aunt about all of that."

"Why?"

He made a helpless, exasperated face. "There's a lot that's not mine to tell," he said.

"Then it's her fault for not telling me."

"I've brought that up with her before." I looked at him with new interest; they'd always presented a united front, but whatever I had started had caused Raoul to split ranks in my presence for the first time.

"Do you think Jack might be—" I was almost afraid to say it out loud. "Do you think he might be my father? I mean, could he be?"

I'd surprised him. "I don't know, sweetheart," he said. "I've never—that's never even occurred to me. But I barely knew Aurora, and I never saw her again after she went—" He paused. "After she went away. I don't know if anyone knew her, to be honest. Maybe your aunt."

"Who would want to know her? She was a jerk."

"You could look at it like that, yes. She was never happy, in the time that I knew her."

"She gave me *away*, Raoul."

"I know, sweetheart. I know. I'm so sorry you've had to grow up with that. But from where she was, it probably looked like the best thing to do."

"Where could she have possibly been that leaving her kid behind seemed like a good idea?"

"She was in hell," he said simply.

I kicked at the floor. "I'm not ever going to forgive her," I said.

"I don't blame you, and you don't have to. But I don't think she didn't love you. I think she knew she couldn't take care of you. She didn't leave you just anywhere; she left you with us. She left you with the most responsible people she knew—"

"The *only* responsible people she knew."

"Probably," Raoul conceded. "But she left you with us because she knew we would love you, and she knew we would take care of you."

"She foisted me off on you."

"I know it feels like that to you. But that's certainly not what it felt like to us—we loved you the moment we saw you. If Aurora were here, I'd thank her every day for leaving you with us. But for her—I don't think that's how she saw it, either, as hard as that might be to believe. I think for her it looked like the best decision she could have made, under the circumstances."

"It was a terrible decision."

"Sometimes all the decisions available are terrible decisions."

"That's not true at all," I said. "Everybody has a choice, all the time—anyone can make good decisions. You just have to want to."

"You might find out as you get older that things are more complicated than that."

"Now you're patronizing me."

"I wouldn't dream of patronizing you, Tally." He paused. "Have you heard from Sh—"

"*No,*" I said, so fiercely that he bit down on the end of the word and looked at his plate.

"I'm sure he'll—"

"I don't want to talk about it."

"Very well," he said. "Can you pass me the salt?"

Long after I turned out the light that night I looked up at the faint glow of my ceiling constellations, wishing there was some map in them that could navigate me like a sailor safely through what lay ahead.

When I finally fell asleep I dreamed of the girl I'd seen in Mr. M's apartment, the girl I'd seen on my birthday: I was running after her, through a forest in the dead of night, running barefoot, leafless branches white as bone clacking all around me although there was no breeze. "Wait!" I called after her. "Please wait!" *However far we've come / you were ever the only one.* But she did not turn or slow, and though I was running as fast as I could she drew away from me, vanishing among the trees. I tripped and fell, landing hard on my hands, panting—and then a terrifying howl split the darkness, once, twice, three times—something coming closer through the trees—"No!" I shrieked aloud, and woke myself up, frantic and tangled in the sheets, soaked in sweat. It took me a long time to fall asleep again.

The night before I left I considered calling Shane, and then squashed that foul treachery of a thought like a bug. He'd find out soon enough, from Raoul or from Henri, that I was gone, and teary goodbyes were for babies, and anyway I had nothing to say to him, or if I did I didn't want to think about what it might be. I was a scientist, and scientists didn't have feelings, and that was what was important, because I did not like feelings, which had thus far only inconvenienced me to no end. I stole an old knapsack of Raoul's out of the hall closet after he and Henri had gone to bed and filled it with a few T-shirts and a couple of pairs of shorts, socks and underwear and a pair of jeans and my favorite old sweatshirt. Running shoes, just in case. I had spent most of my life largely indifferent to the garments with which I garbed myself, and I did not imagine anyone in the country would care much what I dressed like anyway. If Jack wanted to see me in a nice dress he would have to buy me one himself. I looked longingly at my telescope but it was unwieldy, and I didn't know anything about Jack's house—*Where the hell are you going to stay, Tally, you idiot*—but my thoughts went fuzzy again, and the voice subsided. "I'll find somewhere," I said aloud. "A hotel." I'd told Jenn and Molly that I needed a week off from the bookstore because my cousin had died; it was an appalling lie, but if I said anything else I risked them telling my parents. I packed a pair of binoculars instead of the telescope, and my observation journal, and then I was done. I felt like an intrepid explorer.

I took one last walk through the apartment, as if to memorize it—*Just how long do you think you're going for, Tally*—tangly houseplants and well-worn old furniture, battered rag rugs, dried flowers in the windowsills, piles of books in every corner. An apartment, I thought, that looked like what it was: a home where people lived who loved each other. I stopped last in Aunt Beast's room, drifts of Dorian Gray's fur moving in scattered flurries across the floorboards—his fur accumulated like nothing else if we didn't sweep every day—and looked around at her faded quilt, her bookshelf, her dresser-top with its scatter of objects. A sudden wave of preemptive homesickness swept over me, and I snatched the nearest bit of altar detritus—a folding knife, old and scarred, with a long strand of somebody's bleach-blond hair caught in its hinge—and stuffed it in my pocket. It would cheer me to have something of hers, and I'd be back before she came home; she'd never even know it was gone.

Back in my room, Dorian Gray writhing in ecstasy as I rubbed his belly with my toes, I wrote Henri and Raoul a note. Brevity, in this case, seemed the best option, but even so I struggled with what to say. I *was* eighteen, and legally entitled to take charge of my own destiny, but that did not seem the most tactful approach. *Please don't worry about me,* I wrote finally, *I found out where Jack lives and I'm going to see him—I'll come back soon and I'll call as soon as I can. Don't kill me. I love you.*

There was nothing else to do but go to bed. I dreamed strange, restless dreams—the forest again, big black birds flitting through the trees; something howling, lonely and disconsolate, this time safely in the distance; looking for the dark-haired girl, knowing that she was moving farther and farther away from me, that I was losing all hope of keeping up. The night lasted for a long time, and I was almost grateful for the hot insistent blast of sun pushing through my curtains the next morning, because it meant I could give up pretending and get up, drink coffee, bleary eyed, with Raoul and Henri at the kitchen table, kiss their cheeks in a quick goodbye as they left the apartment to begin their days— *Hold on to this, who knows how long it'll have to last me*— shoulder my backpack, think about the sauna-hot stink of the train platform and why was the Q always late and should I eat something now when I wasn't hungry or wait until the airport, when I would be, but all potential edibles were sure to be overpriced and repulsive. The long train ride to the airport, mind empty. And at last, at the gate to my flight west, I turned my back on New York and took a deep breath and walked forward, away from the things I knew about and toward the things I didn't.

LOVE THE
DESTROYER

When I was seven or eight years old, Raoul and Henri took me to Urban Starfest, an annual amateur astronomers' gathering in Central Park. To this day, I don't know what possessed them to do such a thing—neither one has any particular interest in the order of the stars, and I have not known them to do anything like it since. But they were always carting me off to enriching activities as a young person—Shakespeare in the

Park, children's concerts at Carnegie Hall, tours of the Lower East Side Tenement Museum—and so I imagine one or the other of them saw something about it in a paper and thought it sounded promising.

It was the middle of November, and very cold. All day it had been cloudy, but just before dusk the sky cleared, and by the time we stepped off the train outside the park a few stars shone palely against a clean-scrubbed backdrop of velvety purple. From the Sheep Meadow, where the astronomers gathered, the buzzing glare of the city was dimmed, and though we were barely a mile from the frenetic Technicolor of Times Square I could see more stars than I'd ever managed to pick out in the night sky over the city.

We waited to look through a telescope—enthusiastic astronomers nearly hopping with excitement, pointing out stars and planets that could be easily seen with the naked eye, running back and forth with handouts that it was too dark to read—Raoul and Henri patient, me less so, until at last it was my turn. The astronomer stewarding the telescope pointed to a scatter of stars overhead. "That's Orion," she said, kneeling down so our faces were level. "Do you see? There's his belt, and those stars there are his sword."

I squinted upward. "I don't see a belt," I said dubiously.

"Ah," she said, "you have to draw the lines with your imagination. Try again."

I stared intently at the tip of her finger and then, at last, I saw it. "There he is!" I said. I knew who Orion was already; someone, probably Aunt Beast, had got me *D'Aulaires' Book of Greek Myths* as soon as I was old enough to read it. The astronomer pointed to a blurry greenish smudge along the tip of his sword. "That's the nebula," she said. "That's what you'll see through the telescope. Are you ready?"

She adjusted the telescope so that I could look through it, and I put my eye to the eyepiece, and she brought the lens into focus—and then, like that, the course of my life altered. Through the telescope I saw the faint smear coalesce into a cloud of blazing sparks, and I understood in an instant that the world would never look the same to me again. Those distant points of light in the sky were not strangers, but stars; the telescope put me among them, as if they were merely guests at a garden party, cool and aloof but close enough that I could touch the silvery gossamer of their clothes with the tips of my fingers. Prior to that night I had wanted, I am told, to be a marine biologist, an actor, a spy, and the president. "I've changed my mind. I want to be an astronaut," I said to Henri after our turn at the telescope was over, gazing serenely about me at the milling crowds of people, the joyfully frenetic astronomers. "I think you have to go into the military," he said. "They only take fighter pilots." I was, at that time, a pacifist and a vegetarian. "Then I shall become an astronomer," I said. I did not change my mind again.

Later I would learn that the Orion Nebula is a kind of cosmic nursery, a great cloud of gas and dust birthing uncountable infant stars in a nest so fantastically large it would take a half-million years for the fastest imaginable rocket to cross it. The time scale of star birth is nothing like the hummingbird flicker of a human life; we'd have to take a picture every thousand years to track the course of the nebula's shifting, its slow yield of fire and light, but it's enough for me to know that out of a dead cloud particles spin themselves into hundreds of thousands of suns. Our own bodies are mattered out of the same dust: the leftover bits of super-novae billions of years old that time's turned to human heart-beats. Rainwater and skin and bones, the grey sea and the shore upon which it breaks, mountains and snow and Dorian Gray: all of it, quilted out of the hearts of stars. I am not like my family, lost in their superstitious witchery, because the truth of the universe is so sublime I don't need magic or ghosts to teach me wonder. Aunt Beast insists the moon's pull twitches the tides of our inner workings, hooks its mysteries into the movement of our blood, but I knew the first time I looked at the waxing half-moon through a pair of binoculars that its real miracle was the sharp-edged outlines of craters and valleys sprung into sudden relief, its rotation and revolution neatly twinned so that the same sil-very face is always turned toward us.

The moon's unmoved nature meant it was no great work to memorize its landscape—and I did. I learned the map of the moon as I memorized the lines of the subway; I could pick out the Apennines before I could conduct myself to Central Park alone. There was no point in explaining to Aunt Beast that the moon's effect on the movement of oceans was a simple side effect of proximity, not magic, and that we'd have to be thousands of miles tall before we felt any match-ing pull in our saltwater bodies. She lights her candles every month anyway, shut up in her room with crystals and incense that stinks the apartment up like the old head shops in the East Village.

After that night in the park I was a goner. Raoul told me I'd gone home with them and demanded to be shown the entirety of Carl Sagan's *Cosmos* series, which the astrono-mer had mentioned I might find edifying. For thirteen nights in a row Raoul and Henri took turns dozing next to me on the couch as I absorbed, shining-eyed and rapt, the nuances of cosmology and its various theories of the universe's birth and life and possible death. Aunt Beast bought me binoculars and then, when it became clear my madness would not abate, a real telescope, for my thirteenth birthday. I learned to love winters best; when everyone around me lamented the freezing days and muddy grey-white light, the endless months of dirty snow crusting and refreezing, the sodden toes and runny noses, I lived for the season of long nights, when full dark fell by six and the sky opened up to inquiry.

There's no real dark in the city—or most places, anymore, the night world we live in made a dully glowing violet. But the city's worst of all. In Manhattan, true darkness never falls: runny pools of gold light falling from streetlamps, streams of headlights moving from sundown to sunup in hissing white rivers, Times Square clamoring with neon billboards, spotlights spitting forth from police helicopters and news choppers, blue-and-white cop cars wailing, ambulances and fire trucks blaring redly. I only knew the Milky Way existed from pictures in *Astronomy* magazine until the chilly late-autumn weekend I begged Henri and Raoul to take me upstate: me bouncing in my seat on the train north, ecstatic with anticipation, them smiling at me over the pages of their newspapers. The first night was cloudy; Raoul told me that I tantrumed stormy tears and beat my little fists upon the ground. But the second night was perfect, moonless and clear, and I waited in the backyard of the cabin they'd rented as the red sun sank below the horizon and the sky purpled and went black. One by one, the silver stars winked into life above me: steady Polaris marking true north,

Andromeda and Pegasus and Pisces, the friends with whom I was becoming more and more acquainted—and then at last the great white sky-long spill of the galaxy sprawling overhead, a dizzying mass of light.

Raoul and Henri came outside hours later to find me asleep in the grass, murmuring plaintive protests as they gathered me up and carried me inside, and the next day I was so incandescent with joy, talked so incessantly about what I'd seen, that they made a point to take me out to the country more often. Shane usually came with us, waiting outside with me as I fiddled with my telescope and picked out the night's treasures; in the city, he would spend even the coldest of winter nights on the roof of our apartment building with me, swaddled in a down jacket and nested in a pile of blankets, snoring softly while I followed a single star or planet across the heavens until dawn colored the edges of the sky. I collected sightings the way other children kept glass-jarred butterflies or stamps or baseball cards: constellations, nebulae, Messier's chart of objects, the Galilean moons of Jupiter—violent, volcano-ridden Io, icy Europa, massive Ganymede, and cratered Callisto—so named after the man who'd first thought to turn a telescope to the stars instead of on his neighbors, as easy to find in the modern age as they'd been in 1610. And once I realized you could make a career out of looking at the sky, I set a tidily charted course for my future. Physics, calculus, science camps in summers, preadolescent fan letters written to astronomers at prominent observatories and universities around the country—most of them, I'm happy to say, wrote back, and I saved their replies in a box I kept under my bed and took out at least once a week to review the steadily increasing pile.

My family humored my intense and furious drive, their encouragement bolstered by the reports my teachers sent home with me every quarter: *Tally's abilities in math and physics are astonishing. Tally has much to offer the class, although she is often hesitant to share* [disinterested, actually] *and her social skills need developing. Tally is a truly gifted student, although I am concerned about her refusal* [wholly justified] *to interact with other students.* My family did not care that I had no friends, other than Shane. They did not care that I did not invite babbling gaggles of pigtailed girls over for sleepovers, that I did not get myself up in a fetching manner, that boys did not call for me in the evening hours, and that I would rather have run nude through the halls of school at lunch hour than put myself in a dress. If I had cared myself, I am sure, they would have made appointments with guidance counselors or professionals, sent me to therapy, done whatever it is that conscientious parents do when their offspring are bewildered by the various petty traumas of preadolescence—though Aunt Beast and Raoul were unconventional enough that it was hard to imagine them making appointments with psychiatrists or even being aware that such persons existed.

But I didn't care. I had Shane, and I had my genius and my books and my telescope, and I had no doubt that once I entered the environs of the university I should find myself easily among equals and friends. My family was bemused by me; it was not that they themselves were not ambitious, but their passions did not lie in the same direction, and we were in many ways as unalike as people could be. I often wondered if my father had been intellectually inclined; whatever I'd inherited from Aurora, it had been neither discipline nor any aptitude for the sciences. I was satisfied but not surprised when, after a decade of single-minded application of myself to my envisioned destiny, I received not one but several offers of full scholarship to eminent colleges, and the only dilemma remaining to me was choosing the finest among them—and, of course, saying goodbye to Shane, from whom I had not been separated for more than a few days since his family had moved in down the hall.

Up until a month ago my life moved in a route as orderly and logical as if it, too, were governed by Kepler's laws of planetary motion. The only mysteries I tolerated were the marvelously unexplained bits of the universe: What came first? And where were we going? Was the universe expanding endlessly toward an ultimate long, icy silence, or would it tear itself apart in its final hours? I did not like to admit that something so stupid as my uncontrolled affections for a boy had set me reeling, but even the most determinedly stable person could not have helped being sent off course by a discovery like Mr. M's picture. I was hurtling westward toward something I did not yet understand, and instead of elation, I felt only an increasing sense of dread. For the first time in my life, I had no idea what the outcome of my actions would be. All the stories I'd teethed on were plentiful with admonishments about the dire consequences of ill-prepared quests. What was I doing, other than making trouble for myself?

Despite these restless and uncertain thoughts, I fell asleep as soon as I found my seat on the plane, and I did not wake up until the final hour of the flight, struggling out of a thick and disorienting slumber. Below us an endless expanse of flat yellow plain rippled upward into blue foothills, and then we were flying over jagged peaks, cool dark sapphire and edged in snow despite the season. Off in the distance a mountain so enormous it seemed fake towered over the rest of the range, its gleaming white crown shrouded with tattered bits of cloud. I rubbed my eyes and pressed my face against the glass as the mountains gave way and the plane sank toward deep green woods, dotted everywhere with flashes of water that reflected the sun in kaleidoscopic patches. I didn't stop looking until we touched down and the plane whined its way to a halt outside the gate.

I had my resolve and my backpack and two hundred dollars I'd been saving toward a new lens. I was trying not to have any expectations about what would happen next, so I stopped thinking about it as I followed the airport signs to a line of yellow taxis waiting outside. This part, at least, was familiar. The sky outside was a clear summery blue and the air was warm; not the thick, swampy density of New York but something more pleasant and friendly, even on the cement expanse outside the airport—line of taxis idling, buses trundling past with a squelch of exhaust. "Hello there," a man's voice said, and I turned to see a sleepy-eyed traveler in some sort of skirtlike garment made out of pleated canvas with a tool belt around his waist, wearing white socks and sandals and carrying a backpack even larger than mine.

"What?" I said.

"Where you going?" he asked. He was trying to strike up a conversation with me; to what end, I had no idea.

"I know how to get there," I said shortly, and turned back to the line of taxis. In New York there was always a wait, but here the drivers stood outside their cabs, leaning idly against the doors and chewing on unlit cigarettes.

"I was just—" began the man in the skirt, but I ignored him and strode toward a cab in a purposeful manner, and he did not pursue me.

The drive to the ferry took a long time. The taxi driver hummed quietly along to his radio and didn't ask me any questions. I looked out the window as a stretch of industrial buildings and warehouses flashed by, beyond them the round blue arc of water—"What's that?" I asked the driver, and he looked at me, surprised, and said, "The Sound," as if I should have known—and then we were approaching a tiny cluster of skyscrapers. Next to New York this city looked like a dollhouse. The driver dropped me off at the ferry terminal, and I made my way across a broad-planked boardwalk to the ugly white building where he'd told me to buy my ticket. The air smelled salty and clean, and the breeze off the water carried with it the high keening calls of gulls.

I stood on the front deck of the ferry as it chugged away from the dock and out across the Sound, the damp cool wind tugging at my clothes and knotting my hair into salty tangles. Tourists photographed each other all around me, but I did not feel like a tourist; I felt in some strange way as though I had come home, although I had never been here or anywhere like it and could not have previously imagined that a place like this existed. Off on the horizon more mountains made a ragged line against the sky.

"Nice view, isn't it?" someone said next to me, and I put up my best New York wall, expecting another pest like the skirted man at the airport. The speaker was a white woman, tanned so dark I was pale in comparison, her yellow hair clumped into uneven dreadlocks. She wore a shapeless corduroy skirt and a Grateful Dead shirt several sizes too large for her. "Look," she said, leaning on the railing and pointing out across the water. I followed her finger and gasped aloud in spite of myself at the sleek black shapes moving through the waves. "Orcas," she said, in response to the question I hadn't asked. "Whole pod out there." I watched the sinuous curves of the whales' backs as they breached and dove again, their acrobatics punctuated with bursts of spray, their slick dorsal fins making sharp triangles against the blue of the water. The whales were moving away from the ferry, fast and graceful, and their silhouettes faded into the distance until I could no longer make them out.

"You're not from here," she said; it wasn't a question.

"No," I said, irritated.

"Visiting family?"

"Maybe."

"Maybe?"

I almost told her to mind her own business, and then I remembered that all I had were a vague set of directions to my destination in Mr. M's elegant scrawl—something about a bus, after the ferry, and a series of transfers, and then I'd have to find a taxi once I got to Jack's town. My destination seemed very close all at once, and I had no clearer an idea of how to get there than I'd had when I got on the plane that morning. "Do you know anything about the bus?" I asked instead. "To the peninsula?"

"Where are you trying to go?" I told her. "I live out there," she said casually. "Happy to give you a ride." She caught my expression and laughed. "All the serial killers stick to the I-5 Corridor; you're safe out this way," she said. "I can show you the bus stop on the other side, if you want, but it'll take you four hours to get there instead of one and a half. I'm happy to drop you off wherever you're going in town."

Her hand brushed mine, casual but deliberate, and a shock went through me as though I'd stuck my finger in a light socket—whole world tilting, white flash—a glimpse of that girl again, the dark-haired girl from my dream, the dog howling, the white trees—"We've been waiting for you," the woman hissed, in a rough low voice that went through me and through me—I jerked my hand away, and the world went back to ordinary.

"What?" I gasped.

"We wait the whole year for tourist season," she said, her voice normal again and her words light. "And then we complain about it the whole summer. You don't look like much of a tourist, though. Anyway, it's no trouble to give you a ride." *Go home,* wailed the voice in my head, *get on the ferry going back the second this one lands on the other side, go home, go home.* I scowled.

"Sure," I said. "A ride would be great."

"Hekate," she said, sticking out her hand, "but most people call me Kate, these days."

"Your parents, too?" I asked her, and unexpectedly she threw back her head and laughed out loud.

"You could say that," she said, still chuckling. I had no idea what was so funny.

"Tally," I said. "Short for Atalanta. But nobody calls me that." I eyeballed her outstretched hand and took it gingerly, but whatever had happened the first time she'd touched me didn't happen again, and I told myself I must've imagined it—*You most certainly did not imagine it*—and the sleepless night had gone to my head. The rest of the crossing was uneventful; when the boat docked, the passengers filed off it and down a wooden walkway that led to a tiny terminal. I followed Kate out to the parking lot, where an enormous dust-covered pickup awaited us. She opened the door for me, and I clambered inside, moving a tattered Tom Robbins paperback and piles of wilting herbs off the front seat. "Sorry," she said, without helping me. "Meant to hang those up to dry before I left town, but the day got away from me."

There were a thousand questions I could have asked her, but I didn't know where to start, and so I left them all buzzing in my mouth like bees battering a windowpane. We drove for a long time along winding roads through thick woods, sunlight spattering down to land patchily all around us. The trees were enormous and very green and in some places drew so close to the road that it seemed as though we were hurtling through a dim emerald tunnel. We came out abruptly into the blue day, onto a long low bridge resting directly on an expanse of water. I made a happy noise, and Kate looked over at me and grinned. "Hood Canal Bridge," she said. "Third-longest floating bridge in the world. Sank right into the water in 1979. We're crossing over to the peninsula. Not much like this in New York, I'll bet."

"We have a lot of bridges, but it's not the same," I said. (Thinking: the Q across the river, steely glitter of skyscrapers catching the afternoon light, broad ribbon of water below striped white with the wakes of dozens of boats, as far away from this stretch of sky and sea as the Ganges, or the Amazon.) The metal grating of the bridge deck thumped like a metronome under her truck's wheels. On one side of the bridge the water moved choppily; on the other, it was flat and densely silver as mercury, rising and falling in voluptuous movements as if it were breathing. A wooded shore stretched along the far edge of the indigo water, dotted here and there with grey and black specks that must have been houses. "It's beautiful," I added, unnecessarily.

"Yep," she said. "Although if you're ever here in the winter, you might change your mind."

"It stops being beautiful?"

"You can't see shit for all the rain nine months out of the year. You came at the right time. Listen, I can give you a ride wherever you're going, but when we get into town I'll have to stop at work for a bit—I need to open up the bar before the evening bartender comes in."

"I can get a cab," I said. She laughed.

"Maybe," she said. "If he isn't drunk. Where you staying, anyway? You have family in town?"

"Friend," I said cautiously. "Old musician my—" I stalled on the word. "My mother knew. She used to live in LA."

"You mean Jack?"

I looked at her in surprise. "How'd you know?"

"It's a small town."

"How do you know Jack?"

"Everyone knows Jack. I'm just the only person he talks to."

"Oh," I said. There was a silence. "And you, um, work in a bar?"

"I own the bar."

"Which bar?" As if I'd know.

"It's the only bar."

"Oh," I said again. If she was curious why I was visiting Jack, she did not ask. Was she Jack's girlfriend? She wasn't at all pretty, but she looked competent. The muscles in her forearms rippled as she steered, and underneath the ugly clothes she was solid and strong. She looked like someone you would want with you on an expedition to the Arctic. Maybe if Jack had been in love with Aurora he'd decided to move on to a more sensible model. I could hardly blame him. Aurora herself had elected to leave me with a fitter candidate.

After the bridge the road climbed again, into trees and more trees, and then a sprawling valley checkered with farmland, and then more trees. All the extraneous trees of the world seemed to have been gathered here for safekeeping. I wondered if I'd be able to see the sky at all, when we got where we were going; it would be a shame to be all the way out here, a hundred miles from anything like a city, and have all that blessed darkness obscured by a stupid branch. We drove through another green tunnel until the trees opened up to an ugly stretch of road—shabby gas station, dispirited-looking convenience store, my heart sinking in disappointment. (Was this *it*? Why on earth had Jack come *here*?). Then we came around a corner, and I inhaled sharply.

We'd crested a tall hill that spilled downward into what looked like the edge of the world—a tiny strip of town, old red-brick buildings, and past them more blue: blue water, blue sky, blue mountains in the blue distance. It looked like a movie set, not a real place.

"That's the downtown," Kate said. "I'll take you the long way—the bar's down there, but you might as well see a few of the sights first." She turned left off the main road and made a confusing series of turns—more hills, more trees, more long windy stretches. Wooden houses in a row. A field strewn about with tall, jagged-leaved flowers—"Opium poppies, they grow like weeds around here; come September half the town's stoned out of its mind," she said—and a big lagoon. A cemetery with white headstones in perfect lines.

"That's the Fort up there," she said, pointing from a four-way intersection at a big hill that rose behind a huge field lined with Victorian houses.

"Fort?"

"Used to be a military base, up until the end of World War Two. Lot of bored soldiers hanging out with cannons in the bunkers, waiting for somebody to try to attack Seattle. Nobody ever did. It's been a park since the fifties."

"It's pretty."

"Those houses are the old officer's quarters. Up on that hill are all the abandoned bunkers. They have conferences and that kind of thing in the Fort itself and rent out the houses, but the hill's all wild. Some kids broke into the old dance hall on the hill and put on a production of *Marat/Sade* last summer. Cut a hole through the floor and smuggled everybody in at midnight and lit it with candles. They even got a bathtub in there somehow."

"Bathtub?"

"For Marat. Stabbed in the tub? You don't know the story? It's very Greek."

I was not sure if she was telling me this anecdote to illustrate the intrepid nature of the local youth or their level of boredom. "That sounds interesting," I said neutrally. A car honked behind us and Kate waved apologetically and moved forward through the intersection.

How was this place even *real*? How had no one discovered it? "Oh, they've discovered it all right," Kate said, though

I hadn't said anything out loud. "Million retirees moving up from California, buying up all the real estate and sending the prices sky-high. And the whole town depends on tourism. Back in the day it was just a half-dead old mill town—mill's still here—and a handful of people moved out here to grow weed in the woods and live off the land. But now—" She shrugged, in a manner that was apparently meant to convey the entire weight of the town's present tragedies, whatever they might be. I nodded as if I understood and wondered again how the hell Jack had ended up out here.

We'd come to the miniature downtown: a few blocks of pretty old buildings and a gull-dotted wharf. Kate parked her truck and I followed as she unlocked the front door of a building on the water side of the street. Her bar was dimly lit and lovely—I'd been imagining a scraggly dive, but the walls were paneled wood and the long polished bar was wood, too, with a mirror and shelves of liquor bottles behind it like an old-fashioned saloon. The floorboards were broad and ancient. "They don't make 'em like that anymore," Kate said. I was getting tired of her uncanny habit of reading my thoughts. I wandered the bar's length. It ended in a room just big enough for a few booths and a pool table. A glass door led to a balcony that hung out over the water.

"You want anything to eat?" Kate asked from behind the bar, where she was busying herself polishing glasses and counting through liquor bottles. I thought of my tiny stash of cash, already depleted by the taxi to the ferry. "Don't worry about it. On me."

"You don't have to do all this."

She shrugged. "Can't have you starving on my watch, city

mouse. You get too skinny and the coyotes'll drag you off into the woods."

"Coyotes?"

"Big old things. Like wolves, but meaner. They eat people." I stared at her, and she laughed. "Joking, city mouse. Joking."

"They don't eat people?"

"They don't come *near* people. Lots of 'em in the woods around here, though. They do eat cats. And other pets that leave their good sense at home." I thought of Dorian Gray, masticated in the jaws of a ravening wolflike creature, and winced. I sat at one of the bar stools—handsome, leather capped and ringed in brass, heavy and solid—and watched Kate as she bustled about the bar, engaged in various preparatory activities. She disappeared for a while through a set of swinging doors and came back with a hamburger on a white china plate, ringed with a pile of fries.

"Whoa," I said, "you don't have to—"

"Hush," she said. "Ketchup?"

"Yes, please." It was three hours later in New York—Henri and Raoul would have come home by now and seen my note. I thought, *I should call them.* Kate met my eyes.

"Eat up," she said.

*I should—I should—*I shook my head. There was something I needed to do, but I couldn't remember what it was and the hamburger looked amazing, so rare it was almost bloody—"I like it when they're still calling for their mothers," I said happily.

"I had a feeling," she said. I ate my hamburger slowly, savoring each bite. A few people straggled into the bar; none of them so much as glanced at me, and I was relieved, for the moment at least, to be anonymous. The bar door swung open again, bringing with it a sudden heady smell—something wild and sweet, like the dried lavender Aunt Beast sometimes hung up in our apartment in the summer—and a skinny black-clad figure stalked past me, taking a stool a few seats down and slapping a pack of cigarettes down on the bar. Gnawing on a fry, I examined the new arrival.

It was a girl. Not much older than me, from the look of her. She was dressed in tight black jeans, more patch than denim, and a faded black T-shirt, three sizes too big for her and slipping off one shoulder. She kicked at the brass railing at the bar's base with feet shod in decaying black sneakers. She wore no makeup, save for perfect stripes of black eyeliner that extended in matching upward flicks at the outside corners of her eyes; her knuckles were streaked with dirt; and her bare forearms were alive with black tattoos—a crow in flight, an old-fashioned schooner with its sails unfurled, a compass, a constellation I didn't recognize—and crisscrossed with pale scars that stood out sharply against her dark skin. A tangle of black-dyed hair rioted down her back in a serpentine mass. Despite her state of dishabille, she held herself like someone who was used to being paid court. "That's Maddy," Kate said, jerking her chin toward the girl, and the girl lifted her lovely fox-sharp face toward me, and I saw the most striking of all her remarkable features: her immense, hypnotic, lion-colored eyes.

"Did you want to take a picture?" she asked drily. Her voice was low and rough, the voice of someone much older than she looked, and there was something at the back of it that made me think she had grown up speaking a language other than English, although I could not have begun to guess which one. Her yellow eyes gleamed with amusement, and all at once I felt shabby and young.

Flustered, I looked back down at my fries. "Sorry," I mumbled. "Hi." Without being asked, Kate got a bottle of whisky off one of the shelves behind the bar and poured a drink, set it in front of the girl.

"You want a beer?" she asked me.

"I'm not twenty-one."

"So I gathered," Kate said.

"I don't—no, thank you."

Kate shrugged. "Up to you, city mouse." Maddy tilted her head back and finished her drink in one swallow, thumped the empty glass down on the bar, and pointed at it. Kate refilled it, and she drank that, too. Kate refilled her glass for a third time; Maddy pulled a cigarette out of her pack (Lucky Strikes, Aunt Beast's brand), lit it, blew a long satisfied plume of smoke at the ceiling, and sipped her third whisky daintily. I was staring again and so I looked at Kate instead, who was watching me with an expression I could not read.

The door swung open again, admitting a pretty girl with black hair cut to her chin, big eyes, and what Aunt Beast would have called enviable assets. She trotted past me without so much a glance in my or Maddy's direction and slid behind the bar. "Cristina," Kate said, "can you hold down the fort for half an hour or so? I need to give this girl"—she tilted her head at me—"a ride. And *you*"—this to Maddy—"behave yourself." Maddy, in the midst of lighting another cigarette, looked up, yellow eyes narrowed. Behind Kate's back, Cristina rolled her eyes, and a grin flickered across

Maddy's face. I got my bag as Kate came around the bar, half-turning as I followed her out the door.

"Nice to meet you," I said, but if Maddy heard me, she didn't acknowledge it. Cristina was already getting down the bottle of whisky as Maddy held out her glass.

Kate drove us in silence, back past the fort she'd showed me earlier, the blue lagoon, the fields of poppies. We turned, and turned again, and I soon lost track of what direction we were headed in.

"That girl," I said. "Maddy. Who was that?"

"Trouble," Kate said curtly. I flushed. "I've known her for a long time," Kate added, her voice softer. "I try to look out for her, not that I do much good."

"She's from here?"

"No."

"Are you?"

"No." I opened my mouth to ask another question, but I could not think of what I had meant to say. There was a faint buzzing in my ear, like a distant beehive, and I knocked the side of my head gently with one fist. We turned again, onto a long gravel road, rattling around in the truck so that I would have slid into her if I hadn't been wearing a seat belt, and then we stopped. We had arrived at a wide green clearing, ringed with trees; at the far edge stood a modern one-story white house with plenty of big windows and a garden off to one side. Behind all of this was a stretch of twilit sky where the stars were already coming to life. Kate turned off the truck, and I got out.

I had come all this way and now did not know what to do with myself; was struck with the intense and sudden conviction that I had reached the apotheosis of the worst idea of my life. I walked out to the sharp green line at the edge of Jack's yard, where the grass yielded to sky, with some thought of collecting myself, but then I looked down and took a step back, reeling. Jack's yard ended in a cliff, its muddy brown face a sheer drop down to the rocky line of the beach so far below me that the breakers crashing on the shore looked as though they had been rendered in miniature. "Careful," Kate yelled from the truck. I took another step back and turned; she'd gotten my bag out of the truck and was walking toward me. "Don't fall off, city mouse. Nothing left of you by the time you get to the bottom."

"There's no *railing*," I said, and she laughed.

"That's not how we do things out here," she said. She carried my bag to Jack's front door and I followed her, my heart thumping. My anxiety must have been obvious; she gave me a kindly pat on the shoulder. "He doesn't know you're coming, does he?"

"Not technically, no."

"He doesn't bite," she said, almost gently. She reached past me and rapped on the door before I could stop her. After a moment, it opened, and I had to tilt my head up to look at the man who stood in front of me.

He was not handsome in the ordinary, catalog-model sense of the word; he was tall and spare-framed to the point of being nearly gaunt, but his face was striking in the sharpness of its features and the severity of its angles. If I had not known already that this Jack and the man in Mr. M's picture were the same person, I never would have guessed it; that Jack, like this one, was lean and graceful, but that Jack had had, despite the melancholy look in his eyes, a young man's face, and this Jack had the cast of someone wiser and sadder and much older than the intervening decades alone would suggest. That Jack's hair had been long and black, and this Jack's thick, silvering curls were cut close to his skull. His dark eyes were marked with fine lines at their corners, and his forehead was creased in a way that suggested he did not often smile.

But if he had been—or was still—prone to the various excesses of vice said to be particular to rock stars, they had left him otherwise unscathed. He had none of the aging libertine about him. He looked hard and stern, like a fisherman, or a soldier, someone who had spent all his life in repetitive, efficient action. If there was any trace of my own features in the slope of his jaw or the high planes of his cheekbones, those similarities did not give themselves up upon first examination. And it seemed unlikely that someone so dark-skinned would produce someone as pale as me, but my grandfather had been white as a mushroom, and genetics is still a science largely marked by mystery and guesswork. It occurred to me for the first time that I would have benefited considerably from preparing some introductory remarks. Where *had* my brain gone this summer? What was I *thinking*, coming here; how on earth had I ended up on the doorstep of a total stranger, escorted by a bizarre mind-reading hippie I'd known for all of two hours? "Um, hi," I said. "I probably should have called first. But I think you knew—I mean, I know you knew—my—" I could not say the word. "Aurora."

"Aurora," he repeated. His voice was deep, and raspy, as if he did not speak aloud often. He looked at Kate, who remained silent, and then back at me again.

"She was my—she, um, had me. Like, birth." His face was

blank. I sallied forth in the face of his terrifying indifference. "I'm Tally—I know this is unorthodox, but I came a long way and I was hoping to—I thought maybe I could ask you a few questions."

"How did you get here?"

"I found her on the ferry," Kate said. "Take good care of her, understand?" She was looking at Jack with an unnerving intensity; I almost took a step back myself. But he stared her down without flinching, and she shrugged and looked away first. "I have to get back to work now. Come find me at the bar if you need anything." I watched stupidly as she marched back to her truck.

"Thanks!" I yelled after her as an afterthought, but she didn't turn around or acknowledge that she'd heard me. The truck roared to life and she was gone. I took a deep breath. "I was hoping—" I faltered; his expression made me want to crawl under a rock. "Kate said that you wouldn't mind." Kate had said nothing of the sort. If Jack threw me off his doorstep—and I would hardly have blamed him if he did—I was stuck in the middle of the woods, at night, in a place I knew nothing about, with no recourse whatsoever.

"Kate," he said, and his tone was dangerous. He looked at me for the length of another excruciating silence, and then he sighed. "Fine," he said. "Come in."

I followed him into a big open white-walled room whose windows looked out over the water. Huge wooden beams held up the high ceiling, and the floor was made of rough storm-colored stone. It was furnished with a kind of elegant carelessness: a rectangular wooden table that could have comfortably seated twenty people, piled high with books and sheet music and instruments in varying states of string-sprung disrepair; a big low couch, upholstered in desert-hued patterns that made me think of Raoul's Pendleton blanket, littered with beautiful old kilim pillows; a wall of floor-to-ceiling bookshelves opposite the bank of windows, crammed to bursting with more books and papers and here and there gourds and stone statues and smaller, more obscure items that might have been instruments or totems or artifacts of some mysterious and ancient religion. It was the house of someone with a tremendous amount of money and good taste and no inclination to impress visitors; everything in it had been bought for a purpose that was utilitarian, not decorative, despite most of the objects' inherent beauty. The room seemed like an extension of the person in front of me, who was already moving away, arranging a pile of papers on the big table, adjusting a battered old violin where it rested on a chair, drawing the curtains—I almost told him not to, I was so longing to see the stars, but of course it was his house. I had no idea what to say to him. If I had hoped for some teary and melodramatic confession of paternity at the sight of me, a warm and welcoming embrace, impassioned pleas for forgiveness, my hopes should have been dashed against the rocky shore far below us.

"You live in town?" he asked.

"Not exactly," I said. "I came from New York."

"You came from New York *City*? Here? Why?"

"I never met Aurora," I said in a rush. "She ran off, or something, she left me right after I was born, and all this time I never cared, but I'm going to college in a couple of months, and I thought—I mean, it seemed like something to sort out, before I leave. Who she is. And I thought you knew her, and I guess I just . . ." I trailed off. "I just came,"

I finished, "here. To ask you. About her. You *did* know her? That's why you're still talking to me?"

"I knew her," he said. "A long time ago, and not well. How did you find me?"

I opened my mouth to tell him about Mr. M, and my thoughts went staticky again; there was something wrong with the connection between my brain and my tongue. "A—friend," I said. "My friend. Who's your old friend, I think. He looked you up." This sounded absurd as soon as I said it.

"I don't have any friends." There was a dark hum in the air between us, something thick and strange; I thought of Kate's owl stare and Maddy's yellow one, and for some reason Mr. M's own eerie black gaze—his eyes were so dark you could not distinguish between iris and pupil, and it gave him an uncanny look. I made a helpless gesture with one hand. Jack shook his head as if he were trying to dislodge a mosquito.

"I can't imagine why you came all the way out here. I don't have anything to tell you about Aurora." He would not meet my eyes. *You're lying,* I thought. *You're lying, and you know I know you're lying.* I found that I could think clearly again; the air was less odd. I was, more than anything, exhausted. I yawned.

"Where are you staying?"

"I hadn't gotten that far."

"How long are you planning on being here for?"

"I don't know."

He raised one eyebrow. "Your—family? You have one? They know you're here?"

"Of course I have a family," I said, indignant. "And yes. They know. I mean, they will know. When I call them."

He rubbed his forehead with the heel of his hand. "Well," he said. "It's too late to send you packing, and your ride seems to have abandoned you. You can spend the night here, I suppose. And we'll figure out what to do with you in the morning."

"That's very nice of you," I said. "Thank you."

"Are you hungry?"

"Kate gave me a hamburger."

"At least she's good for something," he said. Not his girl-friend, then.

"How do you know her?"

"I've known her for a long time. Look, we can—talk—in the morning. You look tired."

"Kind of," I conceded.

He did not waste any more time on small talk; he pointed me down a wide hallway that led past a kitchen—as beautiful and well appointed as the main room of the house, all gleaming stainless-steel surfaces and burnished copper pots hanging from a wrought-iron rack over a butcher-block counter—several doors in a row that were shut tightly; and finally, another heavy wooden door, this one open, to a small room overlooking the sprawling tangle of Jack's garden. Under the window, a twin bed, neatly made up with a soft patterned grey blanket; against one wall, an old oak chest of drawers; and another door that proved to be a bathroom. A skylight framed a patch of night sky. It was a lovelier room by far than my own beloved but faintly shabby bed-room in Brooklyn, with its familiar but uninspiring view of the side of the neighboring brownstone and its mismatched furniture.

I had never before given much thought to the acquisition and deployment of nice things; Aunt Beast would have been as content with an old barstool as an Eames chair, and Raoul and Henri, though they both loved to brighten the apartment with fresh flowers and were forever bringing home paintings or pretty throw rugs or other small, jewel-like accouterments that made our house the cheery, welcoming nest of disorder that it was, would never have spent real money on something so trivial as furniture. But Jack's house had a cool grace to it that made me feel both envious and awed. I was no stranger to the homes of rich people; it wasn't just money that made this place what it was. It was him. I wondered, with a sudden, delicious thrill, how many stars I would be able to see through the skylight. And of course, there was the whole out-of-doors to make into my observatory. No light pollution here. Assuming Jack let me stay here after tonight, which was assuming a lot.

"Sleep well," he said, and then he was gone.

"Thanks," I said to the closing door.

I set my bag on the floor and dug out the binoculars, and then a wave of exhaustion ran through me, so debilitating that it knocked me onto the bed, and I lay on my back like an upended beetle, staring up at Jack's ceiling. I thought of Raoul and Henri and Aunt Beast, but there was no phone in the room and it seemed a tremendous feat to get back up again and go out into Jack's house in search of one. *I've known her for a long time*—that was what Kate had said about Maddy, too; had they all known—I would just rest for a moment, and then I would take my binoculars outside and survey the constellations—I'd be able to see so much out here—and then I'd find a phone—and then sleep fell over me like a blanket, and all my thoughts ended there.

I woke up to the smell of coffee. *Henri,* I thought, *Henri made me coffee,* and I opened my eyes. The light in my room was not right—too clear and too insistent, and not hot enough. The blue square of sky overhead was all wrong, too, and I turned my head to the window—wash of green, blue water— what had happened to the apartment building next door? *You're not home, you idiot,* said the voice, and then the day before came back to me. I sat up in Jack's guest bed, blinking stupidly, and reached for my clothes, before I remembered I'd fallen asleep in them.

I made my way into Jack's kitchen—I hadn't even taken my *shoes* off the night before—in search of the coffee smell's source, and of Jack. I found the former in a pot, next to a note written, presumably, by the latter:

> *Tally,*
> *Will be on the boat all day.* [The boat? What boat?] *My apologies. Dinner? We can talk then. Stay as long as you like. Bike in the shed behind the house if you want to go downtown. Don't worry about lock, no one will take it.*
> *—J*

I drank my coffee. Jack had said *stay,* but not *pillage the refrigerator,* and anyway I found upon inspection that its contents—a lone jar of hot sauce, a single pickle bobbing forlornly in a jar of brine, the moldy end of a loaf of bread—did not inspire much in the way of breakfasty thoughts. Hopefully he was better at dinner.

The shed was easy to find, half-hidden in the woods behind Jack's garden, which was a tangle of some giant flower I did not recognize: stalks almost as tall as I was, and blossoms of densely packed petals curled into vivid orange and pink tubes. I made a mental note to ask him about them later. The last bits of morning fog were drifting off the grass in sinuous grey tendrils. Unlike his house, the shed was a chaotic nest of grubby disorder: cobwebs thickly netted a tangle of rakes and hoes, and rusty chunks of ancient machinery whose original purpose was undeterminable were half-obscured by a carpet of grey dust. Jack's bike, resting precariously against something that looked like it might once have been a lawnmower, was in better shape. It was too big for me, but after a brief search I found a screwdriver on a workbench, next to a fat black spider that waved one leg at me jauntily before scurrying off, and with some effort lowered the bike's seat to a manageable height.

I more or less remembered the turns Kate had taken the evening before to get out to Jack's house. As long as I headed downhill, I didn't think I could get too far off course. I did not relish the thought of the return trip. I'd been accompanying Aunt Beast for years on her regular laps of Prospect Park—recently, I'd even gotten fast enough to keep up with her, though, despite my namesake, I'd never win any races. But the faint sloping grade of the park road did not come close to the perilous inclines that led to Jack's.

After I'd managed the jarring ordeal of the pothole-laced gravel road, the descent was a delight—flying headlong down hills with the clean summer all around me, fields and salt breezes and a startled, fat old dog that barked laboriously at me from a front yard where it was sunning itself. The main part of town was easy to find. At the far end of the main street was a smallish marina I hadn't noticed the day before and a quaint motel advertising free cable and water views. I straddled the bike and watched sailboats bob in the harbor for a minute before turning around for a closer inspection of downtown.

I had no interest in Victorian antiques, stuffed toy rabbits in a variety of costumes, saltwater taffy, or a 1950s-themed diner whose miserable-looking employees were visible through the window sullenly delivering milkshakes to cabbage-white tourists in visors and garish Hawaiian-print button-downs. On my second pass of the street I discovered a used bookstore tucked between a jewelry store and a boutique offering striped socks, postcards, T-shirts sporting various epigrams on the pleasures of fishing, and scandalous lingerie. A wooden sign in the window bearing the moniker MELVILLE & CO. rested atop a pile of yellowed books. Inside, the store was a jumble; the overstuffed shelves, labeled with hand-lettered signs in crabbed script, had spilled over into teetering stacks of books piled haphazardly on the floor, and the front windows were so obscured by more stacks of books that only a thin slice of sunlight made its way through to illuminate the shop. A middle-aged white gentleman with disordered brown hair and round spectacles sat behind an oak table piled with even more books and did not look up as I came in. It was the sort of place I wanted to bottle and send to Raoul. *Raoul.* I hadn't called them. I would call them later.

I poked happily amidst the stacks, careful not to upset

them. But if I was going to be here a while—how long *was* I going to be here? At least a few days?—it would not do to uncover all the bookstore's secrets on my first visit. Kate's bar was downtown, but I couldn't remember exactly where, and had missed it on my compass of the main street. I had nothing else to do, and anyway maybe she'd have something to tell me about why Jack had vanished into the ether the moment I arrived. I was not thinking about Maddy. I was *not*. I made my way back up to the proprietor's desk.

"Excuse me—do you know where Kate's bar is?" He looked up at me at last, and although his manner was curt, his eyes were friendly, and I found myself liking him immediately. He reminded me a little of Mr. M.

"Scylla and Charybdis, you mean?"

"What?"

"It's called Scylla and Charybdis."

"What on earth is that?"

He lowered his spectacles and looked over them at me with a despondent expression. "What in god's name do they teach young people these days? Nothing at all? Scylla and Charybdis were two extremely unlucky ladies." He got up and disappeared behind a shelf, and I heard him rummaging around for a moment before he emerged holding a decrepit paperback with its front cover missing and several of its pages on the verge of falling out. "With my compliments," he said, handing it to me. "The knowledge that I am lessening the weight of ignorance in the world will be payment enough." I looked at the title page, yellowed and torn: Ovid's *Metamorphoses*.

"My uncle is always telling me to read this," I said. "But

to tell you the truth, I mostly read science fiction and books about physics. I don't like poetry."

"That's like saying you don't like food, or are inconvenienced by breathing," he said, unperturbed, "but you are a child, and so have some small excuse for your idiocy."

"I am not an idiot or a child," I said crossly. "I am eighteen years old and quite intelligent, and anyway that's an unpronounceable name for a bar."

"It doesn't matter. There's only one bar, and so no one has to pronounce it."

"Fine," I said. Aware I was being ungracious, I made an effort to curb my temper. "Thanks."

"You're welcome. The bar is across the street. Surprised you missed it," he said, and returned to his book. Thus dismissed, I went back out into the blazing sunlight.

While I was in the bookstore, an enormous tawny dog with an inky muzzle had draped itself languorously across the stone steps of Kate's bar. "That's Qantaqa," Kate yelled from inside as my shadow fell across the doorway. "Just kick her out of the way and come on in."

"Get," I said uncertainly to the dog, who weighed as least half as much as I did. It looked up at me and yawned.

"Qantaqa!" Kate bellowed. "Get on out of the way, you fat-ass!"

The dog got to its feet with the injured dignity of an old drunk and lumbered a couple of feet to the left, where it resettled itself with its chin on the steps and gazed up at me reproachfully. Going back into Kate's bar, in broad daylight, unaccompanied, made me unaccountably nervous, but perhaps being underage was something like being a vampire;

as long as Kate had invited me in, I ought to be welcome. I stepped past the dog and settled myself on a wooden stool. "Hi," I said to Kate. "That's a funny name for a dog." Maddy was nowhere to be seen, I noted, with a surge of disappointment.

"She went to buy cigarettes," Kate said and, unbidden, pushed a bottle of beer across the wooden bar toward me. I debated confessing what Aunt Beast referred to as my puritan streak ("Unnatural," she said, "in a growing girl, but at least it means I don't have to keep an eye on you") before deciding against it and taking a cautious sip, which I nearly spat out. If people drank this stuff for fun, I could not imagine why. The physicist George Gamow once noted that the quantum principle was not unlike a person being able to drink either a pint of beer or no beer at all, but entirely incapable of drinking any amount of beer in between zero beers and a pint. Kate did not seem like a person who would have much interest in this anecdote. I took another sip; the second one was not as bad as the first.

"How's Jack?" Kate asked. "You have your talk?"

"Absent," I said. "He went to bed right after you dropped me off and I didn't see him this morning." There was something I was supposed to remember about Jack, I thought, something that night—

"He's a hard one to pin down," Kate said. The door to the bar opened again and there she was—same black clothes, yellow eyes gleaming, Qantaqa surging to her feet like a physical manifestation of my own delight. "Down, you goof," she said gently, knuckling the dog—hers, obviously—behind the ears. Qantaqa subsided, remaining on the steps as Maddy slid onto a stool near me in a cloud of lavender-scented black hair, smacking the pack of cigarettes against her left hand. For all the shabby clothes, there was something about her that suggested grace that couldn't be unlearned; her back was as straight as a dancer's and she held her head high. Kate had already gotten down the bottle of whisky.

"Hi," I said.

"Hi," Maddy said. There was a silence. I stared at my beer bottle in a frenzy of anxiety. "It rains diamonds on Saturn," I blurted. Kate and Maddy both looked at me in astonishment.

"Does it," Kate said politely.

"Because of the lightning storms," I said. I had dug my hole; might as well keep going. "They turn methane into carbon and then it hardens in the atmospheric pressure. I mean, no one has seen them, obviously, it's just a theory, but it seems . . ." I trailed off. "It seems possible," I finished weakly. I took another drink of my beer.

"Imagine that," Maddy said. I thought at first that she was making fun of me, but her yellow eyes were clear and she'd tilted her head in my direction. There was something almost tendrilly about her voice, like the wisps of fog that had crept through Jack's yard that morning, something grey and breathing that slipped under my skin and wrapped ghostly fingers around my heart. I forced myself to look back at my beer; without noticing, I'd picked off most of the label in a fit of nervous energy. All I wanted was for her to keep talking to me.

"You and Kate know each other from the bar?" I asked.

"Oh, we go way back," Maddy said.

"Few thousand years," Kate said. Maddy shot her a

strange, incomprehensible look, and then smiled, but I thought, *She doesn't know what that means, either.*

Some tourists entered in a noisy babble; I didn't have to be from here to recognize what they were immediately. Tourists are the same the world over; I could imagine these exact people, in these exact clothes, shrieking with laughter and photographing themselves going through the subway turnstiles in Union Square at rush hour while people clotted up behind them, apoplectic with rage. Kate was polite as she took their orders, but when she turned her back on them I saw her expression was tinged with menace.

"We're thinking of relocating here," the tourists' patriarch informed us.

"How nice for you," Kate said.

"It's so lovely," agreed his wife, spray-tanned a virulent pumpkin color, batting lashes mascaraed into unnerving spikes.

"This time of year," Kate agreed.

"The winters can't be so bad," said the patriarch. In startling contrast to his wife, he was pasty as a block of tofu, save a fluorescing patch of peeling sunburn that spread unevenly across his cheeks; it was not hard to imagine him clammy to the touch.

"No," echoed his wife. "Not so bad. What's a little rain? Forty or fifty degrees sounds downright balmy." She giggled.

"The winters here have destroyed far better men than you," Maddy said in a conversational tone. The patriarch looked at her, puzzled. I hid a smile behind my hand.

"Sure," he said. "I bet you're right. I bet we'd just love it here." The tourists collected their beers, eyeing Maddy nervously, and transported them to a table by the windows overlooking the water.

"Dipshits," Kate said under her breath. "Can't shoot 'em, can't stay in business without 'em. It's enough to make me take up secretarial work in the city."

"Is it really that bad here in the winter?" I asked when I was sure the tourists were out of earshot.

"It's like living with a rain cloud ten feet above your head," Kate said. "It gets dark at four. It's so damp everything molds. The wind comes in off the water and freezes you straight through. The only colors you'll see are fog and wet tree. For nine months solid."

"It can't be as bad as where I'm from," I said. "We have blizzards. It gets down to ten or twenty degrees sometimes. If you spend the night outside without a coat it can kill you."

"What we have out here," Kate said, "is despair, which is a different thing than cold, and a much slower and more miserable death."

"The reason Kate does so well," Maddy said, "is that everyone who lives in this town year-round is an alcoholic. Where are you from?"

"New York," I said. "How about you?"

"A lot farther than that," she said. I waited, but that was apparently the closest I was going to get to an answer. If she was curious what I was doing there, she didn't ask, and I didn't feel like offering. There was something about her that was as unsettling as it was compelling; those eyes, that face, the way she moved, like an animal that had been in a cage too long. I couldn't stop looking at her, but she did not seem to have anything else to say—had lost interest in me altogether, as far as I could tell. She lit a cigarette and looked out the window, away from me.

"Want another one?" Kate asked, nodding toward my bottle, which I had emptied without noticing.

"No," I said, "thank you." I had no excuse left for sitting at her bar, so I got up. I dug in my pocket for my wallet, but she shook her head.

"On the house," she said. "Welcome to the country, city mouse."

"Thanks," I said again. Everyone I came across seemed committed to giving me things for free; I could not imagine anything more unlike New York. Maddy did not say goodbye—did not so much as look up—when I left, and I did not like how this fact made me feel. I had had just about enough feelings for the rest of my life. The beer had made me stupid, but I found I did not mind.

I wasn't ready for the silent loneliness of Jack's house, and so I wheeled his bike to where the main street dead-ended into the harbor, leaned it up against a telephone pole—so far, he'd been right about no one trying to steal it—and walked down a narrow, sandy path through sharp-bladed grass that came to my knees in green spears.

The beach here was alive with unexpected things, nothing like the syringe-strewn and admittedly filthy sands of Coney Island, where Aunt Beast had taken me to ride the Cyclone and eat cotton candy in the summers when I was small, and where Shane and I would sometimes go when we were older with pilfered beer (for him) and Dr Pepper (for me) to bake ourselves in the hammering July sun. Drifts of seaweed were heaped up and down the shoreline, miniature clouds of bugs humming over them and hopping madly on various bug errands. I was alarmed by some slick emerald-green animal I didn't recognize, long and skinny and snake-like, and jumped back in fright; but it didn't move as I got closer, and I thought it must be dead. I turned over a rock and a tiny crab, no bigger than my thumbnail, brandished its miniature pincers at me before scuttling away to safety.

When I tired of adventuring amidst the flora and fauna I sat on the beach and looked at the distant mountains, all a purple smear save a single white-sided peak that stood taller than its fellows—the mountain I'd seen from the plane? But no, the direction was wrong, and that one had been even bigger. It had begun to occur to me that the objects we were accustomed to referring to as "mountains" on the east coast much more closely resembled large hills, and that "forest" had something of a different definition in this part of the country as well. I caught a flicker of movement out of the corner of my eye and looked up, expecting another beachcomber; instead, it was a deer and her tiny, drunken-legged fawn, spotted white and stumbling along at its moth-er's heels as though it had just learned to walk the day before. I sat forward to see them better and both deer turned to look at me, the doe calm, the fawn wide-eyed and panicked. It scampered after its mother, who sauntered away from me in a desultory manner, nibbling at a low-hanging branch before picking her way daintily back into a stand of trees that grew down to the stony shore. The fawn, with one last look in my direction, huge ears flicking back and forth, leapt after her with an endearing, inept lurch.

The back tire of Jack's bicycle had gone flat. I remem-bered the way to his house, at least—it would be a long walk, but not an unpleasant one, and I could do with the exercise. I didn't have much choice but to make the best of it. I wheeled the bike away from the businessy bits of town and back uphill, past houses with big, pretty gardens. Raoul would have loved all these flowers—*phone call*. I hadn't called them yet. "I'm sorry!" I said aloud, as if that would help. They were likely killing themselves with worry, no matter what sort of note I'd left them—even if I *was* eighteen—and then I thought, unbidden, of Maddy. Yellow-eyed girl and her yellow dog; the tangle of her hair; her brown hands on the bar—long slender fingers, knuckles dotted with white scars—and as if I'd summoned her with the force of my will, a truck pulled up next to me, big yellow dog with its head out the open window, yellow-eyed girl in the driver's seat, and I forgot all about calling my parents. "Hey," she said. "Need a ride?"

"Yeah," I said. "That would be great." *Keep it cool,* I thought, *keep it cool, keep it cool.* Her truck was, like Kate's, a battered old thing that looked as though someone had driven it to the moon and back again several times, at least once through a dust storm. I put my bike in the bed and climbed in the cab next to Qantaqa, who listed up against me happily, panting in my ear. Her breath was not pleasant; neither was Dorian Gray's, of course, but he had a lot less of it and a much smaller head besides. I found myself unaccountably panicky and wiped my sweaty palms on my shorts.

"He lives up on the bluffs," I said.

"Off Cook?"

"Yeah, I think so."

"It's pretty up there."

"It's kind of lonely," I said.

She looked over at me. "I live just on the edge of town," she said. "You're welcome to come over for dinner, if you want. I can give you a ride back afterward."

There was something I was supposed to do about dinner, but I couldn't remember what it was. It occurred to me that I hadn't eaten all day, and was in fact ravenous—another indication that something had gone wrong with my reasoning skills; I had never missed a meal in my life. "Sure," I said, hoping I did not sound as eager as I felt. "That would be great."

Maddy lived in a clearing at the end of a long dirt road through the thick woods at the outside edge of town. She parked and I got out, Qantaqa almost knocking me over as she leapt free from the truck. I stopped to admire Maddy's huge garden—neat rows of emerald-green chard with its rubine stalks, broad-leaved kale, something anise-smelling and wispy that must have been fennel. Onions and the cheery tops of carrots, broccoli and cabbages nestled close to the ground, a tidy line of butter lettuce and red-leaf lettuce and green lettuce. At the far end she'd planted a circular garden of herbs; I could pick out sage and rosemary and basil, but most of the rest I didn't recognize. "Wow," I said.

"It's easy to grow things out here."

"It's amazing."

"Thanks. My landlady lives through the woods," she said, pointing. "In a yurt."

"A what?"

"It's a thing out here. Sort of like a cross between a cabin and a tent. She's a witch. Not a good one."

"Like she's evil?"

"Like she's inept."

"Oh," I said, disappointed. "That's not as exciting."

"Be careful what you wish for," Maddy said. "Come on inside."

Her house was tiny and neat as a ship's cabin: a single small room with a miniature kitchen, a round table and two chairs, a bookshelf, and a loveseat with an old quilt thrown over it. In the far corner a wooden ladder led to a square hole in the ceiling. "You can look," she said. I half-climbed the ladder and poked my head into the second story, a loft whose ceiling slanted at the far end nearly to the floor. Her bed was just a mattress on the plank flooring, but it was tidily made with another quilt. Bunches of drying plants hung from the ceiling beams. Her house smelled like her— lavender and clean air off the water, with something headier underneath it; incense and sweat and girl. There were lanterns everywhere, old-fashioned ones with glass chimneys and bases full of lamp oil. There were no electric lights in her house, or outlets—did she live out here with no *electricity*? There wasn't a bathroom, either.

Downstairs, she'd put a big pot of water on the stove— which she lit with a match—to boil. "Pasta okay?" she asked. "I can use basil and tomatoes from the garden, and I have mozzarella from the farmer's market."

"That sounds amazing. This place is great. How long have you been here?"

"Oh, you poor hungry thing," she said to Qantaqa, who was lying on the floor making pained noises. "Has it been a thousand years since anyone fed you? Hold on," she said to me, "let me take care of the dog." She filled a bowl with kibble from a bucket next to the kitchen sink. Qantaqa whined eagerly, but she didn't eat until Maddy set the bowl on the floor and pointed to it. "Go pick some basil, why don't you, and a couple of tomatoes," Maddy said to me.

When I came back in from the garden she had the water boiling, and garlic cooking in a pan of butter on the stove. The kitchen was too small for me to be of much use, and so I curled up on her couch and watched her, humming to herself as she cooked. "Where's your bathroom?" I asked.

"Outhouse," she said. "Out behind the garden."

"A what?"

"Outhouse?" She turned around to look at me and whatever my expression was, it made her laugh out loud. "You better go before it gets dark."

Alarmed, I obeyed, but the outhouse—a half-moon carved in the wooden door, like something out of a pioneer movie—was not as traumatic as I feared. Back in her kitchen, she was spooning pasta and sauce into two bowls.

We ate outside, cross-legged in the grass, our knees almost touching but not quite. It was later than I had thought and the sun was sinking, the sky deepening into twilight. The pasta was delicious, the tomato sauce warm and tasting of summer, and with it cool slabs of mozzarella drizzled with olive oil and sprinkled with fresh basil. As I was finishing the last bit of my second bowl an unearthly howl echoed out from the woods behind her house, and I jumped. Qantaqa lifted her head, sniffing the air and whuffing softly, before resting her chin back on her paws.

"Coyotes," Maddy said. "There's a ravine back there where they spend their nights. When the moon is full the whole pack of them sets to singing; it's something else. You'll have to come back and hear them."

She was looking straight at me, but I didn't have the nerve

to meet her uncanny eyes. Whatever I'd thought I would find out here, it sure hadn't been this girl. "Sure," I said. "That would be—fun."

"A lot of old magic, out here," she said, still looking at me.

"Is that why you moved out here?"

"I moved out here to forget."

I did not know what to make of this. "I don't believe in magic."

"No? I wouldn't have guessed."

Was she teasing me? Flirting? I couldn't have begun to tell. "I like science," I said.

"Ah," she said, "a little Aristotle."

Now she was definitely making fun of me. "Aristarchus," I said, nettled, "more likely."

"You want to study the movement of the stars?"

I did not often come across people who knew who Aristarchus was. "More or less," I said.

"I see," she said. In the long shadows the tattoos on her arms flickered, the crows' wings shifting as though in flight. "You're here visiting family?"

"I don't know, exactly," I said. And though I had just met her I found myself telling her the whole story, leaving out the part about Shane: Mr. M, and the newspaper picture, and Jack, and Aurora, and what I was here for. She was quiet while I talked myself out, and when I was done, she stretched—me trying not to stare at the long graceful lines of her body—and leaned back on her elbows in the grass, one hand terrifyingly close to my thigh. I swallowed and looked up, anywhere but at her. There was Vega, springing to life against the twilight—though of course we imagine the stars' heat backwards; it's the blue stars that burn the hottest and most bright, and the cooling red giants who are nearing the end of their massive lives. To astronomers, stars don't look like stars at all; for all the time I'd spent memorizing constellations, the stories of stars' violent births and blazing deaths, when I got to the real work of astronomy I'd look not at the stars themselves but at the spectrographs that mapped the elements of their making, graph after graph and table after table—not at the heavens, but at the raw data of their hearts.

"You think he's your father?" I had no idea what she meant for a moment, and then I remembered what we'd been— I'd been—talking about, and flushed at the thought that I'd spilled out my whole history to this glorious girl I barely knew. She must have been bored senseless. With effort, I met her molten-gold gaze in the gathering dark, and realized she was waiting for my answer.

"I don't know. But it seems likely. He disappeared last night before I could ask him anything," I said. There was something else he had—"Oh *shit*," I said aloud. He had told me to meet him that night for dinner.

"What?"

"I keep forgetting things out here—I was supposed to have dinner with Jack."

"This is a strange place," she said.

"Strange how?" But she only shook her head, and that was all I got out of her; for a moment, in the setting sun, she had seemed, if not ordinary, at least approachable, but now the aloof wall was back up again.

We finished our dinner. She heated water on the stove and I did the dishes for her, acutely conscious of the warmth of her body as she stood behind me and dried them, the dizzying scent of her skin. I missed Shane, with an unexpected pang; I wondered what he would think of this half-feral girl, inscrutable and imperious and gorgeous, and then I wondered why I cared. He was the one who had bailed on me, after all, and here I was in her house, and if she had any interest in me I couldn't yet tell, but I knew I wanted to find out. She moved around the room, lighting her glass lanterns, but instead of brightening the cabin they seemed to bring darkness crawling out of the corners, and in their murky, dim glow her house took on an eldritch air. The shadows deepened and liquefied at the edges of the room and the walls dissolved—I was standing in the forest from my dream, white branches clacking in the hot night and the dog howling once, twice, three times—the girl just ahead of me again, moving too quickly for me to keep up, and her name was at the tip of my tongue but I could not remember it, could not remember anything; the darkness swallowed me up like a great mouth and something touched my shoulder, burning white-hot as a brand. I yelped aloud and jerked away from it, and the thick black night whirled upward around me like a tornado of wings—and then I was back in Maddy's house again, holding a clean plate and panicking. She was very close to me, one hand hovering over my shoulder, the tattoos on her forearms alive in the low light. The flames of her lanterns flickered in their glass chimneys and outlined the curve of her neck in liquid gold. She was so beautiful I did not know where to look. "I'm sorry," she said. My heart hammered in my chest.

"Where was I—what *was*—" But whatever had just happened to me, I was no longer sure I wanted to know. Her mouth was so near to mine that I would have had only to lean forward to kiss her. She took the plate from my hand and moved her dishtowel across it, and the moment was broken.

"Let me take you home," she said. I knew a dismissal when I heard one, and I followed her out to her truck.

On my way back into Jack's house I nearly tripped over a black bundle in his yard, and it was only the bobbing flicker of Maddy's headlights as she pulled away that caught out whatever it was before I kicked it. I knelt down in the grass for a closer look. It was a crow. Its eyes were dull and its beak gaped and it did not move away from me, and I knew immediately that it was dying. Around me the darkness rustled, and when I looked up I caught the glittering black eyes of a dozen of its kin, ringed around us in a half-circle and watching, alert. "Hold on," I said to them, "I won't hurt your friend." I ran into Jack's house and flipped open cabinets until I came up with a silver bowl and the bread I'd found that morning; I tore off a chunk of the least moldy end of the bread, filled the dish with water, and brought these offerings back out to the crow. It did not move as I knelt over it again, but looked up at me, unblinking. "You're much more attractive than a pigeon," I said, and then worried that I had offended it. *Look at you,* I thought, *only in the sticks for a day and already talking to birds.* The other crows, still in their formation, stared at me unnervingly. "I'll check on him in the morning," I said. "Her? Do crows go to the vet? I'm sorry your friend is sick." They seemed to be waiting for me to do something else. "I'll, uh, pray for him," I said, vaguely aware from books that this was a service one performed for the nearly deceased. "Her." The crows did not move when I went back inside. The house was dark and still, the only lights the one I'd turned on in my search for the crow's succor. If Jack had made dinner, or sat around waiting for me, or come home at all, there was no sign of it. But there was no note telling me to pack up or get out, either, and my bag was in the guest room where I'd left it, untouched. I brushed my teeth and put on an old T-shirt and decided to leave any further mystery for the morning. *Call your family,* said the voice in my head. *Later,* I told it.

I had never prayed before and was not sure how to go about it. "Dear universe," I said into the cool darkness of my room, feeling more than a little silly—but I had promised. "Please take care of my—friend. The crow," I added, for clarity, in case the universe thought I meant Shane. The universe did not respond. I had not expected that it would, but could not help a faint tinge of disappointment as I climbed into bed. I had imagined my first foray into the world of the spiritual would be marked with more fanfare. Aunt Beast would have swooned to know that I had called upon nonrational forces for assistance. *Call home. Tally. Call home.* "Later," I said aloud, and resolutely closed my eyes.

That night I dreamed that I had known Jack all my life and we did not have secrets from one another. We were walking along a stream somewhere in the mountains, although I have never been in the mountains in the waking world, and I could hear the high clear call of some bird that was unfamiliar to me, and a quiet breeze moved through the needles of trees I somehow knew were fir. *It was never easy to be a father to you,* he said. His lips did not move but I could hear his voice somewhere deep in my bones, humming through me like a chord, and then he spread his arms wide and his soft shirt flapped open into black wings and his features sharpened and lengthened into a black beak and his skin sprouted glossy black feathers and like a rent across the sky he rose upward, a great crow beating its wings and inking out the sun until I was standing alone in darkness. The stream at my feet went viscous and black as oil, and the bark fell away from the trees around me, and they glowed bone-white against the sudden night. In the distance a dog howled, deep and mournful, three times. *If you follow me here,* the voice that was no longer Jack's voice said, in the hollow of my chest where my heart beat a staccato tattoo, *there will be no one to lead you out again—*

I woke in a tangle of sweat-drenched sheets, my mouth open as though I had been gasping for breath. All around me was an unfamiliar room in an unfamiliar and too-quiet dark, and then I remembered I was in Jack's house above the sea, and my pounding heart slowed to a normal rhythm. The silence in the room was like another person waiting. I pulled the blankets over my head and cupped my hands over my ears and listened for the faint soothing echo of my own blood moving in my veins, and it was a long time before I fell asleep again.

In the morning, Jack was gone again, and the crow in his yard was dead.

Jack was never, ever home. I had no idea where he went during the day; if it had always been his habit to stay away for hours, for days, or if my presence had chased him out to his own devices; or if he was indeed home, shut away behind the firmly closed doors I did not have the courage to knock against. Sometimes, late at night, I'd hear the soft creak of footsteps, the snick of a door closing, and blink awake in the dark, uncertain whether it was him I'd heard or some polite, unobtrusive ghost. If he was not home, I could not ask him about Aurora; but he couldn't ask me to leave, either, and so this bizarre impasse continued without detente.

In town, everyone said hello and no one was anyone I wanted to talk to. I found a bike shop down by the harbor, where a friendly blond girl with blackberry vines tattooed across her shoulders and a charming gap between her front teeth helped me patch the flat back tire of Jack's bike. I rode around downtown and went for two-hour walks and waited for the dark to come and give me something to do. I read Newton's *Principia*, which even for me was slow going, and I often found myself with one finger tucked between the pages to mark my place, staring off into space with no memory of how much time had passed or what I had been thinking about. A hateful restlessness took hold of me, an unsettled, anxious boredom that had never besieged me in New York, where I could go to museums or eat dumplings in Chinatown or fall asleep in Shane's bed as we listened to music or make Raoul and Henri tell me how to be a grown-up or go to meetings of the Amateur Astronomers' Association or poke through a dozen different bookstores or sit on my stoop and watch a hundred different kinds of people— shapes, sizes, genders, nationalities, ethnicities, political affiliations, religions, language families, possessed of equally myriad types and quantities of pets—amble past in the space of an afternoon. Out here there was nothing to distract me from the essentially displeasing heart of myself.

I meant to call my family; I really did. I would remember it unexpectedly in the middle of an epic ramble, miles from town, and then forget again as soon as I was back at Jack's. Or I'd remember in the middle of the night, thrashing awake in a panic—what was I thinking, they'd be killing themselves with worry, had I lost my mind—but it would be three or four in the morning in New York, and if I called at that hour they'd think it was the police telephoning to inform them I was dead. My thoughts grew slippery as fish, and I could not hold anything in my head for more than a few seconds at a time; not the impulse to tell my family I was, if not entirely content, at least quite safe; not my desire to go outside and look at the stars; not even my reason for coming in the first place, the conversation I'd traveled three thousand miles to have. The tiny voice of reason, barely managing to keep itself alive in New York, had faded to a faint mumble almost as soon as I had stepped off the plane. It did not help that I could not seem to make it through a single night without falling into some version of the same awful dream: the howling dog, the white forest, the dark-haired girl with her huge, pleading eyes. Wine-dark sea and cold empty apartment with its tall windows looking out into darkness. Sometimes the girl would be speaking to me in a language I did not understand, or in words I could not quite make out; sometimes I would be running after her—to catch her, to warn her, to tell her we were not safe—but always she would move away from me, faster and faster, until I was left alone in the dark, sobbing into Jack's pillow and only slowly coming back to myself again, to his quiet house and the low continuous hum of the sea moving endlessly against the beach below.

The only things I did manage to think about for any length of time were Maddy and Shane. Maddy was a mystery that I was hell-bent on unraveling, and Shane—I hated myself for caring and then hated myself for hating myself. Of course I should care. Of course I shouldn't. Of course he was terrible. Of course I was being stupid. What had happened between us was nothing, how could he possibly have behaved as though what had happened between us was nothing, we were growing apart anyway, we were growing up, we had been too old for each other ages ago, we were only neighbors, he was tearing apart my life with his heartlessness, he was an awful friend, I was an awful friend, I had embarrassed myself, I could never look him in the face again, I didn't want to anyway. Everything would be better at college. Except that Shane wouldn't be at college, and I had made a mess of everything. Around and around and around. The circle was made out of a wall, and its circumference was marked out by me at its center, caged with my own stupid self.

There was very little to do at Jack's, and the weather was so magnificent it seemed almost sinful to be indoors anyway. I was used to the sticky, clinging summers of New York, perspiration and the city's filth mixing into a grey sheen on my skin, cold showers three times a day just for a brief respite from the misery, drenched in sweat again before I even turned off the water. Summer out here was a revelation. People wagged their heads over the raging heat wave if the mercury topped seventy-five, the sky was a crayon-solid blue, and the beaches were so clean you could eat off them. Every morning I woke up around eight or nine and made myself coffee in Jack's spotless kitchen and then rode his bicycle into town, where I went and got coffee again at a shop I had found down by the marina, and ate a bagel with butter—the cheapest thing on the menu; I was determined to make my meager savings last. After, I would stop by Melville & Co., and although its gruff and crotchety owner did not offer up any further overtures of friendship after that first day when he'd given me the *Metamorphoses,* one day after I mentioned my investment in the heavens I went in to find that he had gone through the stacks and set aside all the books about astronomy, and I smiled to myself in quiet triumph.

Mostly, though, I wandered around. I ranged far afield, traversing beaches and tramping through woods; I hiked into the hills, where the old labyrinth of sinister World War II bunkers Kate had told me about on my first night in town erupted out of a tangle of creeping ivy. Closer in to the park, they were just eerie, but the farther afield I ranged, the creepier they got: lightless cement mouths yawning into the hillside, rusted iron doors, low cement ceilings, cement walls sprayed with decades of layered graffiti: mostly quasi-Satanic and ineptly spelled ramblings of bored teenagers (HILE SATAN), romantic declarations (MEG C + DAMON S 4EVR), and total nonsense (PETLET AND CAKELING VERSUS THE UNLIGHTS).

When I got spooked by the bunkers I walked down to the harbor and looked at all the boats tethered in their moorings, or sat on the beach and basked in the gentle sun. Time had a different quality out here than it did in the city, slowing down or speeding up of its own volition, so that a ramble I'd thought had taken me hours would turn out to have been a short stroll, or a few minutes leafing through paperbacks in Melville & Co. would slide away into an entire afternoon. I lost track of what day it was completely within hours of arriving at Jack's.

The thought of seeing Maddy again was equal parts terrifying and elating. She had told me, when she dropped me off at Jack's, that she would see me soon, but she had left me no way to get hold of her, and someone who was willing to live without electricity was not likely to have a telephone anyway. The thought of turning up at her house, alone and unasked, was unthinkable. But after a day or two I gave up pretending to myself that I was not looking for her and took to lurking at Kate's in the afternoons, sipping the single bitter-tasting beer for which Kate never charged me and gazing morosely at the dark polished wood of the bar, hunkered on my stool in the dim light while outside the sun buttered the sidewalks and a cool lively wind filled the white sails of boats, tiny sharp triangles against the blue water. I had no doubt Kate knew why I was there, but she did not mention it. Maddy did not come.

The crows from Jack's yard had begun following me around. Not all of them, and not all at once—there was one fat black one in particular, larger and more gregarious than its fellows, who seemed especially to like me, and often in the mornings I would find some small silver thing—a nickel or a quarter, a wadded-up ball of tinfoil, the glinting wrapper from a candy bar—left conspicuously in my path, and one of the crows watching me from a tree. They did not like downtown, but whenever I was out in the woods they were not far behind me, and though at first I found them discomfiting, after a while I got used to their presence, and even grew to like them. I had buried their dead friend while they watched, and said over its grave some paraphrased lines from

Hamlet ("Goodnight, sweet prince / and flights of, um, crows sing thee to thy rest"), while they watched from the branches above, and when I was done they cawed amongst themselves and then flapped off in a flurry of black wings. These days, they were the closest thing I had to friends.

I carried my copy of the *Metamorphoses* everywhere, stuffed into my pocket like a talisman, but I did not open it once.

I had been at Jack's for days before I finally found the will—and the mental acuity—to call Raoul and Henri. I'd remembered on the bike ride back from downtown, and remembered too that I had a pen in my back pocket—I was supposed to be making notes in the margin of the *Principia,* which had not proven a successful resolution—and I dismounted from Jack's bicycle and wrote CALL HOME in block letters on the back of one hand. And a good thing, too, since I'd already forgotten again by the time I got back to Jack's. He was, as always, nowhere to be found; I went on a brief expedition in search of a telephone, and discovered an old-fashioned rotary phone wedged inconspicuously between two stacks of books in the main room of the house. I looked at it for some time, curious as to why I had been so intent on finding it, and then reached for one of Jack's books and saw the letters on the back of my hand and remembered again. *I am losing my mind,* I thought.

It was with no small amount of dread that I dialed my number—I had gone an unforgivable length of time without calling them, there was no excuse for it—and when Raoul's familiar "Hello?" answered on the second ring the worry in his voice was like a knife to my gut.

"It's me," I said.

"*Tally.* Where in god's name are you?" There was so much at war in that handful of words—relief, fury, exhaustion, anxiety—that I took a deep breath before I said anything else.

"I'm sorry," I said. "I know it's been—"

"Where *are* you? Do you have any idea how worried we've been? I thought you were *dead,* Tally, I can't even tell you what you've put us through, Henri's beside himself—"

And then, in the background, I heard Henri crying out "Is it her? It's her?" and a muffled exchange between the two of them, and then Henri's breathless "Tally? Is that you? Where are you? Tell us where you are and we'll come get you—" and then another jumbled exchange.

"Do tell us, Tally. Where are you?" Raoul, this time— Henri was no good at discipline; I could talk him out of being cross with me in a matter of seconds. I really was in trouble, then.

"I'm in this little town—I'm outside of Seattle—it's a long story. I found Jack."

"You're on the *peninsula*? How the hell did you get out there?"

"I flew—"

"When did you get a plane ticket? When did you plan all this?"

It seemed best to leave Mr. M out of this conversation; I already had enough explaining to do. "I, um, found this old newspaper article with a picture of Jack and Aurora. And I thought—I know it sounds crazy, but I thought he might be my dad. Or at least he could tell me about her, or maybe he knows where she is, or something. Anything. And so I, um—" I thought fast. "I went to that record store that you and Shane are obsessed with, and they had a—a magazine that had an article about him, and it said he was out here, and I bought a plane ticket and just, um, went. I didn't plan it ahead, I swear, I knew you wouldn't let me go and so I just—I knew it was dumb but I couldn't—I just had to."

"Where are you staying?" Raoul's voice was deadly.

"With Jack."

"With *Jack*? Is he *there*? You put him on the phone *right now*."

"He's not here much. Mostly I just, um, go for walks."

The silence following this remark was excruciating. "Why didn't you tell us?" Raoul asked finally. "What were you thinking?"

"I thought you wouldn't let me go. I mean, you wouldn't have, would you?"

"Tally, that's not even the point. I don't know. Probably we would have, yes. But running away like that—" He sighed. "It does seem to run in the family."

"That's low," I said sharply.

"Not Aurora. Your aunt. A long time ago. And don't distract me from my lecture."

"You hadn't even gotten going yet." Silence. "I'm so sorry. I am. I didn't think."

"You always think. We had gotten used to it."

"I know. It's a big step, doing something totally irrational."

"When are you coming home? *Are* you coming home?"

"Of course I'm coming home. I just want to talk to him. I just want to know. If he's my dad. If he can tell me anything about Aurora. I know this was a stupid thing to do, and I shouldn't have scared you, but I'm okay, I promise, and this is—I need to know this stuff."

"I just wish you would have told us, Tally. We've been worried sick."

"I know. But I'm here now. It would be just as stupid to turn around and leave again without finding out anything. It's my—" I was seized by inspiration. "It's my quest. Going after the Golden Fleece. Jack even has a boat." I paused. "Aunt Beast is going to kill me, isn't she?"

"Your aunt is not in a position to point fingers in this case, but Henri and I certainly are," he said tartly. "Oh, Tally. I understand why you went. But don't ever do anything like that to us again. If something happened to you—it doesn't bear thinking about. Is that clear?"

"Yes," I said, humbled.

"Do you need anything?"

I had not given much thought to how I was going to get home, but I could deal with that later. "I'm okay. This nice lady downtown gives me hamburgers. And Jack has coffee."

"Please tell me you are not subsisting entirely on caffeine and charity fast food."

"Jack has a garden," I said, which was not technically a lie. Raoul made a disgusted noise.

After I had made a number of other conciliatory remarks, and asked after Dorian Gray's health, and submitted myself to be lambasted by Henri and made the conciliatory remarks a second time, I was allowed to get off the phone with the promise that I would call every day until I returned to New York, that I would put Jack on the phone the second I saw him, and that I would arrange for my return trip the instant I had gotten anything resembling information about Aurora or after another week had passed, whichever came first.

I meant every one of the promises I made; too bad I forgot them all immediately upon hanging up the receiver.

I had been at Jack's for about a week before I saw him again; I came in from where I'd been reading in his garden, late one morning, and he was standing in the kitchen, drinking coffee and looking out the window. He turned when he heard me come in. "I was just about to go sailing," he said. "Would you like to come?"

"I don't know anything about boats," I said, and then amended it. "Very much about boats." I had *read* about boats.

"I do," he said. "You'll be fine."

"Sure," I said. Now, at last, I could accomplish what I'd come here for. I envisioned the afternoon rolling out neatly before me, like a well-plotted movie. I'd find the perfect way to phrase my question, he'd confess that all week he'd been searching for a way to tell me—though it wasn't necessary, we might even embrace—and, secure in the knowledge of my paternity, I'd return home to the bosom of my real family, to resume my actual life, patch things up with my errant best friend, make him fall in love with me as he ought, and then go to college. I could write Maddy letters; perhaps she would be interested in a visit to the city. This plan suited me so immensely that I barely paid attention on the drive to the harbor—Jack, like everyone else I'd met so far in this town, had a truck—or as he parked in a gravel lot and pointed me down a ramp to where the boats were parked in neat rows along a floating walkway. It occurred to me that you probably didn't park a boat. "Slips," Jack said, when I asked. "The spaces for the boats are slips."

Jack's boat was made of wood, clean-lined and a little weather-beaten but scrupulously tidy; where the vessels to either side were some of them stained with algae, the canvas sail covers spotted with mold or oil, his boat glowed with obvious love and good care. He leaped agilely from the dock to its deck. "Untie that, please," he said, pointing to a rope looped around a metal bar attached to the dock, and I did. I tossed him the rope, and he looked back to catch my uncertain face—I wasn't *clumsy,* exactly, but I did better on solid ground, and the boat kept moving in an alarming sort of way—but I ignored his outstretched hand and grabbed the deck railing and hauled myself aboard, smacking my shin painfully on the side of the boat. Jack was gracious enough not to comment on my ungainly method of entry. I tucked myself out of the way in the bow—*obviously* I knew the front was called a bow—while he busied himself untying lines and doing a lot of complicated-looking things that I tried to follow but soon lost track of.

"Do you need help?" I asked, and he shook his head.

"You'd only be in the way," he said, not unkindly. He dug a blanket out from a storage compartment under one of the seats and tossed it to me. "Gets cold out on the water," he said.

He motored us quietly out of the marina, and when we were clear of the rocky jetty he pulled furiously at a set of ropes until the sail unfurled and snapped to life, and he turned off the engine. Once we got away from shore there was a brisk enough wind to send us flying over the water, and I was glad of the blanket. The years seemed to fall away from him; behind the wheel his face was suffused with boyish glee and he looked so at home that he was hardly recognizable as the distant, reserved, and disinterested person I'd met that first day I came to his house.

"This is a nice boat," I said, although I would not have been able to tell if it wasn't. It was the right thing to say.

"*Affair*," he said. "She's a beauty, all right—hand-built wooden ketch—" He launched into a short but comprehensive monologue detailing the boat's specifications, which did not seem all that interesting to me but in which he obviously took great pride.

I had no suitable response to his sailboat's résumé. "It's pretty out here," I said instead when I was sure he was done.

"Yes," he said. "Are you having a nice vacation?"

His face was serene. He couldn't possibly have forgotten why I'd come here—as far as I could tell, he hadn't guessed the real reason I'd come looking for him, but I'd told him I wanted to ask him about Aurora, not spend a relaxing week seaside working on my tan. "Yes?" I said, cautiously.

"What do you do, back in New York?"

"I just graduated," I said.

"College?"

"High school." If he was surprised he hid it well. "I'm going to college in the fall."

"What for?"

"Well, physics to start. But I don't know what I'll do my doctorate in, yet."

At that he did look momentarily startled. "My," he said. "Ambitious. You want to be a physicist?"

"No," I said, "I want to be an astronomer, but physics is

the best way to get there. To the kind of astronomy I want to do, anyway."

"Which is?"

"I'm not all the way sure yet. I'm only eighteen, you know."

"Ah," he said. "Of course."

"But I think—there are a lot of different things you can do, you know; if you're interested in the planets you can do chemistry or meteorology or a whole bunch of other things, or you could even go into astrobiology, which I think is cool, but I'm interested in the really theoretical stuff. Like cosmology, which people used to think was sort of woo-woo, but in the last few decades it's come into its own as a science—I'm quite interested in the origins of the universe, but there are already so many people tackling that problem, and it might be too overcrowded by the time I'm ready to do my postdoc work. . . ." I trailed off; Jack was staring at me as though I had started speaking Farsi. "I want to study dark matter," I said. "Probably. Or dark energy."

He cleared his throat. "I'm not entirely sure what that is."

"I mean, you know about baryons, right?"

"Pretend I'm very, very stupid," he said. "Pretend I barely even know what the universe is."

"Oh," I said. "Okay. Well, we have equations that can tell us—you know what an equation is?"

"Yes," he said drily, "those I've heard of."

"You said pretend you didn't know anything."

"My fault. Carry on."

"We have equations that can tell us how much matter is supposed to be in the universe. And we have equations that can tell us how much matter *is* in the universe. Matter we know about. Like gas, or stars, or planets. Tangible stuff.

We can tell from the way that galaxies move, from their velocities, that they should have more mass in them than what we can observe. Vera Rubin proved this, from their rotational speed, decades ago. And the thing is, the amount of stuff we know exists is only about four or five percent of the stuff that *should* exist. So there's all this other stuff out there, and we have no idea what it is—if it's particles we haven't discovered yet, or black holes, or—"

"Or ghosts," he said, "or magic."

"It's certainly not ghosts."

"You never know."

"There is no empirical evidence whatsoever to suggest that ghosts exist."

"Hmm," he said.

"You don't believe in ghosts."

"There are more things in heaven and earth than are—"

"Thanks, I've read *Hamlet* too."

"A scientist and a Shakespearean scholar," he said. "You are a formidable young lady, indeed."

"But that's not even the crazy part," I said, ignoring him. "Dark matter is weird, but it's only about thirty percent of the universe. So that's not even the biggest missing piece; there's also dark energy, which we think is something like seventy percent of the universe, and we have no idea what it *is*. You know the universe is expanding, right?"

"I'll take your word for it."

"Well, it is. It's been expanding ever since the beginning—"

"The Big Bang?"

"See, you do know *something*. For a long time we assumed that the expansion of the universe is slowing—that would make sense, because of gravity, right? Eventually all the mass in the universe would counteract the expansion, slowing it down, maybe even causing it to contract. But it isn't slowing down at all. It's accelerating. There's something pushing the universe outward, and we have no idea what it is. It could be a property of space—Einstein predicted that, but we have no way of knowing yet. I want to know. But there are a lot of things I want to know. We're learning more and more about the beginning of the universe, we have images of light from the earliest moments—not the *very* beginning, the universe was just opaque plasma at first—but once things cooled down enough for light to escape. But you have to specialize, is the trouble, and I want to do observational astronomy, not necessarily theoretical particle physics—I mean, I don't want to spend my career underground at CERN. I want to be in front of a telescope. I have a while to decide, I guess."

"There are a lot of questions I would ask you," he said, "but to be honest, I have no idea what you just said."

"I'm trying to explain it as simply as I can."

"I appreciate that." His tone and his face were so studiedly neutral that I began to suspect him of mockery.

"But you shouldn't feel too bad," I conceded, and at that a flicker of a smirk did cross his face, which I generously overlooked. "I mean, the calculations involved in the particle stuff are beyond me, even, at this point. It'll take me a few years of undergrad at least before I have enough physics to tackle them. Which is embarrassing; if I were a real genius, I'd be able to manage it." This was the closest I had ever come to a confession of weakness, and I was wasting it on a virtual stranger. "Wheeler had a doctorate in quantum physics by the time he was twenty-one. So honestly, I'm pretty far behind."

"It must be a bit of a rough road, for women," he said. "Astronomy, I mean."

"There are plenty of women," I said, "and they do good work, it's just that usually men take the credit for it. Vera Rubin couldn't even attend the talk George Gamow gave using her research on the orbital velocities of galaxies, because women weren't allowed in the lab. Or, like, Kepler. You've heard of him, right? Johannes Kepler?"

"Sure," he said.

"But not Maria Cunitz, who rewrote all his equations so that they were easier to use, and then wrote a whole book of her own, and had to pay to print it herself—she was the greatest mathematical astronomer of her time, and the only people who have heard of her are a handful of print history nerds who are more excited about her book than they are about her."

"I haven't heard of her, no."

"Nobody has. She didn't even make it into *Coming of Age in the Milky Way*."

"I don't know what that is."

"It doesn't matter. I'm just saying, it's not that women aren't smart enough, it's that they don't get credit, or they get written out of the story. These days they end up in some fucking 'Ten Hottest Astrophysicists' article in a magazine with nothing at all about their research. Jocelyn Bell discovered pulsars when she was a graduate student in the sixties—*discovered* them, *herself*—and her professors won the Nobel Prize for it. Her name wasn't even *mentioned*. Annie Jump Cannon developed the system we used to classify stars;

Henrietta Swan Leavitt catalogued half the known total of variable stars in the late 1800s, single-handedly. Margaret Burbidge figured out how all the elements in nature can be synthesized in nuclear reactions in stars in the 1960s. Beatrice Tinsley took on Allan Sandage when she was just a *graduate* student, and she was right, too, and he wasn't, but nobody wanted to talk about it, because he basically invented observational cosmology, and she was just some girl. I could keep going. You get the point."

"If it is any consolation to you," he said, "I think people will find it difficult indeed to write you out of any story in which you are a participant."

"Things are getting better," I said, "but there's a long way to go yet."

"So you like mystery," he said, after a thoughtful silence. "And darkness."

"You make it sound like I'm *goth* or something."

At that, he smiled. "I just think it's interesting, that's all," he said, "that someone who is so insistent on the empirical is so invested in the hypothetical. Not to mention Shakespeare."

"Shakespeare doesn't have anything to do with science."

"I don't know that I'd agree," he said mildly, "but I'm sure you know better."

I did not much like the turn the conversation was taking, and so I subsided into a haughty silence. It was beautiful, anyway; I felt as though I should be memorizing the air out here, the water, the light, to take back to New York with me as a talisman. I loved my home, and I did not wish in any way to relocate to this backwoods pinpoint populated with near-savages and obsequious cretins, but even I had to admit there was a certain advantage to its loveliness that my own best-beloved city, for all its civilized, fast-paced majesty, did not have to offer. Jack was as content to be quiet as I was, and eventually I let go of my sulk enough to let myself enjoy the wind in my hair and the light rise and fall of the boat as we moved across the water.

"You knew Aurora," I said. We had not spoken for so long that at first I thought he hadn't heard me, but as I gathered myself to ask him again, he cleared his throat.

"I did."

"Well?"

"No." He was avoiding my eyes. "I only knew her for a summer, years ago. Before I went to Los Angeles."

"And became a famous rock star."

He laughed; it was a bitter sound that cut across the wind. "If that's what you want to call it."

"What was she like?"

"I can't tell you much."

"Do you know where she is?"

"How would I know that? Can't you ask your father?"

"No," I said. "I never knew my father."

"Neither did I," he said, with no apparent irony.

I tried another tack. "Why did you move all the way out here?"

"To forget," he said, without hesitation.

"Forget what?" He did not bother to answer. "Do you practice somewhere else? I never hear you play." *Because you're never home,* I could have added, but elected not to. I had often been told that discretion was the better part of valor, although it was not an approach that I myself employed regularly; but there is no time like the present for frolicking in undiscovered country.

"I don't play anymore."

I was dumbfounded. "At *all*?"

"No."

"Why not?"

"Because it was . . ." He trailed off, and something complicated passed across his face; I thought I recognized a hint of the fuzzy confusion that clouded my own thinking out here, the weird blurry wall that made it impossible to remember anything for any length of time, or say out loud the thoughts that scampered fleetingly through my skull and then vanished again. "It brought too many bad things," he said in a tone that did not encourage further enquiry. The sail snapped in the wind and Jack jumped up to adjust it, and I looked out over the water—black, sharp-beaked birds, diving neatly before the boat as it flew across the water; a tangle of seaweed, which Jack deftly maneuvered past; a slick log bobbing in the waves. I pressed one thumb against my shoulder; pale flash, then pink. I was getting a sunburn. Jack sat back down again, the sail safely negotiated, his face serene—we'd been talking about something, something that I felt certain was important, but it had slid out of reach again, and I did not know how to get it back.

"Everything okay?" I said.

"Oh, sure," he said. "You know, I don't know anything about astronomy, but I know most of the constellations. We've been navigating at sea more or less the same way since the ancient Greeks. More technology now, obviously, but I like to do it the old way."

"Jason was supposed to be the first person who navigated with the constellations."

"Jason?" His voice had gone strange.

"Of Jason and the Argonauts."

"I know the one," he said. Something about his expression made me stop talking at once, and he looked out over the water, refusing to meet my eyes. I had no idea what I'd said to upset him, but we were silent for the rest of the afternoon.

After the day on the boat Jack disappeared again, leaving me to my own devices. I went back to prowling around and pretending I wasn't lonely. Early one afternoon I came into the cool quiet of the bar to find a slim girl in a black jacket on Maddy's usual stool, and my heart flip-flopped in my chest like a fish; but she turned at the squeak of the door's hinges, curious, and I saw at once that she was someone else, less scruffy and with none of Maddy's fierce, animal shimmer. She had shiny dark hair pulled up in a high ponytail on her head and hammered silver hoops in her ears, and the feet propped on the bar stool's rung were shod in fashionably battered boots that she had certainly not purchased here. The natives ran toward clogs and rubber-soled sandals with nylon-and-Velcro straps worn with white socks. I did not much myself care about clothes, but that did not mean I did not miss being around people who did. And even I should never have stooped so low as *athletic sandals*.

"Hi," she said; maybe she was from here, then. Nobody else would have been so friendly. The bar was empty, and it seemed unnecessarily rude to stalk off to a spot by myself, so I climbed onto the stool next to her and ducked my head in what I hoped was a convivial manner.

"Hi," I said. Up close she was older than I'd first thought, maybe in her late twenties or early thirties, with a sharp, clever, pretty face. She raised a hand to Kate, pointed at her empty glass to signal another; the way she moved made me think of the crows in Jack's yard. The fat crow had left me a quarter that morning; I fingered it in my pocket and thought about going home.

"You just move here?" she asked.

"No," I said, "only visiting. You live here?"

"From here. My dad owns the movie theater"—she pointed out in the general direction of the street—"down the street, the Rose. But I live mostly in New York."

I was as happy as if she'd told me she had a winning lottery ticket in her pocket with my name on it. "I'm *from* New York," I said.

"Really?" she said, with a flash of recognition that I knew at once: that strange and funny solidarity of New Yorkers, as though we were anthropologists from the same place who had spent too much time alone amidst a pleasant but ineffably foreign people and had at last stumbled upon a kindred spirit with whom to exchange commentary on the inscrutable customs of the native population. ("Can you *believe* what they *eat*? Everyone has a *car*! There are washing machines *in their houses*!") "What part?"

I told her, and she told me where she lived, in a fifth-floor walk-up in a part of Brooklyn I knew well ("Do you get the falafel at that place on the corner?" "Oh, and that bodega on Twenty-first and Fifth that has the most *amazing* tacos!"), and we spent a happy fifteen minutes chattering at each other about all the places we had in common, the overlapping Venn diagram of our New York circles. She was an actor, mostly stage work but more and more television ("It's not rewarding intellectually but god, it *pays*"), and I knew most of the places where the shows she had been in had filmed.

"It's funny," she said, taking a sip of her drink—her second now—"things were going badly there for me for a while, couldn't get work, shows canceling everywhere, and I almost threw in the towel and came back here. Of all places. It's been hard a lot, you know—I think sometimes all that kept me there was refusing to admit I'd been bested, and then things always got better—but that time was the worst, and I was so tired, it was winter and I was living in this terrible apartment with no heat, landlady on the first floor who was this crazy old Polish woman who didn't speak a word of English and would come into our apartment when we weren't there and steal the *lightbulbs*, if you can believe that, and then one morning I was in the shower and part of the tiled wall just *fell* on me, and there was this great gaping blackness behind it, this huge hole, and I screamed and almost broke my leg jumping out of the tub"—we were both laughing—"and I was like, 'Jesus god in heaven, *fuck* this. No career on earth is worth this.'" She looked thoughtfully at her glass.

"What happened?" I prompted.

"I called my psychic," she said.

"Your psychic?" I echoed, certain I'd misheard.

"This woman in Colorado," she said. "They're all different, you know, how they access you—this woman I used to see channeled an alien being called Kotak, and she was good—she told my friend one time to check the right front tire of her car and she went outside and there was a nail in the tire, can you believe that? But she only told me practical stuff, so I found this other woman who talks to your angels. 'They have so much to tell me about you, they're so excited, they've been chattering at me before you even got on the phone,' she said, and then she went on to tell me all these things about how I was going to have a great career, and I had a gift, and—oh, it's embarrassing, you don't need to know what they said. I was crying within minutes. But anyway, I stayed. I come back every summer for a few weeks to run the theater so my dad can have some time off, but I'm so glad I didn't move back here for real."

"You stayed in New York because your angels told a psychic in Colorado that you were going to have a good career," I said. Everyone here, I thought, was utterly batshit, even this totally normal-seeming person, well put together and smart, who had managed somehow to get herself off the peninsula to a civilized place like New York and yet still took the advice of people who thought they were talking to angels. She laughed.

"You haven't seen the bumper sticker yet," she said. But I had: WE'RE ALL HERE BECAUSE WE'RE NOT ALL THERE, plastered on decaying VW buses and battered station wagons captained by decrepit old hippies who looked as though they'd be likely to fumigate you with patchouli. "But I tell you what, she was right."

She finished her drink and dug some bills out of her wallet, left them on the bar with a wave to Kate and a nod to me. "See you around," she said, and I waved back as she left.

"How's Jack?" Kate asked, sliding another bottle of beer across the bar to me.

"We went sailing once," I said, and stopped. When had we gone sailing? Yesterday? Or had it been days ago already? Time was sliding away from me, messy and strange. "But otherwise he's never around and I never see him. Do you know why he doesn't play anymore?"

Kate gave me a sharp, unreadable look. "No." *You're lying,* I thought.

"It seems strange, doesn't it? I mean, who does that? Wasn't music his whole life?"

"You'll have to ask him."

"I did." But some people had come into the bar and Kate was already turning away from me, overeager to greet them, and by the time she came back to me I had lost my train of thought, and so I told her about my crows instead: the circle they'd made around their dying friend, the way they'd watched me, the way the biggest one had taken, now, to leaving me gifts and trailing me as though I was the cor-vids' Pied Piper.

"They do that," Kate said, "keep vigil over the dying; I've never heard of them following anyone, but they're clever birds. You must have impressed them."

"Speaking of animals," I said, "I keep meaning to ask— what are those animals? On the beach, the long green ones? They look like snakes? I think they must be something that only lives in the water, because they all seem like they might be dead?"

Kate raised a quizzical eyebrow. I found a pen and drew the serpentine thing with its odd flat ribbony crown that I'd seen on the beach. Kate peered down at my drawing and hooted with merriment, laughing so hard she had to prop herself up on the bar. "Oh, city mouse," she said. "That's *kelp*."

I blinked with embarrassment. "I'm *not* stupid."

"I'm sure you aren't," Kate said, chuckling. I kicked sullenly at the rung of my bar stool, thinking up ways to ask about Maddy. "She'll come in again," Kate said. "How much longer are you here for, anyway?"

"I don't know," I said. "I have to—" What *did* I have to do, anyway? It didn't seem likely I was going to get any more out of Jack than I had already. I could confront him, but that seemed overly dramatic. But I did not like the thought of going back to Mr. M empty-handed, after all he had done to send me out here, and I did not like the thought of failure, either. And if Aurora was still running around somewhere, and Jack knew—did I want to know? I chewed on this for a moment while Kate watched me with her keen eyes. Which was worse, an Aurora who was gone forever or an Aurora who didn't care enough to look me up? It was a question I'd given surprisingly little thought to over the years; I hadn't even known I cared until Mr. M had given me that picture and set my adventure in motion. "I have to talk to Jack more, I guess," I said. "I keep forgetting things out here. It's weird."

"That's why people come out here," she said. "To forget."

"That's what—" I frowned, thinking. "Jack said that, I think. And Maddy."

"Maddy has more to forget than most people."

"What does that mean?"

The door opened and we both looked up; there she was,

wild-haired, in the same clothes she'd been wearing the first time I saw her, as if Kate had conjured her up.

"Well, well," Kate said. "Speak of the devil. We were just talking about you."

"I know," Maddy said. "I thought you'd be here," she added, to me. "Are you doing anything? I'm on my way to the beach to get oysters, if you want to come."

"Okay," I mumbled, ecstatic.

"You be good to her," Kate said.

"I'm good to everyone," Maddy said.

"That," Kate said, and her voice was sharp and cold, "is not true." Maddy stared Kate down, and Kate looked away first.

"Let's get out of this dark old place," Maddy said to me, and I was only too happy to follow her outside.

Qantaqa barked happily from the truck as we approached, both paws on the windowsill, tail waving madly. She nearly fell out the door when Maddy opened it. The passenger side was unlocked, and I got in. "You have a coat or something?" she asked. "It'll get cold when the sun sets. We can stop by where you're staying on the way."

"Sure," I said, "that would be great."

She found the way to Jack's again without my directing her, followed me into his house and paced the circumference of the main room like Dorian Gray when we let him out of his carrier at the vet's; I could almost see her bristle and sniff, her hackles raised. She picked things up off Jack's shelves and turned them over in her hands and put them down again, carefully and in the same place. I heard a door close and a second later Jack appeared, leaning easily on the doorframe to the hallway.

"I haven't seen you in a while," he said to me.

Not my *fault,* I thought. "I made a friend," I said instead. "Do you know Maddy?" He looked past me; she was holding a clay pot from one of the side tables, and when their eyes met her whole body went rigid, and he froze. The whole room went electric with the force of their locked gazes, her yellow eyes suddenly wild and the air around her bristling with a staticky charge. I took a step away from them, putting out one hand as if to fend off an unseen attacker.

"We went sailing once," Maddy whispered.

"I don't think we've met; you must be thinking of someone else," Jack said, but his eyes did not leave hers.

"You sang to us over the water, and everything was blood—but it was such a long time ago—" Maddy shook her head. "I don't want to remember!" she cried, her voice full of pain. The pot slipped from her fingers and shattered on the wooden floor, and we all jumped. "I'm sorry," she said quickly, and Jack said, "It's no trouble," which did not seem like the right thing to say, and so I said, "I'll get a broom," but I didn't know where Jack kept one, and he went to fetch it instead, and in all the jumble the strange moment was forgotten and the weirdness went out of the room like a guest sent home for being too unruly. Maddy shook herself like a cat who had gotten its paws wet by accident and went back to being a girl again—not ordinary, but not sparking with terrifying electricity, either—and then Jack, blinking and slightly confused, wished us a pleasant afternoon and went back into the room he'd come out of. It was not until Maddy and I were back in her truck and driving away that I realized I had altogether forgotten to fetch my sweatshirt.

Qantaqa panted happily in my face for the rest of the

drive to the beach, as much of her front end as she could manage wedged into my lap. I patted her head. She was the sort of dog you had no choice but to get used to. "Don't let her boss you around," Maddy said. "She's already spoiled rotten."

We drove for a while through a labyrinthine network of narrow two-lane roads, thick green woods occasionally giving way to the bald scars of clear-cuts dotted with smoking piles of brush and splintered trees. Here and there the trees would part enough for me to see a cobalt flash of water, and there was nowhere we went that the smell of the sea did not come in through the truck's open windows. Maddy turned off on a potholed dirt road that rolled bumpily down to a gravelly dead end. She parked the truck, and Qantaqa barked happily.

"Here we are," Maddy said, reaching over to ruffle her behind the ears, "your favorite place. You can let her out, Tally." Qantaqa nearly squashed me flat in her gleeful scramble out the door. I followed more slowly, wincing as the circulation returned to my legs. Qantaqa was already crashing through the underbrush. Maddy got a bucket and two pairs of knee-high rubber boots out of the back of the truck, and we went after Qantaqa with slightly less enthusiasm. We came through a stand of evergreens to a rocky half-moon of beach, sheltered on one side by a high bluff and on the other by forest. The tide was out, muddy flats stretching half a mile before us. "Perfect timing," she said.

We pulled the boots on over our shoes, and Maddy led me out onto the tide flats as Qantaqa bounded up and down the beach and crashed off again into the woods. At first the ground was firm, but soon we sank up to our ankles in thick, viscous mud that smelled of rot and salt and something deeper. *Sex,* I thought, and blushed. The feeling of it was disorienting, the sucking mud pulling at my boots and making each step a laborious struggle to keep them on my feet. The tide was coming back in by the time Maddy decided we had enough oysters, and we took turns carrying the heavy bucket back to the beach as the water obscured the tide flats behind us.

Maddy sent me to collect firewood and went back to the truck, returning with blankets and a bulging cloth bag. She showed me how to make a pyramid of smaller twigs and dried grass and coax it into flame before gently adding bigger pieces of driftwood. "This time of year, the oysters aren't as good," she explained, "so they're better cooked. Come back in the winter and you can eat them right out of the water." Despite the sun, the afternoon was chilly, and I was glad of the fire. Maddy dumped out our oysters and refilled the bucket with salt water to wash them. I was used to oysters from a restaurant, halved and neatly arranged on a bed of ice; these seemed a different thing altogether, over-large and muddy and crusted in barnacles. We both cut our hands washing them, and Maddy pressed her bloody palm to mine. My heart thumped frantically in my ribs, and I licked my dry lips. She watched me, her huge yellow eyes unblinking. I was the first to look down. "Palm to palm is holy palmer's kiss," she said, and took her hand away. I curled my fingers around its absence, her blood drying on my skin, and thought I might never wash my hands again.

She showed me how to shuck the oysters with a short-bladed knife, but I was hopeless at it and cut myself again and so she did them all, laying them out in a tidy line by the fire as she revealed their quivering grey-pink meat. While the oysters cooked she spread a blanket out for us and pulled a bottle of wine and two cups out of her bag, filling one and passing it to me. I wrinkled my nose and took a sip and was surprised to find that I liked it; it was crisp and cool and tasted of apples. Aunt Beast would be proud of me, loosening up at last. Qantaqa settled behind us with a sigh and put her nose on her paws, and Maddy reached back absently to scratch her ears. "I think they're done," she said.

The oysters were delicious, firmed by the fire's heat but salt-tangy and rich with brine. We ate them all, the whole bucketful. Qantaqa watched sadly as our hands moved over and over to our mouths and Maddy fed her the last one, which she took gently from Maddy's outstretched fingers and gummed rapturously. Maddy built the fire up again and poured us more wine, and we stretched out on her blanket. She'd pulled her hair back, but wisps of it had escaped and framed her face in a dark halo. The sun was low on the horizon, and the sky was streaked purple and rose, the water gone flat and silver. "Listen," Maddy said, and after a moment I heard it: the low mournful hoot of some bird in the woods behind us, followed by a ragged caw. My crows. I remembered what I had been meaning to ask her all afternoon.

"You know Jack?"

"Jack?" She blinked, slow and uncertain: stuttering flicker of black lashes, wisp of black hair fluttering against the soft skin of her cheek. I swallowed. "I don't think so."

"But you said—in his house you said—" The words were just out of reach, and I fought the murky wave threatening to overtake me. "You said you went sailing, a long time ago—did you know him in California?"

"I've never been to California." She took my hand and brought my knuckles to her mouth without looking at me, and my whole body went live-wired and frantic. I could hardly breathe. "Do you miss the city?" she asked.

"No," I whispered, and she laughed and looked at me at last, her yellow eyes big enough to drown me, and then she leaned over and kissed me. Her soft mouth tasted of the oysters' salt and the wine's tangy sweetness, and we fell into each other, her hands in my hair, running the length of my spine, soft on my skin underneath my shirt, her mouth on my cheek, at my ear, against the line of my throat. Qantaqa gave an aggrieved huff and rolled over, and we broke apart long enough to laugh at her as she panted at us, and then Maddy kissed me again and I thought of nothing but the taste of her skin and the smell of her hair. I shuddered, and she said, "You're cold," her mouth at my ear, the low throaty rasp of her voice alone sending me ecstatic, and I said, "No," but that was a lie; I was shivering, and not just from her touch. The stars were coming out.

"The Dippers," I said, and could have kicked myself as soon as the words were out of my mouth. She wrapped me up in one corner of the blanket and sat up. *Kiss me more,* I thought desperately, but she did not seem to have Kate's psychic proclivities; or else—and worse—she did not care to kiss me any longer.

"Do you know them all?"

"Most of them," I said, but I did not want her to think I was showing off.

"I used to," she said, looking up at the sky. "There's Thuban." She pointed north.

"That's Polaris."

"The North Star? That's not what we call it, where I'm from. Anyway, we can go," she said, remote again.

"If you want," I said, wishing more than anything for her to turn back to me, to say that of course that was not what she wanted, what she wanted was to throw me back down on the ground again and take off all my clothes and do to me whatever it was she did to people, this astonishing girl who seemed to know so much more about the world than I did, who had undone me with a handful of kisses and some heavy breathing. But she was already standing up and gathering our things, kicking dirt over the embers of the fire, clucking Qantaqa to her feet. I was out of my league; I had no idea what to say to her or what to do to make her kiss me again. Was she kissing anyone else? Was kissing strange girls just her standard operating procedure? Did she like me? What was happening between us? What was I, to her? Why had she brought me out here only to bring me home again, like a child up past her bedtime? I was not used to not feeling special, and I found that I did not much like the experience. And as I followed her back to the truck, carrying the blanket, I did not ask her the other question burning in my mouth: where could she possibly be from, to think that Thuban was the polestar? Thuban had shifted from that place in the heavens three thousand years ago.

We were quiet in her truck, quiet as she drove back toward town; her walls had gone back up, and I tangled my fingers in Qantaqa's fur and tried to think of something witty and clever to say, something to make her look at me again the way she'd looked at me on the beach before she kissed me. The light turned red at the intersection on the edge of town, and she sighed from some deep place and shifted in her seat, and the feeling in the truck changed in some way I could not precisely articulate. "Do you want to come over?" she said. I did not know what she was really asking.

"I—sure." She did not say anything else until we were inside her house. "Do you want tea?" she asked, with her back to me, and I said, "No," and she turned to me again at last, and smiled. "Do you want to come upstairs?"

"*Yes*," I said, and she moved toward me again, putting her hands on either side of my face, and my breath caught in my throat.

"You are so young," she said softly, "you're just a child—look at you, you're shaking."

"I am not," I said, although I was, and then she kissed me and I kissed her back, fierce and hungry, and she took my hand and tugged me to the ladder, and I followed her.

"This is not what you came here for," she said into my ear, the hum of her voice going all through me. "Is it what you want?"

"Yes," I said again, although I was not entirely sure what she was asking me, what she was asking of me; I was not sure, either, that I cared.

Underneath the black shirt she was all over scars, a faded latticework crocheted across her skin; and over that again, more tattoos: the flight of crows, winging from one forearm and across her back to the other, lines written in languages I did not recognize, old star maps, a swarm of bees scattered down her spine. "What happened to you?" I whispered, tracing a knotted line of white tissue where it crossed the sharp edge of her shoulder blade and turned to follow her spine, and she turned her yellow eyes on me and said, "No pasts." I could have fallen forever into those honey-colored depths: sun on white sand, ocean blue as a swimming pool, white sails snapping in the wind; a man with yellow hair and brown eyes, tanned dark; Jack with his lyre—with his *lyre*?— and then drawn all across it, a curtain of blood—I yelped and jerked away from her, my mouth flooding with the sour iron taste; I had bitten my tongue. Buzzing in my ears. And then she kissed me again, hard, and I forgot what I had been thinking about because it didn't matter, none of it mattered, the only thing that mattered was her—her hands on my skin and her mouth at the hollow of my throat. At first I could not help compare the feel of Maddy's body under my hands to what I had known before her: to Shane, the marvels of his own body offset by the familiarity of his heart, so that no matter what new places we found together we could still only ever be two people who had known each other long before we had even known how to be people. But the unmapped landscape I had crossed with him that night in his room compared not at all to the country in which I now found myself, to this girl who moved beneath me and above me like a serpent, lithe and strong, her muscles like cables snapping beneath her skin, the exquisite softness of her mouth a sweet counterpoint to the hard planes of her body; and then all around us a sound rose out of the dark like a swarm of bees humming, and I looked deep into the bright honey of her eyes and found that I had lost myself altogether, that had she not whispered my name over and over as she kissed me, as she made her way from my throat to my breasts to the flat slope of my belly, had she not murmured it against that place that only Shane had ever kissed before her, I should have forgotten it altogether, and it was only the sound of my own name in my her mouth, her tongue shaping it as she shaped me, that brought me back to myself, and not long after that there was nothing left for her to say at all, and I was nothing more than a body singing, a body reborn and born again, utterly hers in the dark.

In the morning I remembered my name and Maddy was still real. She had fallen asleep, finally, after I had done with her all the things I had ever imagined doing with another person, and a few more things that had only just occurred to me, and then she had shown me again and again just how little I knew and how small my imagination was. I had stayed awake after she finally fell asleep, hardly daring to breathe, certain that if I drifted off she would vanish and none of this night would have happened. The sky outside grew light, her lean body coalescing out of the shadows as the dawn crept in. I touched the tall ship etched in black over her heart, its sails billowing. She opened her eyes and smiled at me, and I discovered in that moment that, inspired by her inventiveness and the stunning depth of her knowledge on the subject, a number of new projects I might essay had just occurred to me, and we were occupied with each other for a while after that. In the morning light I mapped out all her tattoos with my hands: more boats and star maps and bees, and a sextant across her ribs, and a bird I didn't recognize.

"Halcyon," she said, in answer to my unasked question. "A kind of kingfisher. Alcyone lost her lover Ceyx at sea, and threw herself into the ocean after him; the gods changed them both into birds out of pity. The halcyon is a lucky bird, if you see her when you're sailing."

"You like sailing," I said, though I couldn't remember how I knew this, or if it was fully true—something about her out on the water, a beach with white sand, hot merciless sun—

"I used to sail."

"Out here?"

"No. It was a long time ago."

"You met Jack. In California?"

"I've never been to California." A strange flash of déjà vu stuttered through me and was gone again. She yawned and stretched—tangle of dark hair, bright eyes, black tattoos. Overcome, I bit her shoulder, and she laughed and pushed me away. "You like boats?"

"I've only been in Jack's boat. But I liked it."

"Get dressed, then. I'll show you something. Coffee?"

I did not want to get dressed, and I did not want coffee, and the only thing I wanted to be shown was the miracle of her, over and over for the rest of my life. I should have been happy to starve to death in her bed, redolent of sex and sweat and even still after all our labors the sweet smell of her skin, so long as she was there with me; but she was aloof again, pulling on her clothes with her back to me, ripple of muscle and ink disappearing under her billowy black shirt. I tried to keep my disappointment off my face, but it didn't much matter; she wasn't looking at me, anyway, was already half-way down the ladder to her kitchen. I could hear her filling the kettle, lighting the stove. I sighed heavily into her pillow and got up myself.

Fog had rolled in late the night before. Outside was a grey world through which mist swirled so thick I could barely see thirty feet in any direction. Even Qantaqa clambered into the truck in a subdued manner. I pulled on one of Maddy's sweaters and took the steaming mug of coffee she handed me, and she drove us down through town to the spit of beach that reached out from the fort. A low mournful noise echoed across the water—"Foghorn," she said, when I asked—as she parked up by the bluffs, where several people stood looking down at the beach. I followed her as she joined them.

The cool dreamy light leached away the closeness of the night before, and I was too shy again to touch her or even stand too close; in her black clothes, in the real world, she was as inscrutable and inapproachable as the day I'd met her. She hadn't put on a coat, despite the chill; the crows on her arms flickered in the mist that beaded on her skin. A rough caw from the trees behind us and a swoop of black: my own fat crow landed in the grass and hopped toward us, its head cocked. "Hi," I said. It eyed me thoughtfully, cawed a few more times in a distinctly imperious manner, and flapped back up into the trees again. I bit my thumb and chewed miserably at my knuckles, pretending not to notice Maddy refusing to notice me. I could not imagine how she got her eyeliner so perfect; I hadn't seen a mirror anywhere in her house.

On the sandy beach below us, six or seven canoes lay parallel, with a scatter of people surrounding each one. A line of more canoes stretched out across the water and disappeared into the mist, each of them big enough to hold ten or fifteen people paddling in unison.

"What are they doing?" I asked.

"It's the annual canoe journey. The Northwest Coast tribes started organizing it in the eighties, to revitalize the tradition, and now they paddle all the way into Canada, and down almost to Oregon. That's the Klallam, down there." She pointed to where a tent was set up, with people milling around under it. "This is their tribal land. Each tribe along the coast hosts the travelers as they make their journey."

"I got two kids in one of those canoes," said the woman next to us. Her clear grey eyes were startling against her brown skin, and she wore a red sweatshirt with a canoe logo. Her features were drawn with worry but still striking in their harmony, and her heavy dark hair fell sleek and glossy past her shoulders. "It's so foggy out there, I'm a basket case. My youngest is twelve; she was so excited last night she was talking in her sleep."

"Did you paddle?" I asked her.

"Not today," she said. "Twenty-four miles yesterday. And tomorrow, even farther, when we paddle to Quinault. That's where I'm from. The fog was nothing like this yesterday. I heard you can't even see the front end of the canoe from the back out there. That's a nice dog you got there." She bent down to pat Qantaqa, who gazed up at her happily, pleased someone had realized she deserved to be the center of attention.

As each canoe drew close to shore someone would leap out and run up toward the tent pavilion and, panting for breath, ask permission to land on behalf of their tribe. They'd pass the mike over to a rotating member of the Klallam, who welcomed them in a language I didn't know—"Klallam," the woman said—and English, crying, "Come ashore! Come ashore! Come ashore!" The paddlers steered their canoes to an open spot on the beach before jumping out, hoisting the canoe to their shoulders, and carrying it carefully ashore. "That fifth one in is cedar," the Quinault woman said, pointing at the biggest of the canoes; it was beautifully painted, with red and black figures winging across its bow. "The ocean dugouts weigh sixteen hundred pounds, some of them—Oh, thank the Creator, that's them out there with the flag," she said. "I better get down to the beach." Some white tourists were playing volleyball next to the nearest of the canoes, oblivious; a girl in hot-pink short shorts lobbed the ball at one of the kids climbing out of the canoes and shrieked a falsetto, giggling apology. A few of the paddlers were wearing flat, circular hats and beautiful black coats sewn with vivid patterns of birds and fish outlined in white disks—"Buttons," Maddy said—but most of them were wearing sweatshirts and athletic shorts. All of them looked happy.

We stood for a long time as the canoes materialized out of the mist, one by one, and glided toward the shore, the people on the beach calling to each in turn: *Welcome, welcome,* and then the echo in older, richer languages, unfamiliar in their music and pattern. The heavy fog lent the whole beach the weighty, hazy quality of a dream. Grey beach, black boats, silver water. We watched in silence until the last of the canoes was drawn ashore, the last of the paddlers greeted and folded into the circle of family and friends, and then Maddy turned away and, after a beat, I followed. She was careful to keep her face hidden from me but still I caught the snail-traced glint of tears tracking their way down her cheeks.

When the fog cleared Maddy drove us to the farmer's market downtown, and we bought raspberries in a pint box and cider, salmon out of a cooler full of ice and a lettuce as big as my head, because the lettuces in Maddy's garden were done for the year. I picked up a bunch of deep velvety purple-green kale as big as a baby. The vegetables here did not look anything like the vegetables at the farmer's market in Prospect Park, which seemed shabby cousins in comparison. Maddy laughed at my big eyes.

"We don't have vegetables like this where I'm from." She looked at me as though she was on the verge of asking me something, and I would have given anything to know what it was—since I'd blurted out my whole history to her, that first evening at her house, she'd asked me nothing about myself or what I was doing here or what I planned to do next, as though to do so would be to violate some unbreakable, unspoken rule, commit some trespass against me, or against herself. If she was not curious about me, I thought, it was because she did not wish to evoke any answering curiosity about herself.

"There are a few perks to living in the middle of nowhere," she said.

"Maddy? Why did you move out here? To forget what?"

But she was walking too fast, and I had to half-run to catch up with her—"Oh look," she said, "we should get some of this pesto, too." We bought the pesto, and coffee, and I did not ask her any more questions.

"That's my landlady," Maddy whispered with a jerk of her chin toward a stall full of brown glass bottles and baskets of herbs. The woman behind the table didn't look much like a witch; she was short and stout, with long, curly dark hair and a sour expression that looked to be more or less permanent. I knew, from living with Aunt Beast and Raoul, that the bottles were tinctures; Aunt Beast had gone through a dreadful phase of making her own herbal salves, which involved a lot of melting things and burning pots and stinking up the kitchen. The witch landlady gave us a basilisk glare, and I collapsed into giggles. Maddy grabbed my hand. "She'll hex you!" she hissed, laughing, and pulled me away.

I did not much feel like going back to Jack's, and Maddy did not suggest it. Time had lost all meaning, and I had no idea if I had been at her house for days or for weeks; nor did I care. At Maddy's house my dreams were even worse than they'd been at Jack's. Over and over, the dark-haired girl, the bone forest, the dog. And uglier things, now, too: a ship full of men with hard mean eyes; a one-eyed monster the size of a house; a child, eyes wide in terror, screaming wetly even as a crimson fountain poured forth from its cut throat. All my dreams ended in blood: hot red rivers of blood, blood poured over me, blood washing across a white-sand beach; I'd wake up screaming, Maddy's hands knotted in my hair, her mouth at my ear, hushing me in a language I did not know. When I was too afraid to go to sleep she'd keep me up, telling me stories about old gods while she drank whisky out of the bottle and smoked cigarette after cigarette, or in other ways: her fingers inside me and her mouth on my skin, the salt taste of her body its own ocean mapped in scars, until my nightmares were forgotten and I could not think of anything other than her lavender-scented skin, her raspy voice, her bitten-nailed fingers, cigarette hanging loosely between her knuckles.

One afternoon she sent me out to the garden to pick kale, and when I walked in the front door of her cabin I smelled the metallic tang of blood. She was in the kitchen, where

I'd left her, her arms red to the elbows, a knife in her hand, a rabbit on the counter in front of her cut open from its throat to its tail. Its guts spilled across the counter, the red kernel of its heart pulsing fast as a hummingbird's wings. It looked up at me and blinked, its nose twitching in panic. "Come in, sweetheart," Maddy said. "What's the matter?" I stumbled back out the door and made it ten feet before I threw up in her garden. I sank to my knees, doubled over, but there was nothing left in my stomach, there'd been barely anything there to begin with, and so I retched spittle onto the rich dark earth, my stomach still heaving long after my mouth was dry. There was nowhere for me to go, so I went back inside. She was in the kitchen still, thumping out dough on the cutting board, her hands white with flour. The counter was clean save a dusting of flour where she kneaded.

"Where is it?" I asked thickly.

"Where's what?"

"The rabbit," I whispered.

"What rabbit?" She came toward me and I let her kiss me, her soft mouth tasting of raspberries and salt. She tugged my shirt over my head, and my body came alive under her hands. Everywhere she touched me she left a dusting of flour across my skin. Something stirred inside me, some memory— dark night, blood all over, a child in her arms. What child? Maddy didn't have a child. I was dreaming again, dreaming while I was awake.

That night we ate lentil soup and fresh-baked bread and went to bed early. She fell asleep before I did, and I watched the bone ladder of her ribs rise and fall as she breathed. She slept like a child, curled in on herself away from me, and if sometimes she seemed a thousand years old, at night, like this, after we had come together and then she had fallen into sleep, she looked even younger than me. "What are you?" I said to her softly, but she did not stir, and even if she had heard me I was not sure I wanted to know the answer. I got out *Metamorphoses* for the first time since the man in the used bookstore had given it to me and opened it at random.

Gods of the dark-leaved forest and gods of night,
Come to my call. When you have entered me,
As if a miracle had drained their banks and courses,
I've driven rivers back to springs and fountains.
I shake the seas or calm them at my will;
I whip the clouds or make them rise again;
At my command winds vanish or return,
My very spells have torn the throats of serpents,
Live rocks and oaks are overturned and felled,
The forests tremble and the mountains split,
And deep Earth roars while ghosts walk from their tombs.

I did not much want to read any more after that. I put away the book and blew out the candle and curled myself around Maddy, my face buried in the hollow between her shoulder blades, my belly cleaved to her bony spine, and when I finally fell asleep I was grateful beyond measure that, for once, I did not dream.

I asked her, once, about her tattoos: they moved, I could almost swear it, under my mouth when I kissed her, slipping across her belly—bees buzzing from flower to flower, constellations tracking across the map of her skin, crows' wings outstretched in flight. The halcyon's sharp eyes watching me. She only laughed.

"Who did them?" I asked again, insistent, and she shrugged.

"I don't remember. People all over. I did some of them myself. Do you want one? Is that why you won't leave me alone?" And that was how I came one night to let her dip a thread-wrapped sewing needle in black ink and pick out a tattoo on the inside of my elbow. It hurt like hell, but I thought it might help me keep her. I was so drunk on her I would have let her do anything to me by then, any number of things; I would have gone anywhere she had asked, if it meant more time in her company. Even in those brief days when all my life was her some part of me understood that I could not possibly live like that forever, in her house in the woods, surrounded by coyotes and crows; but as long as she was willing to make me forget myself over and over again, as long as she did not tire of me, I could pretend that I had dropped whole cloth into a world that consisted solely of her. When she finished with the needle I had a black crow of my own, standing with its head cocked, so lifelike it seemed about to leap off my arm into flight. "It's beautiful," I said when she'd wiped away the blood.

She kissed me, soft and full. "Not as beautiful as you," she said.

Maddy thought we should leave her house; Maddy thought I should learn to drive. "I'll teach you. You're not in the city anymore," she said, unmoved by my protests. "Everyone here drives. What if I get too drunk at Kate's and you have to drive me home? What if Qantaqa gets sick and you can't find me?" We had not been to Kate's in—how long? I had no idea how many days I'd been at her house, but we'd barely left it since the night I'd first slept with her. No matter how much Maddy drank her disposition remained unmoved, her movements as precise and controlled as a queen's. And I could not imagine any situation in which Qantaqa would be sick, I would be anywhere near Maddy's truck, and Maddy herself would be nowhere about. But this logic had no effect, and so we put Qantaqa in the back of the truck, she drove me to a gravel lot out by the paper mill—"Generations of teenagers have mastered the clutch on this very ground," she said cheerfully—and made me switch places with her, and she taught me to drive.

I killed the engine a dozen times—"Lovely, you are not trying to end a cockroach, less with the stomping"—and sent the truck forward in jolts that made Qantaqa bark anxiously, her wet nose pressed against the glass window between the cab of the truck and the bed as she looked in on us in confusion, the order of her world gone askew. But Maddy was a good, patient teacher, never alarmed by my mistakes, and after a couple of hours she pronounced me fit to try driving on the back roads.

"I don't even have a license," I said, horrified.

She waved a hand. "I know all the cops," she said. "Just don't hit anyone. You'll be fine."

At first I drove at an old-lady crawl, hunched over the wheel, but at her urging—"We could walk faster than this, come on, be brave"—I sped up. I drove down the mill road and back up again several times, executed left- and right-hand turns under her directions, made a seventeen-point U-turn. "See," she said, "nothing to it. Let's go out on the highway."

"No," I said immediately. The speed limit on the highway was fifty; twenty-five was frightening enough.

"Yes," she said, imperious. "You can write a postcard home about it." Alternately threatening and cajoling, Maddy got me to turn onto the highway, Qantaqa barking excitedly at this change in our progress. "She thinks we're going to the beach," Maddy said, and I blushed. How many girls had she taken to the place where she'd first kissed me? My own jealousy shocked me. It was late in the day by now, nearly twilight, and the road was deserted. "Faster," Maddy said, "you're going ten miles under the speed limit," and I gritted my teeth, my knuckles white on the wheel, and floored the gas. The truck leaped forward—and then an amber flash out of the corner of my eye, a grotesquely fleshy thud, the truck jerking—

"Oh shit," I screamed, "oh shit oh shit"—the truck veering into the other lane and back again. Maddy's voice in my ear, cool and calm: "Slow down, slow, slow, hands on the wheel, pull over, there you go." Somehow I got the truck to the side of the road, shaking so violently I thought my teeth would come out of my head, one of Maddy's hands on my back, the other on my hand, shifting the truck into park.

"It's okay," she said in my ear, over and over again, "you're okay, everybody's okay," until I calmed down and unknotted my hands from the steering wheel and put them, trembling, in my lap.

"What happened?" I whispered.

"You hit a deer," she said.

"Oh, fuck."

"It could have been a lot worse. You did great."

"Qantaqa—"

"Is fine. We're all fine. I promise. I want you to wait here, okay?"

"Where are you going?" But she was already out the door of the truck and walking back down the road. I watched her in the rearview mirror, long legs in the dim light, and then I opened my door and got out, too. My legs were so shaky I almost fell, and I had to stand for a moment with both hands on the truck, holding myself up, Qantaqa nosing me worriedly. I scratched her behind the ears and she whined.

"I'm okay, too," I said, more to myself than her, and I followed Maddy.

She had walked a long way already and was hunched over something by the side of the road. When I got closer I saw what I had done, and had to stop and look away. The truck had done a lot of damage; its legs were splayed at unnatural angles and its intestines spilled out of its split belly in a steaming, slick red mass. The ground around it was covered in blood. "Oh god," I said brokenly, and Maddy looked up, her yellow eyes intent.

"I told you to stay in the truck," she said.

"I couldn't—"

"Then come here." I walked over to her and made myself look down at the deer. Impossibly, it was still alive, its dark eyes rolling in terror, jerking its useless legs in an effort to get away from us.

"Can you finish what you began?" Maddy asked, and when I didn't answer she bent over the deer again, whispered something to it and touched its trembling head with one hand. It calmed instantly, looking up at her, its bloody sides heaving.

"There's a knife in the glove compartment," Maddy said. I stood rooted to the pavement and she looked up at me with a flicker of impatience. "Go get it." I walked back to the truck in a daze, opened the glove compartment, saw it: a dull-handled knife in a worn leather sheath, longer than my hand. I walked back to her. She took the knife from me and unsheathed it. The blade was some dark oily metal, with a lethal-looking edge. She said something to the deer again, in the secret language she used to calm me in the dark, and it looked up at her with trusting eyes. She pulled its head back and cut its throat in a motion so fast I did not see her hand move. The deer's blood geysered over her, but she did not flinch or back away.

The world around me shifted violently, the trees spinning away from us and fading into green blurs, the road flickering under my feet; a roar filled my ears like waves rising and in the distance a dog howled—once, twice, three times. The woods were gone; I stood on bare rocky ground under a low, hot yellow sun, the air desert-scorched and clear. Maddy knelt in front of me in a white dress that left her arms bare, and the face she turned up toward me was younger somehow, less wary. But her wide gold eyes had a spark of madness in them, and her expression was awful. Instead of the deer she held a child, asleep, its peaceful face slack.

A passion drives me greater than my will, she said. The oil-dark knife flashed in her hand and I cried out but it was too late: red crescent gaping where the child's throat had been and its blood pouring out over her, soaking her dress and pooling beneath her in the hard pale earth where she knelt. I felt bile rising in my throat and the world spun again, and I staggered, putting one hand out to steady myself, but there was nothing there—I was falling, falling through darkness and heat, the dog howling again and again and again, a madness of crows' wings flapping around me. I hit the ground with a thud that snapped my teeth shut and brought tears to the corners of my eyes. I rolled over onto my side, a lone crow cawing from a tree somewhere above me, my fingertips touching something rough and warm. Pavement. I was next to the road again. Maddy cradled the deer's head, singing to it softly as its blood ran out and the light in its eyes dimmed, her voice sweet and sad, rising and falling.

I watched stupidly as the deer died, as she wiped the knife on her pants and sheathed it again, then stood up. "I'm going to move her off the pavement. It is better for creatures like her to go back into the earth." I felt as though I had fallen into tar, the air so thick that I could not speak or move my limbs. Maddy did not ask for my help as she dragged the deer's carcass away from the road, and I did not try to get up. When she came back I saw that there was no blood on her clothes or her hands, though I'd watched the deer bleed out all over her. None of what had just happened seemed in any way real. With a flap of dark wings the crow, my crow, fluttered out of the trees above us and landed near me, hopping toward me with its head cocked.

"Come on," she said, offering me her hand and pulling me to my feet. "You going to be sick?"

"No," I whispered, although I wasn't sure if this was true.

"Good girl." Her hand, firm on my back, gentled me back to the car: *One foot in front of the other, one foot in front of the other, one more step, come on sweetheart, that's right, one more step.* I sank into the passenger's seat with a shuddering sigh, Qantaqa's cold nose pushing inquisitively at my palm; I petted her instinctively, and she clambered up and over me, whuffing, and settled next to me on the seat. Maddy got in on the other side.

"Let me take you to a party," she said.

I couldn't think of anything I wanted less, but I shrugged and she started the truck. Trees flashed by in a darkening blur. I rolled the window down to feel air on my face and Qantaqa readjusted, draped herself heavily across me and thrust her muzzle upward. I tangled my fingers in her fur. *You hit a deer,* I told myself, *you hit a deer, and it was the worst, and it's normal to freak out, and nothing else happened, you hit a deer, and Maddy killed it because it wasn't going to live and you weren't brave enough to put it out of its misery. You hit a deer.* I was still shaking. Qantaqa whined and pushed the top of her skull into my hand, and I scratched behind her ears. The deer's panicked eyes and then its eerie calm, the hypnotic lull of Maddy's voice. She was good with animals, that was all, she was good with animals. "We should have taken it to a vet," I said aloud.

She was humming to herself as she drove, and now she reached over and turned on the ancient radio, fiddling with the dial until she found a song she liked, her eyes still on the road. "The first death is always the worst," she said.

"I don't ever want a second."

"It gets easier," she said.

We drove in silence for a while, past the edge of town, farther than I'd been since I first came. Down a long winding road, edged on one side by a steep drop to the water and on the other by more woods. I curled over Qantaqa and put my face in her soft fur. She smelled like Maddy's house: rosemary and lavender and incense and underneath it a not-unpleasant chemical tang of the kerosene Maddy put in her lamps. Qantaqa thumped her tail against the seat. The glistening mass of its guts, red blood dark on the pavement, its black eyes rolling, the smell—oh god, the smell, the smell, I had done that, I had done that—I sobbed into Qantaqa's coat, my shoulders heaving, and she licked my ear. We turned again, and I felt tires crunching on gravel, more bumpy dirt road—god, how I missed New York and its own streets riddled with sinkholes and craters—the truck slowing to a stop. The clamor of voices and outdoorsy scent of wood smoke drifted in through the open window. I didn't move. Maddy put her hand on my back. *I want to go home,* I thought.

"Tally, my lovely girl," Maddy said, her voice in that low, sweet register, the voice she'd used on the deer; I could feel it winnowing in through the cracks of me, filling me with a balmy warmth. Shane, I thought, Shane, his smell, his room, its haze of pot smoke, a record on the turntable, bologna and Wonder Bread sandwiches, my own home, familiar as the skin I live in. His raspy voice, telling me about some effects pedal. A rush of homesickness, a flash flood tumbling me down a chasm. *Make it be normal again, just make it be normal—*

"Tally, lovely, lovely," she said again, and her gentle voice drove all thought of anything else out of me. She pushed Qantaqa gently to the floor of the truck, and I put my head in her lap, and she stroked my hair out of my face, her fingers teasing apart the knots—how long since I'd brushed my hair? Taken a shower? Eaten a meal? I couldn't even think. "Lovely, lovely," she repeated, her voice a deep dreamless sleep falling over me. "Don't think about it anymore," she said, and my mind went blank.

I sat up and got out of the truck. We were at a party. Whose party? Who cared. Qantaqa jumped out of the cab behind me and lumbered off into the trees. I heard a harsh caw and looked up: a ragged black patch flapping against the less-black night, a black glint that could have been a beady eye. The sky was silvery. There must have been a moon. How did I not know the moon's phase? How did I not know what day it was? Buzzing in my ears. I shook my head and it went away. Maddy at my side, her hand slipping into mine, her mouth at my ear. "Good girl," she said.

The party was noisy and alive. People standing around a bonfire, people running in and out of the woods. A few faces I recognized, from Kate's bar, but mostly strangers. Lots of black boots and torn black jeans, like the crust punks who festooned the streets of New York every summer with their backpacks and their dogs, and lots of the logger clothes people wore out here: work pants and billed caps, here and there even a flannel shirt. Maddy's hand at my back, resting on my bare skin underneath my shirt. I shivered. I wanted to grab her and throw her to the ground, eat her alive, tear her to pieces.

I tugged her into the shadows, away from the circle of people where the bonfire's light didn't reach, shoved her against a tree. Her yellow eyes met mine, and she grinned and pulled me into her. I kissed her hard and she kissed me back harder, hungry, her thigh wedged between my legs, her fingers undoing the buttons of my jeans. She bit my lip with her sharp little teeth, so hard I tasted blood, and I yanked her hair. She worked her hand into my jeans and shoved her fingers inside me, and a harsh animal noise came out of my throat, a sound that I had no idea I could even make. I was like a tiny sailboat on a sea mad with storms. I held tight to her shoulders, clinging desperately to the anchor of her body as she moved deeper and deeper inside me until I came in a shuddering wave that I thought would undo me. I buried my face in the curve of her neck and she held me tight, kissing the top of my head, my ear, my forehead, stroking my back until my shaking subsided. If she had not been holding me up I would have fallen to my knees.

"I'm falling in love with you," I said into her shoulder.

"I know," she said.

After that, the party was a blur. How we must have looked—our hair in tangles, our eyes alight, drunk with sex like maenads, like furies. A glittering host of curious eyes. I drank a beer and then another and said nothing, and Maddy was mostly quiet, too. Somebody's toddler was underfoot, running in and out of a forest of legs looking for a mother. I pretended not to see it. The bonfire washed away the dark, made faces lovely in its light, but none so marvelous as hers— her soft skin, the fox-fine bones of her face, her huge yellow eyes. I could not look away from her. I did not talk to anyone, and nobody talked to me; it was as if she'd woven a force field around me, so that anyone who tried to come close would catch fire with the power of the charge she'd set.

"I want to go," I said finally. I couldn't even remember why we'd come here.

"Back to Jack's?" I looked at her, helpless with lust, and she smiled.

"I see," she said, and drove me back to her house instead.

After that was a blur: her body, her skin. Sweat and salt and teeth. I couldn't remember anything from one moment to the next, couldn't remember my own name or hers, or whose hands were between my legs, whose cat-quick tongue, or where I had come to, or how I had gotten here; and then it would come back to me again in a swift flood like a storm surge, and I'd remember—my name is Tally this is Maddy this is Maddy's house—and recede as swiftly as it had risen. I couldn't stop crying. The air tasted of blood, and I didn't know why—white dress silver knife—and I screamed out loud, and she stopped kissing me and held me tight. "Hush," she said, "you're safe now, you're here."

"Tell me a story," I said against her soft mouth. "Please. Tell me something true."

"Long ago," she said, her voice low and heavy, calming the flutter of my heart, "when the gods came down among the people and made trouble, a king who wanted a son had a daughter instead. He was so angry he left her on a mountain to die. But a bear found her and nursed her, and with a bear for a mother, the girl grew up strong and without fear. She could run as fast as any animal in the forest. Finally the bear knew it was time for the girl to go live among her own kind, and so, though it grieved her, she gave her human daughter to some hunters. The hunters taught her to shoot true, to move silently through the woods, to live wisely and alone.

"The goddess of the wild places became angry with a lord who lived in that country because he had forgotten her in his sacrifices, and so she sent a great boar to destroy him. The boar was so monstrous no warrior could defeat it, and it killed many people and laid waste to the land. In desperation, the lord called together a great hunt, and the girl went among the hunters, and they laughed at her. Others were angry, for they thought it beneath them to go hunting with a woman. But she ignored them, and when the boar came and rushed upon them, it was she and she alone who stood her ground, and struck it dead with a single arrow.

"Because she was so strong, and also beautiful, she had a great many suitors, but she had no use for any of them. To get rid of them, she said she would marry any man who could beat her in a footrace; she and everyone else knew there was no such man on earth.

"But the goddess of love dislikes being thwarted by savage young ladies, and so she gave three enchanted golden apples to an aspiring suitor. No mortal could look upon them and not wish to possess them. He challenged the girl to a race. As they started she left him behind easily, but he tossed the first of the golden apples before her. Entranced, she stooped to pick it up, and he passed her. She soon caught up with him, and so he threw the second apple. Again, she stopped to pick it up, and then caught up with him easily. Finally, at the finish line, he threw the last apple, and it rolled a long way off the course. Unable to resist it, she ran after it, and he crossed the finish line first, and she had to keep her promise and marry him, though she did not wish to."

"Whose story is that?" I said, although I knew.

"Yours, lovely," she said.

"I still don't understand why she had to marry him," I said. I was calm again, myself. "He cheated."

"The gods hold mortals to their promises," she said, "but

they themselves are cheats. It's the word and not the gesture that binds. Who named you?"

"My aunt."

"She named you after a girl who refused to fall in love," Maddy said, stroking my hair. "Why do you think she did that?"

"She tries not to. Maybe she didn't want me to, either."

"Some people say Atalanta sailed on the Argo with Jason," she said, yawning. "Before Melanion tricked her into marrying him. But nobody puts girls into those sorts of stories, even if they belong there. Only witches get to travel with heroes."

"Maybe if Atalanta'd been a witch, she wouldn't have ever had to marry," I said.

"Maybe," Maddy said. She propped herself up on one elbow and looked at me. "But even witches are made to sacrifice."

That night I dreamed about a familiar place I'd never been. A flat expanse of stone, the sun hot on my shoulders. A sea as glossy blue as a jay's wing, the smell of salt and scorched earth. A circle of crows surrounding me, motionless in the merciless light.

"If you listen well enough all the stories of the world are written in your body," Maddy said behind me, and I turned around to face her: bare feet, her arms red from fingertips to elbows, the front of her white sleeveless dress soaked in blood. Her hair was a loose cloud around her brown shoulders. "I told you to listen," she said, "I told you, I told you," and her voice rose to a high wordless wail, and I took a step back from her and then another, but she kept coming toward me.

"Let me go," I said, "please, let me go," and she laughed and shook her head.

"As you wish, little bird," she said, and I took another step backward and there was nothing beneath my foot but air, and I tipped backward into a hot blue emptiness, falling toward the breakers that crashed on jagged rocks a hundred feet below me. I jerked awake. She was fast asleep, one hand tucked beneath her chin and the other thrown outward as though she was reaching for something I could not see. I watched the rise and fall of her ribs for long minutes. Outside her house a coyote howled, and another answered it, and then the voices of the whole pack rose in an eerie chorus, yipping wails that looped back on themselves, rising and falling and then subsiding at last into silence again.

"What are you?" I whispered. "What have you done to me? What are you doing?" But she did not stir. In the morning she was just a girl again, kissing me awake, and the dream faded like a ghost in the ordinary light.

"Jack will think I've stolen you," she said one afternoon.

"I guess I should make sure he knows I'm still alive." I thought guiltily of my family: They probably thought by now I was dead, too. I could call them again from Jack's. Maddy dropped me off, kissing me in his driveway for so long I wanted to tell her to turn around and take us back to her cabin, take all my clothes off and make me forget who I was over and over again. With effort I broke away. "Do you want to come in?" A troubled look crossed her face, and she shook her hair out as though she'd seen a bug in the car.

"No," she said.

"You can ask him—" I thought carefully, struggling to remember the words even as I thought of them. "You can ask him about sailing," I said. "Didn't you go sailing with him?"

"No pasts," she said. "Come back to me." I nodded. I stood watching her drive away, willing her to look back, but she didn't. My own thoughts were not comfortable company. I went inside Jack's house; to my surprise, he was seated at the table, hunched over some old instrument I didn't recognize, fiddling with its strings.

"Hi," I said.

"You look terrible," he said. "Where have you been? Are you eating?"

"I eat," I said, ignoring his first question.

"What would your mother think of me?"

"I don't have a mother."

Jack sighed. "Let's go sailing."

He drove me to the marina in silence. In silence we parked the truck and walked to his boat, in silence we climbed aboard, and in silence I sat in the bow while he pulled in the line and raised the sail and guided us out past the breakwater. Out on the open water the temperature dropped. I wrapped my arms around myself and hunkered down in the bow.

"You're charming this afternoon. Are you going to tell me where you've been? Should I send you home in disgrace? I haven't had much to do with teenagers since . . ." He trailed off. "In a long time," he said. "You'll have to help me with the details."

"I've been here for ages, and you haven't told me anything," I said. "Not a single thing. Not about who you are or about Aurora or about where I come from or how you knew her."

The sail snapped in the wind and he did not answer me for a while, frowning in concentration as he fussed with the lines.

"I told you I barely knew Aurora," he said finally.

"You're lying." I was too tired to care anymore.

He shook his head. "I'm not, Tally. It was years ago. A lifetime ago. She was young when I met her. About as old as you are now. She was beautiful, which I think for her was more of a curse than a gift. You look like her."

"I'm not beautiful."

"If you say so," Jack said. "But she was, and there is no mistaking you are her daughter. She was . . ." He paused, trying to think of the right word. "She was heartbroken," he said finally. "I think when her father died he took some part of her with him. By the time I met her she was already lost."

"And then what? What happened to her? How is it that no one knows where she is?"

"She and I lived in Los Angeles for a while at the same time," he said. "But I had lost touch with her by the time you were born. She had fallen into—" He stopped.

"Fallen into what?"

"Fallen in with some bad people," he said. "There was a record producer she was . . . Once he got hold of her, she never had a chance." Another pause. I waited. "I'm sorry. I can't tell you any more. I don't know what happened after that. I played music in LA for a while, and then I didn't want to be a part of that scene so I came here, over a decade ago, and I've been here ever since, and I can't say I've noticed much that's happened in the world since then. Aurora never tried to find me after we lost touch. I don't know—I don't know if she could have, from where she was when I knew her."

Did you love her? I thought. *Did you love her long enough to make me? Long enough to write that song for her? Do you know if I am your child? Do you even care?* He was looking out at the water, not at me, his face inscrutable. I didn't know how to ask him, or what to ask him, or what he would say if I did somehow find the right question, and so I did not ask him anything at all, and he pointed out some otters winnowing quick as laughter through the waves, their heads popping up in unison to watch us as we sailed past, and the moment was gone. "I'm working up to sailing around the world," he said after a while. "Next year, probably."

"Why on earth would you want to do a thing like that?"

"To see if it can be done," he said.

"Obviously it can be done."

"To see if it can be done by me." He looked out at the mountains, where they were going purple against the cooling dusk sky. "People who sail like that," he said, "a voyage like that, alone through all that darkness and terror, are either sailing toward something, or running away."

"Which one is it for you?"

"Sometimes it's hard to tell the difference," he said. "Why did you come here, Tally? To find, or to run? We're not so unalike as you might think."

"You've had a lot longer than me to run away from things," I said coolly.

"Why are you so angry? What good is it doing you?"

I opened my mouth to answer him and found to my surprise that he was right: I was angry, and I had no idea why. I had been angry at Aurora all my life, I was angry at Aunt

Beast for lying to me and Raoul for letting her, at Shane for letting me go so easily, at Maddy for making me fall in love with her, at Jack for being what he was, elusive, evasive, inscrutable. I was angry at myself for coming all this way for nothing. And more than anything I was angry at whoever my real father was, moving around in the world, oblivious or uncaring—and which, in the end, was worse?—or maybe this infuriating chimera of a man in front of me, basically a stranger, who might know more about me and where I came from than anyone else in my life. But here, now, in Jack's boat, the salt wind in my face and gulls eyeballing me from where they bobbed in the water, hoping for snacks, and loons diving quick and sure away from the bow as we sailed, all my anger seemed overlarge and unnecessary and exhausting.

"I've been angry for a long time," I said finally. I had not expected myself to be so honest with him, but here I was. "But I don't think running away is the answer. I don't think I'm running away."

"I never knew my father," Jack said, and I thought he understood at last what it was I was looking for, but he only meant he'd lost a parent before he'd had one, too. "I thought for a long time that it didn't mean anything. I knew who I was and what I wanted. A father seemed like an unnecessary burden. Someone else's expectations for you, someone else's dreams. A mother was hard enough. But the older I got, the more I wanted to know where I had come from. What it was that had made me. If I was a musician because of myself or because of him. If I was always leaving because he was a leaver, too. Things like that. And when I got older still I realized that loss had shaped me in ways I was still coming to understand. It's not the end of the world, you know, living without a parent. It's not like you're half a person while everyone else is a whole one. But there's always a mystery that other people don't have to reckon with. Was he a good man? An awful one? Would we have loved each other? What did he have to pass down to me, that I had lost?" He fell silent, and I held my breath. He'd said more to me in the last five minutes than he had in the last month. He shook his head. "I'm sorry you came all the way out here to find out more about her, Tally. I wish I had more to tell you. She was one of the most beautiful people I've ever met, and one of the most complicated. She was generous and funny and mean. She didn't care about what she was—you know, rich, pretty, famous. She never said anything to me about it, but I think she would rather have been anyone else instead."

"I don't understand how she could have left me," I said. "If her dad dying messed her up so much, how could she do that to me? How could she not know better?" He changed the angle of the sail, and we moved back toward the harbor.

"We don't always see the mistakes we make as repetitions until long after we've made them," he said. "It's getting late. Let's go in. I'll buy you a hamburger at Kate's."

When we walked into the bar together, people turned around to look at us and then sat, staring. He ordered bitters and soda for himself and two hamburgers and raised his eyebrow when Kate passed me a beer but said nothing. Kate's was crowded; some kind of open mic night. An old lady in a purple skirt was singing a warbly but enthusiastic cover of a Bob Dylan song; after her, a pimple-faced black-clad teen played a few morose acoustic compositions; after him, some bearded guys in suspenders played bluegrass. Jack chewed his hamburger and watched, impassive. "Nobody in this town would last five minutes in New York," I said when they were done and carrying their instruments off the stage.

"Ssshh," he said. Three hippie girls were adjusting the microphones—pretty, white, more or less indistinguishable from one another. Long, shiny brown hair and long gauzy skirts in three slightly variant earth colors, embroidered tank tops that made it clear none of them had much use for undergarments. The attention of the bar had shifted to the hippies, evidently the reason so many people were here.

"Thanks for coming," the middle one said in a breathy, sultry voice that made me giggle. She licked her pink lips in an affectedly sexy manner that had a profound impact on a number of gentlemen sitting near me, who were sitting openmouthed and rapt. "We're the Sirens." The other two stepped up next to her and the three girls linked hands—*Cute,* I thought—and looked as one at some point over the heads of the audience, and then they began to sing.

Whatever language they were singing in, I didn't know it, but it didn't matter. Their voices wove in and out of one another, moving like water, like the wind in the sails of Jack's boat, sweet and sad and longing, carrying us all out of that dim room and into a place I had no words for. As they sang they grew more and more lovely, until I had to shut my eyes lest I leap up and throw myself at their feet; next to me, Jack shifted, and I knew he felt it, too. *Sing my name,* I thought, *sing my name and I will follow you anywhere, follow you into the wheeling spheres of the stars,* and each note wrapped itself around my heart in tighter and tighter coils until I thought I would weep from the exquisite pain of it. How long the music lasted, I could not have said—a moment, an hour, a thousand years—and when the last perfect harmony faded into the still room you could have heard a hummingbird's heart beating. Around me more than one person was crying. The girls' unearthly beauty slid away until they were just three chipper hippies standing on a stage again, looking at each other as though they were all in on some private joke, and then they took a bow and left the stage. No one even clapped; we stared, mouths open, speechless and stunned as rabbits.

They were the last act, and it took a long time for the room to go back to ordinary, for chatter to start back up again, people shaking themselves as if out of a dream and getting up to order more drinks. Jack's eyes were closed, and he held his drink on the table as tightly as if it were a lifeline. "Are you okay?" I asked, and my voice sounded strange in my ears, harsh and ugly after the lilting glory of their song.

"Yes," he said, opening his eyes but not looking at me. "I'm fine." I didn't quite believe him, but I didn't know him well enough to say anything else. "Let's go," he said, standing up and stalking toward the door with his long strides without looking to see if I was following.

"Okay," I said to his back, scrambling after him and waving goodbye to Kate at the bar, who was busy with customers and didn't see. Outside, a boy in a baseball cap and a white apron was smoking on the curb; I recognized him as the busboy from Kate's. He was wearing a faded old T-shirt with my grandfather's band emblazoned across the front.

"I like your shirt," I said, and he looked up, a slow shy smile spreading across his face.

"You know this band?"

I almost laughed. "Sure," I said.

"My favorite album is the first one," he said eagerly, "the EP, you know, not the full length. *We drive down the coast all night / count the stars in your eyes / baby's gonna be all right,*" he sang, making drumming motions with his arms.

"That's a good one," I said. Jack was watching us, his eyes sad. About what, I wondered. Me? Music? This poor lonely kid? "My friend's waiting, I should go."

"You have a good night," he said, and I smiled.

"You, too," I said. "See you around." Jack was silent for the entire drive back to his house, silent once we got in the door, and silent as he walked away from me, down the hall, and shut himself in one of his secret rooms without a backward glance. If I wanted to get anything real out of him, it was going to take a while. Maybe more time than I had.

The next morning, I called my apartment from Jack's phone and Raoul answered on the second ring. "You're a week overdue," he said.

A week? I thought. How had I only been at Maddy's for a week? How did I not even know what day it was? I rubbed my eyes with the heel of one hand. "How did you know it was me?"

"The telephone had a guilty ring."

"Sorry," I said.

"I hope your negligence of your loving family is due to an overabundance of joyful exertion on your part."

You could say that, I thought, grateful Raoul could not see my flaming cheeks.

"It's nice here," I said neutrally.

"You promised, Tally."

"I know. I keep—" It did not seem advisable to tell him I kept forgetting. "I'm having a hard time with, um, time."

"Your aunt is furious. Furious, Tally. She almost left her retreat—"

"You can't let her do that!"

"I talked her out of it. But only just."

"I—okay. Thanks."

"Jenn and Molly called."

"Jenn and Molly?"

"Your *employers*?"

Oh shit, I thought. "Oh. That Jenn and Molly."

"They offered their condolences about your cousin but were hoping you'd be feeling well enough to come back to work soon."

"Work," I said stupidly.

"You never told me you had a cousin." His tone was arch.

"Distant cousin."

"Now deceased. Tragically. Cancer, was it? Of the conscience? You still have a job, but I don't know that you deserve one."

"Raoul, I'm sorry. I just . . . I can't even think out here. I don't know what's wrong with me. I have to find out something. Anything. I can't just come all the way out here and then turn around and come back with nothing." *I can't leave Maddy,* I thought, but I could hardly tell him that. "Tell them—oh, man."

"*You* tell them."

"Fair enough."

"How is Jack?"

"Mysterious."

Raoul made a noise somewhere between a snort and a cough. "Nothing new there. Did he take you to the city?"

"Not yet. I mean, I drove through it on the way here from

the airport. But not since then. Maddy might—my friend might take me. We were talking about going."

"Your friend?"

"I met this—girl. Out here."

"Hmm," he said, but he didn't push it. "Tell your friend to take you to the market. Your aunt and I used to work there, once upon a time."

"Okay," I said. "Raoul?"

"Yes?"

"When did you know that you were in love with Henri?"

There was a long pause. "Is this an abstract question?" he said. "Or an immediate one?"

"I just—when did you know?"

"The second day we spent together," he said. "Our first date lasted for a long time; I hope you are not too scandalized."

I laughed. "Surely you didn't sleep together before you got married."

"Oh dear," Raoul said. "Several times, I'm afraid."

"I don't see how I can face you again in person. Seriously, though. How did you know?"

"We went out to breakfast," he said, "the morning after our first date, and then he took me to Central Park, and we sat on a rock and watched the swans paddling around in the lake, and I looked over at him and thought, *Oh shit, here I go*. That was it. I knew I was going to fall in love with him. And then I did."

"Did you love other people? Before Henri?"

"Sure."

"Do you think I could—do you think someone could be in love with more than one person at a time?"

"Yes," he said. "Do you want to tell me what this conversation is about, Tally?"

"I met someone," I said. "This girl. She's—I feel—it's different."

"Than how you feel about Shane?"

"Yes," I said. "No. I mean, yes. He's so . . . solid. He's just Shane. He's always there. I've known him forever. We know everything about each other. This girl, she's like—she's like a wild animal. That's an embarrassing metaphor. Scratch that from the record."

"Scratched."

"She's—I don't know how to explain it. She's, like, old in her heart. I mean, she's not old. Like an old soul." I had no idea how old Maddy was, but I thought if I told Raoul that I would probably worry him unnecessarily.

"You met her through Jack?"

"I met her in a bar," I said without thinking.

"I *see*."

"Not like that. You know me. The squarest square in squaretown. But around her I'm like—I feel—I don't even know. She's like this magnet." Raoul laughed. "What?" I said.

"I would never malign the power of the magnet," he said, still laughing.

"It's not funny," I said, wounded.

"I'm sorry. I'm not laughing at you. Do *you* think you're falling in love?"

"I don't know how to tell," I said. "I just feel crazy all the time."

"Well," he said, "that sounds about right. It's never easy to learn how to love, especially the first few times you try.

Take good care of yourself, Tally. You know we're always here. All of us."

"I know," I said. "I love you a lot." I wanted badly to ask him if anything about the way I felt about Maddy was normal; if it was reasonable to be certain that if someone were to leave you, you might curl up and die; if I was supposed to spend every waking moment of every day thinking about the sound of her voice and the movement of her body; if nightmares were a common symptom of love; if being followed by a pack of crows happened to ordinary people all the time. I wanted to ask him about all of it, but I could not even bring myself to begin, and even as I tried to assemble the words they slipped away from me. It was no use.

"I love you, too," he said. "*We* love you. Oh, here's Dorian Gray. Dorian loves you as well."

"Dorian is dumb as a barrel of rocks, Raoul."

"Did you hear that?" Raoul said, his voice muffled. "Tally doesn't understand you, Dorian. But I do."

I laughed, really laughed, for the first time in what felt like a long time. "You tell Dorian I'll bring him a West Coast rat. They're way fatter and healthier than the Brooklyn ones. He can gnaw on it for days."

"He'll be so pleased."

"Even the raccoons here are different from the raccoons in Prospect Park. They seem, I don't know, more raccoonish. Like they might run you out of your house and take over. I heard them in Jack's yard one night making all these crazy noises, and I thought it was monsters or something before I went out there and saw them. And there's a whole family of coyotes that lives in the ravine behind Maddy's house. They howl at the moon, just like wolves; it's the coolest thing you ever heard in your life. And the gardens here—you wouldn't believe all the kinds of flowers that just grow everywhere. And I ate raspberries from the farmer's market and they were so good. And Jack took me sailing, and I saw otters."

"You're making me miss it out there."

"It's hard to imagine you living here."

"It had its disadvantages," he said. "But there are a lot of beautiful things."

"And a lot of white people."

"A *lot* of white people."

"I love you, Raoul," I said again. "I should go."

"I love you, too, Tally. Call anytime, okay?"

"Okay."

"At least call more often."

"Okay. Give Henri a kiss for me. Tell Aunt Beast I'm still alive."

"Done and done," he said. "Tally?"

"Yeah?"

"Are you sure you're okay?"

No, I thought. "Why wouldn't I be?"

"You'll tell me. You know I'll come out there. Any one of us."

"You can't send Dorian."

"I'm not joking right now, Tally."

"I know," I said. "I'm fine."

"You told me you'd put Jack on the phone. You told me you'd call every day. You told me you'd come home in a week. You promised, Tally."

"I need a little more time. Just a few more days."

He sighed; I could picture him, one thumb rubbing the

worn beads of the wooden rosary he always wore, the phone tucked between his chin and his shoulder, his ink-stained fingers—he wrote poetry in longhand, with a fountain pen, but in him the gesture seemed necessary instead of affected.

"Just a few more days," I said. "Please."

"Fine," he said. "Just a few more days."

I did not see Jack again; I went back to Maddy's that night, and forgot again—her hair, her teeth, her eyes—that I had promised Raoul I'd go home. The next morning I left her in bed, sleepy eyed and tousled, and rode Jack's bike downtown to the bookstore. "I haven't seen you in a while," the proprietor said, looking at me over his spectacles.

"I've been busy," I said.

"I see," he said.

"Look," I said, pulling the Ovid out of my bag and putting it on the table in front of him, "I want to ask you something. This book you gave me." He raised an eyebrow, expectant, and I cleared my throat, feeling stupid. "Do you think—can any of this—I mean, none of this is real, right?"

"Do pissy gods turn women into birds and stones and flowers? Do inventors build wings out of wax and wood and fly too close to the sun? Do kings cut out the tongues of the sisters-in-law they've raped, and shut them away in houses in the woods?"

"Any of it," I said. "Is any of it real?"

"There are historical sources, certainly."

"That's not what I mean. I mean—the things that don't seem possible." He waited. "Look," I said, "I met this girl here and I—she—I think she—" But I faltered and could not finish my sentence. I think she what? I think she's put me under a spell? I think I can't remember anything for more than five minutes at a time? I sounded like a lunatic. "I'm sorry," I said. "Never mind."

"You look unhappy," he said.

"I'm not crazy," I said. "I know I sound crazy. I'm the most rational person—" I raised one hand and dropped it with a helpless gesture.

"This is a strange place," he said. "Stolen land—I mean, of course, all the land we live on is stolen, but some of these places are more full of ghosts. Out there"—he waved his arm behind him—"is some of the last wilderness in this country, and I mean real wilderness, not some game park. You wouldn't be the first person to see a few strange things in the woods."

"She told me she came out here to forget," I said. "And Kate, too, at the bar—Kate said that. And Jack."

"Then perhaps there is something that ties them all together," he said. "All your friends. A quest in which a glamour has been placed upon the key constituents."

"What?"

He smiled. "Why have you come here? To forget, as well?"

He was a stranger; I had barely exchanged a handful of words with him, and I had no reason to trust him with my secrets and wild imaginings. But there was something about him that invited confidence, and all the things I had meant to tell Raoul but hadn't were still built up in me, threatening to spill over, and I thought if I did not talk to someone ordinary, or at least wise, I would burst with what I had been carrying around. I did not tell him the whole story, not by a long shot, but I told him how Jack and Maddy seemed to know each other, except that they didn't, and how I could no longer go outside without being followed by a bevy of crows. I told him that I had been having very, very bad dreams. He did not interrupt, although I had to go back several times and start over when I left out something important, and sidetracked, as was my wont, into a rather more elaborate explanation of the early moments of the universe than was probably entirely relevant to my narrative. I am sure I made very little sense, but it was such a relief to unburden myself that coherence seemed a tertiary goal. "You think I'm out of my mind," I said when I had talked myself out.

"Not at all," he said.

"Really?"

"I think there are different kinds of stories, and different kinds of knowing. And different kinds of sailors, too—you know, the native peoples of this peninsula were great navigators." I thought about the morning Maddy and I had gone to see the canoes land. "They had a lot of stories about Raven, for that matter," he added.

"My crows."

"Perhaps. I think you are in the middle of a story whose ending you cannot yet see; but that's true for all of us, isn't it?"

"But none of this—I mean it can't be—it can't be *real*."

"What is *real,* exactly? You of all people should know that real is relative—we're barely even here, any of us, we're just empty space and particles flying around—"

"That's not exactly—" He cleared his throat. "It's more complicated than that," I said, unwilling to let him get away with an inaccuracy.

"You are willing to make space for mystery in the universe. Why not mystery closer to home?"

It was a valid question, and one I couldn't answer. I could have said any one of a dozen things I'd have said at the beginning of the summer; I could have quoted Shakespeare: *They say miracles are past; and we have our philosophical persons, to make modern and familiar, things supernatural and causeless.* I could have pointed out that science was based on empirical evidence, not baseless conjecture. If he'd known his stuff, which he seemed to, he could have quoted Shakespeare right back—*we make trifles of terrors, ensconcing ourselves into seeming knowledge, when we should submit ourselves to an unknown fear*—and, more relevant, he could just as easily have pointed out that if the empirical evidence is so wild only the impossible theory fits it, the impossible might just, as it had done time and time again in the history of cosmology, turn out to be the truth. I went out again into the sunny afternoon no less confused than I had been when I'd gone in to see him, and a lot less sure of myself, too.

THE
RETURN
VOYAGE

All my life I had let my own stubbornness carry me, that and the gifts I was sure of, the strength I'd been born with. I knew what languages were spoken in the world I wanted to inhabit, and if I was not yet fluent in them, if I needed years still to untangle the grammar and syntax of thermodynamics, the poiesis of astrophysics and particles and the movement of light, I understood nevertheless the alphabets in which they were inscribed. I had thought that I knew exactly what I did not yet know: unlearned equations like missing volumes on a shelf, to be slotted in neatly as I acquired them. I had been unable to bear anything like disorder, and no wonder—the word *cosmology* itself comes from the ancient Greek *kosmeo,* which means "to order," "to organize"—the universe is worthy of study because it operates in patterns, and our understanding of them is, fundamentally, a kind of organization, a fact which suited my tidy nature well.

And then I had come here, and all I had brought with me seemed now nothing like what I needed, what was necessary to make the world clear. I had arrived with a star chart of a cosmos I expected and landed instead in a universe whose physics were nothing like the physics of the world I knew; I had tumbled into a landscape without polestar or cardinal direction, where the tools with which I'd flawlessly navigated my previous life—my memory, my history, my experience of love—were as useless as a compass held over a magnet until its needle spun in circles. Our universe has been expanding since the moment of its fiery birth, and for decades, cosmologists thought that there were only three possible ends to its story: it might balloon outward forever, at an ever-slowing rate; it might one day stop altogether; or its expansion might finally be reversed by the gravitational pull of its heart, leading to its long, slow collapse inward. And then astronomers studying the recessional velocities of supernovae discovered something extraordinary: the expansion of the universe was not slowing down at all, it was *speeding up*. Propelled by some force whose nature we do not understand, the universe is flinging itself outward like a runaway train. The history of science is a history of those moments in which a single piece of information has torn asunder everything that came before. "The years of searching in the dark for a truth that one feels, but cannot express; the intense desire and the alternations of confidence and misgiving, until one breaks through to clarity and understanding, are only known to him who has himself experienced them," Einstein wrote; it was something I had underlined without taking to heart years ago, but now its truth was sunk into my bones.

The obsession with order and elegance at the expense of the truth is a fatal flaw that goes all the way back to the Greeks, who were the first to propose a cosmos constructed out of a set of concentric spheres wheeling about the earth: graceful, harmonious, and totally inaccurate. And the truth—Kepler's discovery of the planets' elliptical orbits around the sun, the elegance of the equations he wrote to describe their sweeping arcs—is itself unimaginably beautiful. But the beauty of the truth does not mean that all beautiful ideas are true. I had wanted desperately to believe in order, but I had learned, in the last month, that order was invariably subjugate to its underlying architecture, and the truth was more, and bigger, than I had ever imagined; that uncertainty can be beautiful too, and the unknowable—like dark matter, like dark energy, like, dare I say it, *magic*—is far greater than the known. If before my mind had been like a warehouse of file cabinets, tidy and organized, Maddy had come along like a cyclone and pulled all the drawers from their casters, scattered the folders to the wide world, and kicked the doors open, and I did not know, any longer, how to put things back in order.

After she took me to the party in the woods, Maddy and I went out more. She drove us back to the ferry, and we took it into the city and wandered around the old downtown. We ate clam chowder from a stall on the creosote-scented wharf, wheeling seagulls shrieking demands at us all the while; we visited the mummies in the touristy curiosity shop on the waterfront, and Maddy bought me a piece of polished quartz on a cord that was meant to bring good luck; we climbed the hilly streets to a big open-air farmer's market—which must have been the one, I thought, where Aunt Beast and Raoul had once worked—and found underneath it a warren of shops. Maddy spent a long time in one in particular that reminded me of the witch store in the East Village where Aunt Beast bought her candles and herbs: rows of tinctures labeled in neat cursive, glass cases displaying tarot decks and silver pentagrams and crystals, shelves of books on Magickal Thinking (witches, apparently, being averse to copyeditors) and Guiding Your Dreams. The woman behind the counter had crescent moons tattooed at the corners of her eyes and runes inking her knuckles; though her face had a kind of ageless, serene quality to it, I thought she must have been nearly my grandmother's age. She watched us both intently as I loitered uneasily by the door and Maddy more enthusiastically perused the herbs and made her selections, reaching for me as the woman measured them out into paper bags; I came to stand beside her at the register and she put her mouth against my ear and her arm around my waist, and I felt her smile at the shudder her breath at the whorl of my ear sent through me. The woman rang her up and then looked directly at me. "Tell Cassandra that Raven asked after her monster," she said, and I said, "Excuse me?" But she only smiled, her keen dark eyes glittering. "Well met, sisters," she said to us as we left.

We only went to the city once, but now we went often to Kate's, and to potlucks in ramshackle houses in the woods, full of people who wore a lot of down vests and had beards and made foods I barely recognized even after a lifetime of Aunt Beast's cooking. They were fond of banjos and washboards and something called "old-time music," which involved a lot of whisky and stomping on the floor and shouting, and not, as far as I could tell, making much effort toward bathing regularly, although I was in no place to pass judgment, since my own hygiene regime consisted largely of sponge baths at Maddy's sink and the occasional shower at Jack's when I got so filthy I could no longer stand myself. The hippies were not friends of Maddy's, exactly; they seemed to regard her in much the same way I did, with a kind of quiet and respectful awe. Her company conferred upon me a kind of invisibility, and I was content to remain so: I ate the hippies' roots and tubers and grilled fishes, avoided their liquors, eschewed their dancing, and fielded their occasional and largely disinterested enquiries as to my nature and ambitions with a discretion that bordered on sullenness. They were the sort of white people who wanted to talk to you earnestly and at length about their compost. "In New York, we put things in the garbage," I said once, when I had gotten tired of this line of disquisition, and this riposte proved so effective that none of them ventured conversation with me again. And anyway, next to Maddy I dimmed into nothing: she was the singularity, and I was just another particle in her orbit.

A few years after the night in Central Park that had made

me into an astronomer, Raoul and Henri had taken me to Cornwall to see a total eclipse of the sun. We stayed in a bed and breakfast in Perranporth, booked up months in advance by people who, like us—well, like me—were obsessive enough to travel halfway round the world or farther in pursuit of a single observation. In the morning the landlady made us toast and sausages and coffee and we ate them, blinking sleepily, with the other guests at the bed and breakfast, all of whom were there for the same reason. "All this way," the landlady said, her accent thick and burry, "for a little spot across the sun."

The morning of the eclipse we went down to the beach. The sky was scuddy with clouds and I wondered unhappily if I had come all this way for nothing, if I'd be standing on this crowded shore with hundreds of other strangers staring up at a patch of grey instead of the miracle of physics and luck I'd come to see. It's only because we are here in this time, this moment out of all the billions of years our solar system has gone flying around the sun's hell-hot ball, that we get to see eclipses at all: The moon is gradually spinning away from us, out into the dark of space, and only at this point in the history of the solar system does the moon's distance from us make its size in the sky appear equal to that of the sun. A handful of millennia earlier or later, and we'd never have known that a lifeless lump of rock and dust whose only glory comes from a light not its own could suddenly wipe the sun out of the sky neat as a gunshot. How cruel it would have been—all this confluence of chance, to bring me to the time and place where such a thing was possible, only to have it veiled by something so dumb and everyday as a rain cloud.

But at the last moment a wind rose up and swept the clouds away, and a ragged cheer rose up from the beach as the sun came out. I'd read about the moments before the moon blocked out the disc of the sun, the way the colors around me would grow richer and more saturated, the way shadows would go crisp and keen-edged; I knew a hush would fall, animals nervous and silent, the whole world still and strange. But being there—thousands of crescents winking into life, glowing like half-moons in the trees; shadow bands, shimmering lines of black dancing around us; the stars flaring into life in the daytime sky—was so alien, so wonderful, that even Raoul and Henri were looking around with their mouths open.

In the dim shadows of Kate's bar, Maddy'd had no real background against which to dazzle, but here, among people, I understood that I was not the only one who found her a degree of magnetic that moved past human and into more transcendent spheres. She would have been as regal anywhere else; I could easily imagine her in the middle of my own city, surrounded by equally adoring and far more sophisticated throngs. She was like the exiled princess in the fairy tale who spends her days scrubbing dishes in the kitchen, only to be transformed at night by a series of dresses woven out of starlight, moonbeams, the sun's rays: She could be hidden away, but there was no keeping her glory secret from the world, no fooling anyone who took a second look— and anyone who saw her once did.

Maddy presided over the hippies, their undisputed queen; though she was nearly as likely as I was to sit out their thunderous dance reels and elaborate courtships, on occasion she would succumb to their entreaties and rise up as they danced;

from the edge of the room I would watch her, the heart-stopping curve of her mouth, the place at her temples where her rich brown roots shaded into the harsher dyed black of her hair, the dangerous glow of her yellow eyes, as she whirled and stomped and around her the room spun into a dark vortex with her its pulsing, neutron heart. I could no more have left her than the earth could skip its orbit around the sun and go frittering off into space.

My irregular calls home were punctuated by Raoul and Henri's increasing despair, and finally resignation, as every time I promised myself to be on the verge of purchasing a ticket home and every time abandoned that promise as soon as it was uttered. I understood, in some remaining rational part of my brain, that I could not remain out here forever, driving around in Maddy's truck and kissing her until dawn and crossing my fingers that Jack would not be home (he was not) on the rare occasions I stopped by his house to bathe or exchange one dirty T-shirt for another—because if he was home he would likely demand to know what I was doing, a question for which I no longer had an answer.

"You're at least going to college?" Raoul took to asking, in a tone that was initially accusing and soon became almost desperate.

"Yes, of course," I said, and then made no move whatsoever to remove myself. Aunt Beast had had to be prevented several times from boarding a plane and coming out to forcibly extract me from my new environs. But the only person who could have sent me home was Maddy, and she did not seem to care about much of anything—how long I was planning on staying with her; what was happening between us (which was, some part of me knew, largely one-sided); whatever the hell was happening to me, a formerly ambitious and upright young citizen-scientist with a promising future who without warning found herself forgetful as an amnesiac and content to spend whole days at the beach, staring mindlessly out over the blue waves while Qantaqa frolicked in the surf and Maddy dozed in the sun.

It was Kate, of all people, who called my bluff. One night Maddy was restless and bored, pacing the circumference of her house like a tiger until I thought I might shake her, and so I said, "Let's go do something." We drove into town in Maddy's rattling truck, and she sat at Kate's bar and, chain-smoking, drank one whisky after another while I nursed a single beer and watched the muscles of her throat move as she swallowed, wishing it would not get me thrown out of the bar to lick the sharp, graceful edge of her collarbone. The other bartender, Cristina, was working, too; she had a boyfriend, one of the hippies, called for some arcane hippie reason "Timber," who regularly visited her for the duration of her shifts, and they would stare moonily at each other over the bar in the moments when Cristina was not serving drinks. I could not help but be jealous of their relationship, which, while it did not appear to be intellectually stimulating, was at least an example of the kind of transparency I found myself longing for. Cristina, I thought, did not sit up nights agonizing over where she stood—over whether her lover had, at heart, any real interest in her at all.

We had been there for a while when Maddy got up to go to the bathroom, and as soon as she was out of earshot Kate spun around like an ungainly top to stare me down.

"What do you think you're doing?" she asked. I tried to look stupid, but she was having none of it.

"I don't know," I said, truthfully. *I'm in love with her,* I thought, though I could not bring myself to say it out loud. Kate gave a disgusted snort.

"You and everyone else," she said. "There should be a global support group for all you poor fools. That's not what you came here for."

"That's what happened."

"*You,*" she said, an accusatory finger coming dangerously close to poking me in the eye, "have a life you left to come here. You have a family. You have a place to go from here, do you not? *You will do what I brought you here to do, and then you will go home.*" As if she'd summoned them, I thought of Henri and Raoul, side by side on the couch in our apartment, holding hands and looking anxious; Shane, staring at his phone—Shane, *Shane.* I remembered with a sharp pang the green-grass smell of the park in summer, underneath the city's swampy stink; the bitten-nailed fingers of Shane's hands as he played the same chord progression over and over again, writing it deep into his muscles until he could play it a final time without thinking; Dorian Gray howling petulantly outside the door of my own room in my own apartment, my family in the other room, doing the crossword and bantering. That girl, that ordinary and lovely girl, that girl who could not turn her face away from the stars—that girl in that life, loved by those people, was me. "You do not have much time left," Kate said. "Do not waste what has been given you."

Maddy came back from the bathroom and slid onto the stool next to me and put her face in the curve where my neck met my shoulder. "Take me home," she said, and my heart skipped at the feel of her mouth there as she pressed her keys into my hand, but I was conscious of Kate's eyes boring into my back as we walked toward the door, and that night my thoughts were clearer and I did not dream, and Maddy, too, was almost distracted as she undid me and put me back together again in her bed. Afterward I put my head on her chest, and she wrapped me up in her bony arms and sang to me, and I said, "What's that song?" and she said, "It's what they sing where I'm from," and when I asked her where that was she fell quiet again.

"A long way," she said.

"A long way where," I said. She moved restlessly, and I sat up and looked down at her. "A long way *where*."

In the lamplight her eyes were very large. "I don't want to remember that," she said. "I want to rest for a while." Her voice had a note in it so heartbroken, so plaintive, that my own heart ached dumbly; I could not bear the thought of anything that had hurt her enough to make her sound like that, but I could not let go of what I wanted, either.

"Maddy. How do you know Jack? When do you know him from?" She did not answer. *Ask her,* Kate's voice hissed in my ear. *Ask.* "Did you know Aurora? How old *are* you?"

"That," she said, "is not a question you want the answer to."

The dark of her room was still and close. *It is time,* Kate said. *No more secrets.* I leaned down to kiss Maddy. "Tell me a story," I said into her hair. A coyote howled once in the dark and was answered in chorus.

"I told you no pasts."

"You don't tell me anything at all."

She sighed and put one cool hand on my back. "Once there was a girl," she said, "who was born in a kingdom on a distant shore, and who taught herself the language of the wind and the song of the earth and the music of the sea. She could make magic out of herbs and a handful of words and call birds to land upon her shoulders and tell her about the farthest reaches of the sky, but she did not know anything about what it was to love. Her father held a treasure so great that no one in his kingdom had ever looked upon it, and guarded it so jealously that he had no room in his heart for the daughter he had sired or the wife who had borne her, and his absence was like a canker in his daughter's heart, though she could not have named the loss that pained her.

"One day a boat full of heroes came to her country; it was the lure of her father's treasure that called them, but though she knew the patterns of the clouds and the names of the stars, she knew too little of the ways of men to recognize the greed that had swallowed their hearts whole. The worst of them, the most beautiful, took one look at her and saw a girl who was a path to what he wanted, and the words of love he spoke to her caught her as surely as a hare in a hunter's trap. *I will make you my queen,* he said, *you beautiful girl, you have only to give me your father's greatest treasure for a dowry; and what little thing is this, compared to the bounty I lay before you?* And she believed him, and so she helped him. But he knew her father's treasure was twofold: the wealth he hid away, and the magic that lived in his daughter, who could undo the hearts of kings with a word, who could sing down the wind and the rain, who could fell whole kingdoms with a breath. But she was very young, and all her power was not enough to keep her safe from love, the most terrible sorcery of all.

"And so for him she distracted her father by killing her own brother, for him she murdered the kings who opposed him, for him she left the only home she had ever known, and when she landed at last on the shores of his country he made her not his queen but his concubine. He would not name her as his wife in front of his people, and the warriors she had sailed with turned their backs on her and laughed behind their hands when she came into the hall where they feasted: at that dark-skinned foreigner, that bloody-handed witch, that whore who thought she could be a queen. She had thrown over everything she loved for a love that betrayed her; she had borne the hero two sons he would not acknowledge; she was, in her new country, wholly alone and unwanted.

"And then that great hero told her he had found a girl to make his wife, a slip of a girl, a fair king's daughter whose skin shone paler than milk. And so the witch wove a dress out of fire and spite that was more beautiful than any garment that child had ever seen, and when the little queen put on her raiment it turned to flames, and her screams drew her father to her side, and he burned with her. And the witch called her children to her and cut their throats rather than leave them, and when all around her was ashes and blood she summoned to her a chariot drawn by serpents and rode it into the sky." Maddy stopped talking, but her hand moved up and down my back in a slow hypnotic rhythm.

"What happened after that," I said, my voice catching.

"She wandered," Maddy said, and the low terrible note in her voice swelled and filled the darkness until her whole room hummed with it. "She wandered for a long time, until she came to a place at the end of the world and tried to forget. But our pasts do not let go of us so easily, in the end."

"Whose story is that?"

"Look at me," she said, and I turned my face to hers on the pillow. "You know whose story that is, Tally," she said. "You know what I am."

"I don't know," I whispered, "I don't," and she said, "Loss burns like a beacon in you. You want to see her. You have wanted it all your life; I see the longing in you the same way I see the curve of your mouth or the color of your skin. I can take you to her. Wherever she is, I can find her."

"She's dead," I said. "She has to be dead. She's been dead for years. That's the only reason"—I would *not* cry—"that's the only reason no one knows where she is anymore. If she was still alive, one of us would have to know. And I'm fine. I've never needed her before. It was a waste of time to come out here." The crow Maddy had tattooed on my arm burned as hot as the night she'd inked it into my skin. Her expression was unreadable.

"As you wish. Sweet dreams, then," she said, and kissed me, and I curled myself into her lanky warmth, and her sweet-smelling hair moved around me, and I closed my eyes and wished more than I had ever wished for anything that I would wake up in my own bed in my own apartment, that none of this had ever happened, that everything she had done to me would unmake itself and let me go.

The next morning I rode to Jack's house and called Shane as soon as I walked in the door, so I would not have time to talk myself out of it, or to forget. He answered on the second ring and a glad rush went through me at his familiar, raspy *hello*.

"Hi," I said.

"Tally?"

"Yeah."

"Where the *fuck* are you? Where the *fuck* have you been?"

"I'm at—" I laughed. "You're not going to believe where I am."

"You're at his house."

"You talked to Raoul?"

"Of course I fucking talked to Raoul, what the fuck do you think? You stopped talking to me, and I didn't know what to do, and it had been *weeks,* Tally, fucking *weeks,* and I went over to your house because I thought maybe at least Raoul or Henri would tell me what was wrong with you or why you were mad at me or, like, whatever, and then Raoul was all serious and told me you were on a *quest* and they didn't even know how to get ahold of you and I was like 'What the hell is wrong with you, you fucking *lunatics,* what the fuck do you *mean* you don't know how to *get ahold of her,* she's my best fucking *friend* and your fucking *daughter*' and Raoul spouted off some total nonsense about how you were on a journey and had I taken careful consideration of how I had mistreated you and you would contact me when it was right for you and I had to respect your boundaries and a bunch of shit I didn't even understand, and then he told me you went to see Jack Blake because he was maybe your *dad* and I couldn't even—I don't—did I *mistreat* you? *Is* he your dad?"

I picked the easier question to answer. "I don't know. I think he is, yeah."

"Why the hell didn't you tell me?"

The old Tally would have lied, or said nothing. The old

Tally would have buried it. But this Tally had come all the way out here, and fallen in love, and started to wonder if she was maybe off her rocker, and a lot of other things besides, and so this Tally said, clear and strong, "Because I was pissed at you, Shane," and surprised herself when it was not nearly so hard as she had imagined it might be.

"Why?" he said, and the genuine bewilderment in his voice made me want to reach through the phone and slap him.

"*Because,*" I said. "Because of what happened. That night." Silence. He was going to make me say it out loud. "Because you—because I—because we—*you* know what we did with each other, and then you didn't come over on my *birthday* for the first time in ten years, and you never even said you were sorry—you never even tried to say you were sorry. You didn't even just pretend things were normal. You disappeared."

There was a silence. "Do you want me to say I'm sorry?" he said quietly.

"For standing me up? Goddamn right I do, you dick."

"For—what we did."

"Oh," I said. "I don't—I don't know. I wanted you to be there afterward, how about that. Even if you didn't"—I took a deep breath and squeezed my eyes shut, as if he could see me—"even if you didn't mean it the way I did. Because I, um, meant it."

I could hear the hoarse rasp of his breath on the other end of the line. "I went to this lecture," he said, "at the Museum of Natural History, on making a candle with a supernova—"

"Standard candle with type 1a supernovae," I said automatically.

"I had no idea what they were talking about, I just went because it seemed like something you would like—"

"But it's not hard to understand at all, it's just a process of finding a variable star with a standard—"

"Tally, I don't *care* what a standard candle is. What I'm telling you is that I miss you like crazy and I went to this stupid lecture and sat through the whole thing just thinking how much better it would have been if you were there with me, and I still wouldn't have understood a word but you would do that thing you do where you act like only a total idiot would have no idea what these guys are talking about, and then I would get mad at you for like five minutes—"

"What do you mean, mad at—"

"—and then we'd forget about it and go look at the dinosaurs and get pancakes after at the Candy Shop—Tally, I think about you every day, and sometimes when I wake up in the morning I forget that you're gone and the whole day is so much bigger because it'll have you in it, and then I remember how far away you are, and I don't understand why you can't just come home." His voice cracked. Was he *crying*? "Tally, come home."

I had no idea what to make of this new, loquacious Shane, or what was veering dangerously close to a discussion of our feelings. "I will," I said. "Soon. I will soon. I just have to—I can't leave until I know."

"What if he never tells you? Are you just going to stay there forever? What about school?"

"I still have time. I'm not going to stay here forever. I promise, okay?"

"Please come home."

All the time I'd spent imagining this conversation, and now that I was having it I felt as though my heart was going to come apart in my chest. It was too much to choose from, too much to think about: Maddy, her mouth on my skin, her laugh in the dark, her witch's hands. Jack. Who he was and who I was and what the fuck I was doing here, among strangers, away from the people who loved me, who knew me—away from the people who were my family. Not blood, but home. And Shane—however Shane felt about me, however I felt about him now, he was still the person I knew best in all the world, the Castor to my Pollux, my twinned, steady-burning star. There was so much I wanted to tell him and so much I didn't know how, and so instead I said again, "Soon. I'll come home soon."

"If you go to college without saying goodbye to me I'll hunt you down and kill you."

"I won't do that. It's me."

"I don't know who you are anymore."

"Don't be melodramatic," I said, and the surge of irritation was wonderful in its homey, comforting familiarity. "That's an asinine thing to say. We're not in a *movie*. You know just fine who I am."

"You've been gone so long I almost forgot what an asshole you are."

"You're the asshole who didn't call me."

"You're the asshole who skipped town."

"Well then," I said.

"I got a show," he said. "A real show, at Brownies. Promise you'll come."

"When is it?"

"Next week. We're opening for some dumb rock band, these total heshers, but I don't care, you have to come."

"Next week? I don't know—"

"You *have* to come. It's my first real show ever. I have a band now. A lead singer. You'll like her. I'll tell them you're in the band, otherwise you can't get in, it's not all-ages."

A hot flash of jealousy raged through me, leaving me breathless. "What lead singer? What band? When did you get a band?"

"A lot has happened since you left."

"Yeah? A lot has happened here, too."

"It's not a contest."

"*You* made it a contest."

"You are fucking *impossible*. Say you'll come."

"I don't know. I'll try."

"Do or do not. There is no try."

"I'll try."

"You do," he said, and hung up on me. I threw Jack's phone at the wall with a satisfying crash.

Jack leaned through the open door, his eyebrows raised. "Everything okay?"

"I dropped something."

"It sounded like you threw something."

"It's fine." I didn't want to look at where I'd thrown the phone, in case I'd dented his wall. "I was thinking about leaving soon." He came into the room and sat on my bed, glancing idly over the various possessions I'd slowly strewn about until his guest room looked much like my own room at home, disorderly and marked as mine. His gaze sharpened suddenly. "Where did you get this?" He picked up Aunt Beast's knife from the nightstand. I'd left it there when I'd half un-packed, that first night in his house.

"It's just something of my aunt's. Why?"

His expression was that of a man who has just been shot in the chest; not so much fear, or pain, but a kind of deep, profound shock. "Your *aunt*? But this was mine—I gave it to—"

I met him at one of Aurora's parties. He loved music more than he loved me. Some scientist I was going to make: It was so obvious I couldn't believe I'd missed it, right there in front of me this whole time—I'd been getting nothing out of him because I'd been asking him the wrong questions all along. I stared at him, dumbfounded with revelation. "That song," I said. "'About a Girl.' That song's not about Aurora at all, is it?"

He looked up from the knife and blinked at me, seem-ing completely at a loss. "Is that why you came out here? You thought—" He shook his head. "Your aunt was Auro-ra's best friend?"

"She's not my aunt, exactly."

"Your aunt was my—" And then he really looked at me, for the first time since I had set foot in his house. "You thought I was your father," he said.

"Yes," I said. "Are you?"

He closed his eyes and put his hands on his knees and sat like that for a long time, as though he had just com-pleted some difficult and draining task—run a marathon, sailed around the world—and was so exhausted that if he did not prop himself up he might fall over, and then he opened his eyes again and looked at me. I had meant to shout at him; it was his stubbornness, his refusal to talk to me, that had gotten us to this awkward confrontation. If he had been honest with me—if he had just *talked* to me— we could have sorted it out the night I arrived. Of course they had all known each other, back then; if I had not suc- cumbed to the hazy amnesia of this strange place—if he had bothered to help me—I would have figured it out im- mediately. But the pain in his face was so deep and raw that I faltered and found, to my surprise, that the only sen- timent I could muster was not outrage, but pity.

"No," he said, as I had already known he would. "I'm not your father."

"The whole story," I said. "You owe me. Please."

He looked down at the knife again, opening it and clos- ing it without speaking; though it must have been old, its hinge still worked smoothly and silently. I waited. He took a deep breath and began. "I lived in Seattle, for a summer, a long time ago—I went there to try and make a living, as a musician, like a lot of other people in those days. It was a strange time. Your grandfather—no one had ever heard of that city, before your grandfather, and then when he died they were everywhere. Producers, record label executives, hangers-on, dreamers. Like locusts. I thought I knew what I was doing; I thought I was quite something, back then. I was very young." He passed one hand over his face and his eyes clouded, as if he were trying to remember something. "Aurora was at the center of it—I don't think she wanted to be, but they wouldn't leave her alone. So many people. As if they could take from her something that would make them into her father. She was even younger than I was, you know, and her mother—your grandmother—was not . . ." He paused, and then said delicately, "was not around. As you know. I went to a party at her house with my guitar and my last five dollars in my pocket; I thought if I could play for the people there, there would be someone to hear who could—I don't know what I thought." He laughed. "Like they would give me a contract and a million dollars right there; that's probably what I thought. I told you I was young.

"So I went. That night. I don't know what I was expecting—I had never met Aurora, only heard about her; I thought she would be awful. Insufferable. You know, spoiled rich brat, daddy's legacy, the kinds of things you think. And she was nothing like what I had expected, nothing at all. She was so human and alive, and funny and ferocious and tough in her own way—you couldn't help but love her, just being around her. She had this radiance—it wasn't just that she was beautiful, she was, but it was something else—you felt that in her company, the whole world might become magic. Anything could happen. If she had had a chance, if she could have gotten away from those people, there's no telling what she might have been. I wish I had done something more for her. I should have taken them both that night and run for the hills, but I didn't know better, then."

"Them both?" I prompted.

"Aurora and her best friend." He paused again. I took his hand and he tightened his fingers around mine. "Her best friend. Your—aunt, I guess. She was nothing like Aurora; she wasn't beautiful, she wasn't charismatic, she wasn't any of those things—she let Aurora do that for her. But she had her own kind of magic, this strength—when I met her, I thought, *That is a woman who will die before she lets go of something she loves,* and I hadn't had much of that in my life up until then—and she was funny, too, and stubborn, and tough. I fell in love with her, which was the last thing I expected to do. And then I did get a record deal, and I left her. I left them both." He took a deep, ragged breath; he was squeezing my hand so tightly I thought the bones of my fingers might crack, but I was terrified he would stop talking, and so I said nothing. "That was a terrible time," he said. "I will carry what I did then with me for the rest of my life. I let them both go even though I knew that what I had signed on with was something far worse than I had imagined. Your aunt survived it, but only because it wasn't after her, not directly; your mother—Aurora—it swallowed her up. They swallowed her up. I didn't even try to . . ." He looked away from me. "I couldn't play anymore after that," he said. "After I knew what I had awakened. I couldn't let anyone else come to that kind of harm. I couldn't stand what I had become. I quit playing and came out here, and I've been here ever since. I'm sorry I don't know who your father is. I loved Aurora, but never like that."

"But you were so good," I breathed. "Music was—it must have hurt, to give it up."

"It has nearly killed me again," he said. "Without it, I am nothing; I am only a sad old man, an empty shell with a sailboat. I am only waiting for the right time to die."

"I don't want you to die," I said. "I want you to—I want you to play again. After all this time? It can't do any harm, now."

He let go of my hand at last, and I surreptitiously tried to shake some feeling back into my fingers. "You look like Aurora," he said, "but you are so like your aunt. So stubborn. I don't know if I could play now, Tally. It's been so long. What came after me then is very patient and very old. I think it is only waiting—but maybe you are right, and it has turned its attention elsewhere. I don't know. I am afraid to risk it, even now."

"Is that why you've been avoiding me?"

"You haven't been around much, either, young lady," he said.

"You can't go your whole life being scared," I said, ignoring that. "Look at you. You just told me—you just told me you want to die. How much worse can it be?"

"You can't imagine," he said quietly, "how much worse it can be."

"You have no idea where she is?"

"I have some idea. But it's not a place you can go."

"What do you mean, you have some idea?"

"Tally," he said, "I am telling you, you cannot follow her there. You won't come back, even if you manage to get to her."

"You threw your whole career away, you fucked over my aunt, you left Aurora, you don't even *play* anymore—what was it all for? Was it worth it, to be safe here? All alone in your big house with all your money?"

He did not answer me, and I thought for a moment I had gone too far. "How is she?" he asked, finally.

"Aunt Beast? She's okay. She's fine. You should ask her yourself. We're in the phone book."

He laughed. "Does she still paint?"

"That's what she is. A painter."

"I'm glad to hear it. I've never stopped thinking—" But he cut himself off and stood up, and stretched: lean arms, bony fingers like mine; if he wasn't my father, who was? If he didn't know where Aurora was, who did? Who was there left to ask?

"I have to go home," I said.

"You can stay as long as you like."

"Thank you. But I—this isn't my life, out here. I keep forgetting, but I have so much else to do."

"It's up to you," he said. "I wish I could tell you more. I'm sorry. I did not behave well then, and I have not behaved well to you since you showed up on my doorstep."

"It was sort of a surprise visit, in your defense."

"That it was," he said. "It's getting late. I believe I promised you dinner, the first morning you were here, and have been remiss in following through."

"There's nothing in your kitchen to eat."

"Maybe you would like a hamburger at Kate's, if you're not sick to death of them." That seemed a fine compromise, and I said so.

Maddy was not at Kate's, but some of the hippies were; they looked me over with disinterest and looked away again. Without Maddy next to me they did not even recognize me. Kate was in a temper and slammed my hamburger down unceremoniously, but Jack raised an eloquent eyebrow at her and she softened.

"Long day," she said; for her, that was almost an apology, and I accepted it. "Nice to see you out among the living." Jack flinched, and the look she gave him was freighted with meaning, and I wondered, not for the first time and with some exasperation, if I would ever sort out what strange threads raveled them together, and then Kate turned to me and said calmly, "You have the book already, child; it's right in front of your face, and the path to what you want, too," and I said, "What?" but she was already moving across the room to the hippies, who were clamoring for more beer.

You have the book already, child. That night back at Jack's I got out the battered copy of *Metamorphoses*. A rustle at the sill of the open window, and there was my crow again, one beady eye trained on me, its head cocked. "Hello," I said, "this is a bit much, you know," and it cawed imperiously, and I opened the book at random. *Now in a ship that had been built at Pagasae, the Argonauts cut through the restless waves. . . .* Golden-haired Jason and his crew: brave Asterion; Erytos and Echion, sons of Hermes; Mopsos the bird-omener; the warrior Oileus, and on and on. And Orpheus, Orpheus the musician, who was said to have charmed rivers from their banks, caused wild oaks to march in order to hear him play— *Supposedly he played one show at the Coliseum in LA, and when he finished the crowd was surrounded by all these animals— wolves, bears, cougars, animals that don't even* live *in that part of California. Like they had come to see him play.*

"No," I said aloud, and my crow flapped its wings at me, and I turned back to the book. *Sharp-eyed Medea, burned with quickening heat.* Medea who waited, alone and lonely, on the far shore of her father's country, with her magic and her herbs and her shrine to Hekate—"No," I said again, but there was no undoing it. It was a story I already knew, the story Maddy had told me, but the Maddy in this book was even crueler and more bloody minded: making daughters cut their fathers to pieces; slitting the throats of kings and flying away in a chariot drawn by dragons; burning Jason's second wife to ash—*even then her blood-red steel had pierced the bodies of their two sons*—and poisoning heroes. And then: *Medea, 'scaping her own death, vanished in a cloud, dark as the music chanted in her spells*—and she exited the story as swiftly as she'd entered it, and there was no word of her again. It was not possible, but there it was. I closed the book and sat looking at it for a long time, and when I looked up again my crow was gone.

Brushing my teeth before bed in Jack's bathroom, I knew that what I had told him was true: My time here, unsuccessful as it was, was at its end. I did not want to think about Maddy. I dug my unused binoculars out of my bag and slipped quietly out Jack's front door with a blanket; the trees were too thick behind me to see anything at the horizon, and the moon washed out most of the sky—Why hadn't I been out here every night? What had come over me, in the last month?—but there was Arcturus, blazing overhead, and Spica in Virgo, and good old Polaris marking out the north, as it would for another few thousand years. *That is not what we call it, where I am from.* Because it had been a different star. A few degrees to its northwest, half-hidden by the horizon, Castor and Pollux in Gemini; I could not look at them without thinking, once again, of Shane. I heard footsteps on the grass behind me, and then Jack folded himself up next to me on the blanket, and I handed him the binoculars. He lifted them to his eyes and fiddled with the focus. "Oh. Wow."

"You've never tried it?"

"I use a sextant on the boat, but binoculars never occurred to me. Navigation is a different science."

"You must know all the constellations, all the same."

"I know most of them."

"It's too bad we don't have a telescope. But look, there's Lyra, you can find Vega, and just a tiny bit below it you can almost see the Ring Nebula—maybe not with the binoculars—"

"No," he said, "I see it. It's just barely there."

"With a telescope it's something else."

"Lyra," he said, handing the binoculars back to me. "The Lyre."

"Orpheus's lyre," I said. "If you believe that kind of thing."

"If you do. The stars fell from the harp in spring," he said. "When I was—younger."

"The Lyrid meteor shower," I said. "It's not that strong anymore, but there are observations on record that go back almost three thousand years." I paused. "There's a Chinese record that says the stars 'fell like rain,' but that was back around 700 BC."

"Like rain." He seemed far away. "That sounds about right."

"I would have liked it," I said. "If you had been my dad."

"I would have liked that, too." We were both quiet, looking at the stars together, and then we went in to bed.

The dream that came to me that night was the worst of them all. *It will have blood; they say, blood will have blood:* Blood all over and the girl again, her dark eyes pleading, and out of the boundless dark a wailing pack of three-headed dogs that set upon her and tore her to pieces as I watched, rooted to the ground in horror. *Tally,* she gasped as she died in front of me, *Tally, you do not have much time—Tally, come to me—* and then a slavering dog with awful teeth tore out her throat, and I tried to scream but no sound came out of my open mouth as a hot red wave crashed over me, and I jerked awake in the dark, gasping and flailing for the bedside light. "I'm coming," I said aloud, into the quiet room. "I don't know how, but I'm coming." I left the light on until the dawn came, and I did not try to sleep again.

Maddy was in her kitchen, stirring something on the little stove. No blood, no nightmares: just her, and the sight of her, as always, enough to make my heart give a dumb, helpless leap—her hands, her mouth, the softness of her skin. I'd kissed her so many times I could taste her now just thinking about her. She looked up as I came in, Qantaqa at her feet, tail wagging.

"I want to go," I said. "I want you to take me to see her." She put down her spoon and stepped toward me, cupped my chin in her hand and tilted it upward, kissed the pulse of my throat.

"I know," she said.

"She's dead, isn't she?"

"Yes," Maddy said simply.

"Did you know this whole time?"

"Your journey is not my journey, Tally."

"Tonight," I said. "And then I have to—go."

"Tonight," she agreed, leaving a line of kisses along my collarbone that made my knees shake. "But that leaves us all afternoon," she murmured, and pulled my shirt over my head and then leaned in to kiss me again. "Come upstairs," she said, and turned off the stove.

At sunset she drove me down to the beach. We left Qantaqa at Maddy's; she whined as she watched us leave, wagging her tail anxiously. "The world of the dead is no place for a dog," Maddy told her. And I thought, *This is crazy,* but I didn't say anything out loud. It was still warm enough for shirtsleeves, and I rolled my window down, stuck my head out like Qantaqa, whooped at the twilight wind.

I'd expected—I don't know what I'd expected. Blood sacrifice or a kettle full of newts and bats. But when we got down to the water's edge she sent me to find driftwood for a fire, got a blanket out of her truck and two bottles of wine and her cigarettes and some bread, for all the world as though we were at an evening picnic. She let me set up the fire and then she lit it with an ordinary match. "We have to wait until the moon rises," she said, and opened the wine. "What's the second bottle for?" I asked, envisioning some ritual bath.

"For me," she said. "While you're gone."

"Oh," I said. "How long will I be—gone?"

"For as long as you go."

"Oh," I said again.

The water went silver, and then a deep violet-blue, and then the summer-swollen yellow moon rose high enough for its light to make a white path on the water. She took off her shoes and nodded when I did, too.

"There are many ways into the world of the dead," Maddy said. "The moon road is only one of them. It will hold for you as long as you can see it on the water."

"If it doesn't?"

"You are a little like me," she said, "but even for those of us who are not wholly human, the way out of that place is hard."

"I don't want to stay," I said. "I just want to see her."

She took my hand and walked me to the edge of the water, where the reflection of the moon lapped at the pebbly shore. "Don't I have to do something?" I asked. She smiled.

"No," she said. "You're with me." She stepped out onto the water and I watched, incredulous, as her foot landed on the silver surface, and stayed there. "The longer you take, the less time you'll have," she said, and I took the first step after her. The water was cool and solid under my bare feet, and her hand was warm in mine—*This can't be real,* I thought, *this can't be*—but she took another step, and so did I, and the white road beneath me held firm. "I can only set you on the path. You must walk it on your own." She let go of my hand. "I'll wait for you here," she said. "Travel well."

"Thanks," I said, although it didn't seem the right thing to say to a girl who had just made an ocean solid so that I could walk across it to drop in on a dead woman. The whole night had a surreal, liquid quality; I wondered if I was dreaming, if I'd wake up in her bed, feeling silly. I began to walk.

White moon, black water, time passing. "The formula for omega is two times the deceleration parameter plus two divided by three times the cosmological constant times the velocity of light squared over the Hubble constant squared," I said, and my voice sounded small in the dark, and so I cleared my throat and tried again. The world at the edges of the path grew darker and darker, and after a while I saw things moving, shadows even deeper than the darkness around them, and I could hear something like the sound of branches clacking in the wind, though there was no breeze on my face. A dog howled in the distance, low and mournful. The darkness shifted, and I looked up.

I was still on the moon road, but the black water around me was not the water I'd started across, and the sky overhead was scrubbed empty of stars. The white strip of light on which I stood led to a larger white blur in the distance ahead of me. I walked for a long time, and the white blur grew larger and larger until I could see at last that it was an endless bone-white plain, out of which rose a towering black palace covered in doors that lay open to the night. One step after another, the palace looming ever larger and more awful, and then I took the final step, off the moon road onto the hard white earth. The ground was so cold I winced. The soles of my feet were raw from walking, and I left red-stained footprints behind me on the pale ground. I had seen light like this before—I remembered, during the eclipse in Cornwall, the way the shadows' edges had grown sharp enough to cut like knives—and then I thought of Raoul and Henri, and Aunt Beast, and the icy grip around my heart lessened. *You are Tally,* Maddy said, and for a flash I saw her, too: leaning against a log, her long legs stretched out toward the fire, a cup in one hand and a cigarette in the other. *You did not walk so far to fail now, lovely.*

I could not have said how long it took me to reach the black palace. I stood before one of the open doors, waiting, but the world around me did not change. There was nothing else to do but go inside, and so I did. The doorway's frigid maw made the cold of the plain seem tropical; it seared the back of my throat and wrapped itself around me until it was all I could do to move forward, down a long greenish-lit hallway cut into the black stone—another door, this one closed, at the end of it, and when I laid my hand on its surface to push it open, the cold burned me and I cried out. The door swung open silently and I walked through it, beyond fear, beyond caring, beyond the memory of ever having been warm.

I was in a big, high-ceilinged room, clean angles and sharp

lines, floor-to-ceiling windows all around me that looked out on the white plain, the black sea where the white stripe of moonlight still glittered. It was important, but I could no longer remember why. The girl from my dreams was sitting in a black chair at the far end of the otherwise empty room, and next to her stood a tall man with ice-colored eyes and a face that was so cruel I held my breath when I looked at him. She raised her head when I came through the door, and I crossed the room and stood before her.

I had been told all my life that Aurora was beautiful, but beautiful was not the word for the woman in front of me. *Beautiful* was a word for human beings. She was something else entirely; next to her, even Maddy would have seemed some shabby copy of the real thing. She was terribly thin, but the planes of her face were smoothly cut, and her skin glowed with a radiant inner light. Her dark eyes were very large. She was still and straight backed in the black chair, which was, I saw up close, cut from some glossy stone. *Obsidian*, I thought, *the word for that is obsidian*. Heart, lungs, my own human hands. In this place I had nearly forgotten already what I was.

"I have been waiting for you for so long, my Tally," she said, and I dropped to my knees before her and put my head in her lap, and she wound her cool fingers through my hair, and I felt a great shuddering sob rise up through me and burst in my throat as I wept into her bony thighs. She let me cry for a long time, saying nothing, only stroking my hair over and over, until at last the gentle, rhythmic motion soothed the last hiccupping sob out of me and I could raise my head and look at her. Her eyes were fixed on my face and the sorrow in them was awful to see.

"It was brave of you to come here," she said. "But you cannot stay long." The ice-eyed man watched us without blinking. "Leave me alone with my daughter," she said, but he did not move. She turned her head away from us both to look out the window, where the white scorch of the full moon burned in the dead black sky and glittered on the flat black sea. There were so many things to ask her: who my father was and why she had left me, and how she had come to this terrible place, and what could possibly be better about sitting in this ugly chair in hell than spending all her life with me. I did not know where to start, and so I said instead, "I came here to get you," which I had not realized until I said it out loud, and then it seemed obvious; I had come here, and that was not possible, and so it was surely no more impossible for me to bring her away again.

"I left once," she said, "and it was all I could manage. I cannot leave again."

"When?" I said, and then I thought about it. I lived in an apartment in New York with people who had come together to be my family. I looked through telescopes. I was going to study the origins of the universe. She had taken me out of this place and into that one, that world of gardens and summers and too-furry cats, that world of music and light, and heartbreak, and sweat and real death and pancakes and love. "You left to bring me to Aunt Beast."

"He wanted you, too," she said, as if the ice-eyed man were not standing next to us, listening; but maybe she had spent so long at his side that she no longer cared. "But I would not let him have you." He must have been furious, I thought, that she had so defied him, that she had somehow found the strength to escape him long enough to deliver me from his reach. She shifted in her chair, and I saw a glimmer of silver at her foot, a thin cruel line of chain that circled her ankle and trailed off into the darkness behind her, and she smiled again at my face.

"It's not so bad," she said. But her lightness could not hide the tapestry of pain woven into her words, and I understood in an instant that all the time I had spent hating her, all the life I had lived refusing to admit her as mine, I had been wrong, and more than wrong: she had given up any chance she had ever had to get away from this place herself in order to give me a life outside it, and she was trapped here now like a ray of light sucked into the maw of a black hole. "It's not so bad," she said again, putting one cool hand against my tearstained cheek. "I came here first of my own will. I would have liked to see you in the daylight, just once, but to see you here is enough. Tally, you brave and wondrous thing—you are so much more like her than you are like me, and it's her strength that will carry you away from me again. You must go on being brave. You must not look back on me here, in darkness."

"Why did you come here?" I cried. "How could you leave—how could you leave the green grass? And the water? And all those trees? How could you leave the stars—and Aunt Beast—and me? How could you give all that up?"

"Because I was lost in the past before I came here; because I was lost in loss. Not all of us are made for the world above, sweet child—but I would release you from the mistake I made of looking only backward, of living in regret over what is already done. 'What is to give light must endure burning'—"

"That's a physicist, who said that," I whispered.

"That was a poet," she said. "I could not bear the fire. But you are made of stronger stuff than I. You are so much more than the sum of the mistakes I have made—you are yourself, Tally, your own bright and wild star, the best thing I could have hoped for. I have watched you in dreams; I am so proud of you. And you must go back to the world above and carry your light wherever you go—there is so much that is still possible for you. Do not spend your life in the sun weeping over me."

Was there no one in the world who had not been unraveled by the past? Jack and Maddy trying to forget it, Kate erasing it, Aurora lost in it, Aunt Beast refusing to speak of it, Raoul heartbroken by it. And I saw, finally, that how I lived with it would come to define me, too, but it did not have to be a trap so much as one of the many stories I would someday learn to tell. Like looking at galaxies at the far edge of the known universe: The light of what has come before can show us where we are now and how we got here, but it is no place to return to, no place to call home. The ice-eyed man shifted, his cold stare laden with menace, and I knew I could not stay any longer if I was going to make it back to the world I wanted to live in. "I love you, Tally," she said. "I have loved you every day of your life, and I will love you long past the end of it," and I thought the sobs that came out of me then would tear apart my whole body. I shook in her arms, and she let me cry myself out, and then she said, "You are loved by more, and better, than me. Go back to the world I gave you. Go home."

"Not better," I said. "Only different." I would not let go of her hand. *Home*, I thought—home. Shane and Raoul and Henri, Aunt Beast, sad old Mr. M. My family, my real family, the people who had let me come here, who had woven a ladder for me out of love all the way to the stars, the people who would be waiting for me always, on the other side, when I came through this place and back to where I belonged. And Maddy. Maddy was waiting for me, too. All of my life in front of me and all I had done, to come here, lay behind: I remembered, remembered my own name and who I was and that I was alive and whole and the next step in the story was mine to choose.

"I love you, too," I said. "Thank you. And—goodbye."

"Goodbye, Tally," she said, and I let go of her hand at last. She let me stand on my own, without helping me, and when I was sure of myself I turned my back on her and walked, proud and strong and whole, out the black door and across the white plain, back to the cold dark sea and the white scar of the moon road home. My heart quailed when I took the first step. The moon was low in the sky, and I could not see my way out of the dark. I began to run, faster and faster, willing all my laps of the park with Aunt Beast to matter, but the moon was sliding toward the horizon fast and merciless, and the white road began to break up below me. My foot plunged through it into searing death-cold water, and I tripped and fell forward, staggered to my feet again. *Run, fucking run, oh god oh god,* my heart pounding in terror and exertion. *Don't let me die here, please don't let me die here alone in the dark*—I thought of that awful place, locked in my own frozen chair next to Aurora for the rest of all time, under the cruel uncaring gaze of the ice-eyed man—*Don't fucking let me die*—but it was too late, the road dissolving below me, I was sinking into the frozen nightmarish depths of the black sea. "*Maddy!*" I screamed, "*Maddy!*" And then my mouth filled up with water and I choked. Hands wrapping around my ankles, pulling me deeper, the empty sky gone mad with howling, whirling demons, laughter rising up around me and impossible things winking in and out of life around me—a bull-headed man roaring, a three-headed dog with teeth as big as my hand, triplet mouths open and howling, a huge swan beating a terrified girl bloody with its wings. *I will not die,* I thought, and fury welled up to replace my terror, a fury so hot I thought it would burn away the dark water around me. I thought of Maddy, her yellow eyes, her skin, her mouth, her magnificent strength: Maddy, beloved, for all of what she was, for what she'd given me and what she'd taken away. I willed her into life before me, reaching my hands out to touch her, the tattoo on my arm blazing with light—and there she was, in the white dress I'd seen in my dreams, blood soaked, her knife in one hand and the other hand held out to me.

"*Fight,*" she said, her voice a huge bell tolling. "*Tally, fight,*" and I kicked my legs and swam toward her—*naked girls, bloody limbed and screaming, tearing a man who looked like Jack to pieces as he bellowed in pain*—and there was Maddy, waiting for me, and I was not going to die. I *refused* to die. Our fingers touched and at last her hand closed around mine and pulled me up, up, up out of the dark water into the less-dark night.

She'd dragged me up onto the beach—the fire still burning, all around us quiet, the mad visions behind me. I took a huge gasping breath, and it turned into a cough, and then, heaving, I threw up salt water, coughed, breathed again, coughed. "Come here," she said in my ear, helping me to my feet. "Let's get you dried off before you freeze to death."

She sat me down by the fire on a blanket, and I hugged myself while she built it up again and then found me a dry shirt and pants in her bag, helped me out of my wet clothes, night air cold against my colder skin. I couldn't stop shivering. She held me tight while I shook, and when I began to cry again she did not say anything, but she held me even tighter and kissed my cheeks where the salt of my tears mixed with the salt of the water. When at last the shaking subsided she kissed my mouth, my throat, my shoulder, and I felt hunger coming awake in me where moments before there had been only loss, and I kissed her back, still crying, and let her take off the clothes she'd just helped me into and kiss her way down the plane of my belly and bury her face between my legs, and her hands were everywhere and all of her through and through me, all the light in the universe splintering—in the first moments of the birth of the universe, the hot plasma of its origins ballooning outward in waves of light faster than anything before or since—and when I came again, again, she held me, pulled herself up to kiss me again with her mouth that tasted of the salt tide of my own body, and I was still crying, I thought might cry until the final moments when the universe rent itself into nothing at the end of time. She wrapped me in the blanket and murmured nonsense into my sweaty salt-drenched hair, and I clutched at her even as she rolled away from me, pulled a cigarette out of her pack and lit it, blew smoke at the lowering fire. She had a flask of whisky, too, in the bag she'd brought down to the beach, and she fed it to me in sips, and I did not even mind the burn.

I did stop crying, eventually. I was so tired I thought I might die of it. I rested my head on Maddy's shoulder and thought about how to say goodbye. "I saw her," I said finally.

"Was it what you wanted?"

"I don't know. I wanted—I thought I could bring her home."

"That's not how it works."

"I know. But I thought maybe—I thought I could. If I tried hard enough."

She was quiet for a while, her breath warm against my ear. "You don't have to be like me," she said. "Living as a memory of loss. Alone with all the demons I made and the demons I've chosen. Becoming a monster is only one way to survive."

"I don't think you're a monster," I said, and I felt her smile.

"I like being a monster," she said. "But you are young, and there is still room for you to be a girl instead."

"It's time for me to go home," I said.

"Yes."

"Maddy?"

"Yes?"

"Do you love me?"

She lit another cigarette. Inhale, slow exhale. Inhale. "Anything I love I bring to ruin," she said.

"That's not a no," I said, greatly daring.

"It's not a yes, Tally." She let me go, and I sat up, and she smoked in silence while I laboriously put on my clothes again. I was so exhausted I could barely move, and it took me a couple of tries to stand up and feebly shake out her blanket. She stood, too, but made no move to help me as I handed it back to her.

"You went a long way," she said.

I thought of Aurora in that cold empty room, looking out eternally on an endless black sea, and squeezed my eyes shut before I started crying again.

"I came back," I said.

"Not many people do."

"Maddy? Why did you move here?"

She opened her yellow eyes wide and looked at me. Overhead, Ursa Major was sinking into the sea, and I knew it was almost dawn.

"Sweet thing," she said, "I was waiting for you." She offered me her hand, and I took it, and we walked back to her truck.

She drove me to Jack's and made no move to get out of the truck when we got there, didn't even turn off the engine. I stared at her dashboard, gathering myself, wanting to ask and not wanting to ask. I thought of the plants hanging in her house, of the mornings she had kissed me awake in her blankets and brought me coffee, of all the times she had made me certain I was the only girl in the world only to turn away again. She was more herself than anyone I had ever met: more sure, more fearless, more capricious, more reckless—and all across it, the girl that she was, the wash of blood: *the rabbit the deer the knife, the child with a red gape where its throat should have been*—but I was strong now, I'd always been strong; I wanted her to see it. I'd been to hell and back in a single night, and I was still walking around. "Will I see you again?"

"The ocean is a vast thing," she said, "but all its drops are connected, one to the other."

"That's not a yes."

"It's not a no."

I forced myself to look her in the eye. "I love you," I said. "Thank you." Yellow eyes, tangle of dark hair, crooked grin. "Say goodbye to Qantaqa for me."

"Qantaqa doesn't believe in goodbyes."

"But you do."

"I've been around for a long time." I waited for her to say something else, but she didn't, and so I got out of her truck and shut the door and stood there, squeezing my hands into fists and then dropping them helplessly again by my side, and I waited for her to turn around and look at me as she drove away, even though I knew better, even though she never did. The sun was coming up, and my old crow flapped out of a tree and came to land next to me.

"I came back," I told it. "But now I have to leave again." It ducked its head—I saw a glint of silver, and then it was flapping away again, cawing hoarsely. I leaned down to pick up what it had left me. A silver heart locket on a chain; inside, a tiny picture of a cat that almost looked like Dorian Gray. "Someone's going to miss this," I called after the crow, but if it heard me it was not interested in my commentary. I smiled to myself, put the necklace in my pocket, and went inside.

Jack was in his kitchen, making coffee. He turned around as I came in and started. "What happened to you?" he asked.

I considered and discarded various explanations and finally settled on the truth. "I went to see my mom," I said.

He studied my face, saw that I was serious, and nodded slowly. "Why don't you have some coffee," he said. "You look like you could use it." I almost told him no, that I was tired of him and all his bad memories and his sorrow, that I still had not decided whether to forgive him for leaving my family—*all* my family—behind, that what I really wanted was to sleep for a thousand hours and then wake up and get on a plane and never come back here again, but then I thought, *Why not.* I sank into a chair at his kitchen table and he brought me a mug of coffee and poured one for himself and sat across from me. I took a sip. He made his coffee strong, like Henri.

"Do you want to talk about it?"

I frowned into my cup. "I don't know. I don't think so. I want to go home."

"I decided to play a show," he said unexpectedly. I looked at him with new interest.

"A big show?"

"I thought I'd start with the open mic in a couple of days and see how it goes. If you want—if you're not angry at me—I mean, even if you are angry at me, I don't blame you, but I'd like you to come." I thought of Shane, a continent away, and what he would say if I called him up and told him I was going to see Jack Blake play, for the first time in decades, in a bar at the edge of the world, with a bluegrass band and an old lady who did terrible Dylan covers, and I laughed out loud.

"You're not off the hook," I said. "But yeah, I'll go."

I was so tired that I could not get out of the chair on my own, and Jack had to help me back to my room, and take my shoes off for me over my sleepy protests, and heave my legs up onto the bed as though I were a very small child. I was asleep before he had even covered me with a blanket. I did not sleep for a thousand hours, but I slept for a long time, all through that day and most of the next night, and when I woke up Jack's house was dark and still and so I went back to sleep again. When I woke up for the second time it was morning. He wasn't home, but he'd left me a note in the kitchen.

*T: Checking the boat. Meet me down at the harbor later?
I'll take you for a farewell cruise. Bought you a ticket home
for tomorrow. —J*

The coffee in the pot was still hot and he'd left me a croissant (From where? Who knew?) on the counter.

I ate my croissant and drank my coffee and tested out my limbs. There was no part of me that did not ache, but the sleep had done me some good. My mouth still full, I called home. Raoul answered on the second ring. "Tally," he said, and the relief in his voice nearly undid me.

"I'm okay," I said. "I'm fine. I'm coming home. For real this time."

He sighed. "Good," he said. "We miss you."

I heard something behind him, and then Henri's voice: "Is that her? Is that her?" I felt terrible.

"I'm so sorry," I said. "I should have—I didn't think—"

"You're okay," Raoul said, "and that's what matters, but if you ever do anything like this to us again at least one of us will skin you alive."

"I won't," Henri said indistinctly from behind him.

"Is Aunt Beast home?"

"She's at the studio. She's worried sick about you, too— but I'll tell her—god, it's been more than a *month,* Tally, you're *unforgivable*—when are you coming home?"

"Tomorrow."

"*Tomorrow*? Are you sure?" Henri behind him: "Tomorrow? She's coming home tomorrow?"

"Jack bought the ticket."

"Did you find . . ." Raoul paused. "Is he?"

"No," I said.

"Ah," he said. "Well."

There wasn't much to say, after that. They made more disapproving noises, and I made apologetic ones, and I told them about Shane's show and how we were all going to go to it, and if they were surprised to hear that I'd talked to him they didn't say so. When I hung up I was so homesick I could feel it inside me, heavy as a pulsar. *Tomorrow,* I thought happily, *tomorrow tomorrow tomorrow tomorrow.* But I still had today to get through.

I went into my room and packed my things, which did not take long, and then sat on my bed and watched the light move across the wall of Jack's room, the way the shadows almost looked like black wings. *Maybe I can be just a bit monster,* I thought. *Just enough.* I went out and got Jack's bicycle and rode down to the harbor.

He was on his boat, sitting on the deck in the sun with his eyes closed like a cat. I studied him again, seeing what I'd chosen all summer not to see: There was no mark of his face in mine, nothing about him that suggested we were blood. Was I mad at him? Happy we'd come to some kind of peace? Had we, even? And then I decided I wasn't sure, and it was fine not to be sure, and maybe I would see him again after today and maybe I wouldn't, but I had come here for something other than what he had to give me, and anything after this was up to him. "Hey," I said, and he opened his eyes and stood up and reached out to me, helping me onto the boat. I thought, belatedly, that I ought to have made him give me sailing lessons, while I was out here. But I'd been distracted. I did not want to think about Maddy, and so instead I thought about whether there would be otters again.

Jack did not talk about anything like family, or history,

or what had happened to me in hell. Instead he pointed out the mountains on the horizon. "That's Baker, those are the Sisters—that range is the Cascades. The Olympics are the ones behind us." He paused. "If you come back next summer, I can take you hiking, if you like," he said without looking at me; offhand, trying not to make the words matter too much.

"That sounds nice," I said, and he relaxed.

The hippie girls were at Kate's again, giggling softly together at a table in the corner. Jack—who'd dug his guitar out of his truck, wedged carelessly in its case behind his seat—did not acknowledge them, but they looked up when he came in, and then at each other. The Bob Dylan lady, dressed in an eye-searing purple full-length skirt, a blouse spackled with tiny mirrors, bells, and an enormous appliquéd daisy, and a floppy velvet hat, gazed eagerly at the makeshift stage. I had tried, without success, not to hope that Maddy would be there. She wasn't.

The Bob Dylan lady went first—Neil Young covers this time, and rather more of them than I would have preferred—and then some more teenagers, and then the bluegrass band again, who were giving Jack unmistakably nervous glances, and did not do well with any of their songs, although it was hard to tell, with bluegrass, whether or not they were supposed to sound like geese. And then it was the hippie girls' turn again; they rose from their table as one, and looked at Jack, and to my surprise he took his guitar out of its case and joined them onstage, pulling up a barstool and settling his guitar in his lap. You would not guess, to look at him, that he'd spent the last twenty years or so refusing to play music, that tonight was anything other than one more ordinary night in a series. I heard a dog bark outside, and my traitor heart seized in my chest; there she was, in the doorway, backlit by a streetlamp, her black hair a halo, and I didn't know what to do with myself. I kicked my chair and thought about going over to her and sat on my hands and didn't.

Jack played a single chord, as if he were thinking about something, and then another, and the notes settled softly around us, and the hum of conversation in the bar died until we were sitting in total silence. I recognized the song immediately; I'd been carrying it around in my head all summer, thinking it was for someone else—*You were ever the only one,* he sang, and if his voice was older and even more weary and soaked in sorrow than the voice on the record Mr. M had played for me what felt like a lifetime ago, it was no less beautiful. He played with the same surety and careless grace with which he sailed, each movement economical and precise, and the rich timbre of his voice filled the little bar like a golden cloud until every corner glowed with the light of it. I thought of Aunt Beast, solid and practical and entirely devoid of the quirks and eccentricities said to be endemic to artists (save, of course, for her tofu scrambles and sage smudges), her unremarkable countenance and workmanlike body, and I thought of the man in front of me so wrecked by the loss of her that he made music this heartrending, and I thought, not for the first time that summer, that there was very little I understood about love. It was strange to think of one's parents as they might once have been, foolhardy young people very much like oneself; stranger still to imagine Aunt Beast such a creature—but this song was about a woman who'd stitched her way into the fabric of Jack's heart, and that woman had been Aunt Beast, and the way he played it now left little doubt in my mind how he still felt about her. When the song was over I was far from the only person in the bar furtively wiping my eyes. He looked over at the hippie girls and nodded, and they began to sing.

I had never in my life heard anything like that music and I knew, even as I listened to it, that I would never hear anything like it again. In their singing, in his playing, was all the longing in the world: decades of wandering, of unfulfilled searches and lost and broken hearts, a yearning so immense it swallowed whole the night, the hushed bar patrons weeping into their beers—and I saw them as they once were, on the broad-planked deck of a boat at sea, under a hot yellow sun—saw the halcyon circling, the white sails full of wind, Maddy with a girl's gentle face, her yellow eyes full of hope and Jack playing ballads for the open sky, all around them the open horizon, the whole world new and possible, before everything she had once loved was gone and drowned in blood. He played for her, for me, for all of us, for every regret that hung behind us in a shimmering curtain of loss, and the Sirens' voices spiraled and dove and soared again through the aching chords, and I thought I could not bear it if they played for another second, any more than I could bear it if they stopped. I had no idea how long they played; it could have been a moment or a year, so enraptured was I by the spell they wove, and I would have done anything that song asked of me—flung myself off a cliff, taught myself to fly, gone running out toward the wide horizon where the blue bowl of the sky met the grey-blue plane of the sea. I was half out of my chair, ready to give myself up if they asked it, the flawless bell jar of their music dropped over me and sealing me in; instead of oxygen, I was breathing sound, my blood turned to song, my heart beating one note after another, and still they played.

When Jack's final chord dropped into the still air at last, I opened my eyes and looked around me. The bar was full of crows and coyotes; I blinked, thinking I was seeing things, but they were still there. I turned to look back at Maddy; her cheeks were streaked with tears, gleaming in the low light of the bar, and the naked anguish on her face was enough to break my heart all over again, but she wasn't looking at me. She was looking at Jack, and he was looking at her. "I remember," he said to her from the stage, his voice rough and low in the quiet of the bar, and she raised one hand to him—a farewell or a benediction—and then she was gone. I got up to go after her, but beside me one crow stretched its wings, and then another, and then all around me they rose, turning the still-silent air into a blur of black, and moved out the door in a whirl of feathers, and the coyotes went after them, slinking out one by one, and I sat back down and wiped my eyes and let her go.

The next morning Jack drove me to the airport and I went home. I thought the journey should be more momentous: mythical creatures to slay, deserts to cross, a quest to fulfill. But that's not how airplanes work. We said little during the long drive to the ferry. I asked him if he was going to play real shows again, and he said he would think about it. "I have this friend," I said, "who would be excited if you did." He only smiled.

When he pulled up under the DEPARTURES sign and got out to hand me my bag, we stood looking at each other awkwardly, and then we both lurched forward at the same time, and instead of hugging him I hit him in the chest with my bag, and he laughed and so did I, and we tried again with more success. He held me tightly, and I felt tears well up as I seized him in return with a force that surprised me. When he let me go I had to pretend I had something in my eye, and he pretended not to notice. "Thank you," I said. "For everything."

"Thank you," he said. "For coming all this way. For reminding me—" He stopped and cleared his throat, and I realized his eyes were not any drier than mine.

"It's okay," I said. "I think I know what you mean." We regarded each other, and then he swept me up in another hug.

"Come back," he said. "Anytime you like. I mean it."

"I think I will," I said, and then he let me go, and we smiled at each other, and he gave me a little push.

"Go back to your bright future, young lady," he said. "Tell your aunt I said hello."

"Tell her yourself," I said, and went into the airport.

I had meant to stay awake on the plane, to think about what I had learned, maybe write myself an essay about it in my journal, "What I Did on My Summer Vacation," with lessons bullet pointed or flowcharted in a scientific manner, but I fell asleep instead. I did not dream about my mother; I did not dream at all.

Raoul and Henri and Aunt Beast were all waiting for me at the gate. I was surprised how glad I was of it. They hugged me all at once, and I hugged them back, and we were stiff with each other and did not know what to say. Walking out of the airport was like walking into an open mouth full of unbrushed teeth, and I winced; I'd forgotten what real heat was like, and the stink of the city. Back at the apartment we milled around in uncomfortable silence until I took my bag into my room and shut the door. I could imagine them, sitting on the couch, hands folded on their laps, waiting for me to emerge again.

At dinner that night we were mostly quiet. Raoul had made enchiladas, with the mole sauce his mom sent him sometimes from the desert. Even Dorian Gray was uncharacteristically subdued; he'd been aloof and disdainful since I came home, largely ignoring me until I gave up making overtures. "He thinks you should have called more, too," Raoul said. After dinner we sat without speaking for a moment. Henri got up to clear the table.

"I don't understand why you didn't just *tell* me," I blurted. Aunt Beast and Raoul looked at me, and Henri looked at the three of us.

"I think I'll leave you to this," he said, and took a load of dishes into the kitchen, and then he went into his and Raoul's room and shut the door gently.

Aunt Beast got up and poured herself a glass of whisky. "Come into the other room," she said.

They sat on the couch, and I sat in the shabby old armchair—after Jack's house, our furniture looked particularly dilapidated—and pulled my knees up to my chin and glared at them.

"You're angry at me," Aunt Beast said, "and I understand why. You think I lied to you."

"You *did* lie to me."

"I didn't tell you the whole truth. But you have to understand—Tally, some of the things that happened then, to me and Aurora, they're not the kinds of things most people believe in. I told you what I knew was true, which was that we had lost touch." She paused, and I saw the tears welling up in her eyes, and it was hard to stay angry at her. *They're not the kinds of things most people believe in.* I knew about that. It was too much to tell them, too much to say out loud; I didn't know how much of what had happened to me out there I believed in myself, from the safety of my homely apartment, surrounded by my family's love. I had never kept secrets from them before, but this did not seem so much like keeping a secret as telling the story a different way.

"I dreamed about her," I said, "when I was out there. In this apartment by the ocean, with this man. She was so alone, and sad. But it was like—it was like I could finally let her go. Like I knew what she was, finally, like what all of you kept telling me about her—that she just couldn't make it work, as a person. It hurt her too much to live in the world the way she was, and so she went somewhere else." Aunt Beast wiped her eyes—I couldn't remember the last time I'd seen her cry, Aunt Beast hated crying even more than I did—and I went over to the couch and curled up between them the way I'd done when I was little, although I was so tall now that I had to push them to both ends of the couch to fit, and even then I was half in Aunt Beast's lap. She stroked my hair out of my eyes and sighed.

"That sounds like her," she said.

"He told me he'd never loved her," I said. "Jack. Not like that. Not like he loved you."

She didn't say anything for a moment, and I wondered if I'd said the wrong thing, and then she smiled down at me.

"I know," she said. "I doubted it, back then. But I always knew, somewhere."

"No more secrets," I said, and she nodded. But I was lying, too: I had secrets from them already, and I knew, whatever she was telling me now, that there were a thousand pages of her own story I would never be able to read. Before, that knowledge would have eaten at me, but now I understood the thing I'd never been able to see before: that our stories are our own, even when they overlap with other people's, and that sometimes keeping them safe is a part of keeping ourselves whole. Maybe someday I'd tell them about Maddy, tell them about what I'd done out there, tell them about falling in love with a tidal wave, a monster, a monster who was also a girl. Tell them about what it had felt like to be with her, the whole world blown wide open, the smell of her skin. But probably I wouldn't. I caught Raoul looking at me thoughtfully, and I smiled at him, and he smiled back.

"Sweet dreams," he said.

"You, too."

That night I dreamed about her. The two of us in her house, in her bed. Coyotes singing in the ravine beyond, her yard ringed with a circle of crows. She was not bloody, not monster, only girl, in her black shirt and black jeans, looking at me the way she used to: not with love, or hunger, but something older and larger than both alone. *I love you,* I said to her, *I love you,* but she only shook her head and said, *There is more to this story, lovely, there is more for you to find.* I woke up with the dawn. *Once he got hold of her, she never had a chance,* Jack had said. And Maddy: *Even for those of us who are not wholly human, the way out of that place is hard.* Those of us. All the pieces of the story, coming together at last.

I slipped out of the house before anyone else was awake, walked down the street to his apartment; though the sun was barely up he was, as ever, unsurprised to find me at his door. I followed him into his living room and looked around at his shelves for the last time before I sat down across from him. He looked at me, and I knew he knew.

"I see," he said.

"Why did you send me all that way?"

He raised one shoulder, dropped it again. "We do not know how to do things straightforwardly," he said.

Pale as bone and thin as wire knotted together, in his red chair, in his black clothes, his dead eyes; I did not know, now, how I could have ever mistaken him for human. But the answer came to me as quickly as the question: I had loved him, and love makes us more than willing to see the best self the beloved has to offer. He had left the place he was from to come here, to wait quietly down the street for me to find him; he had kept all the secrets of my history from me, unraveled my family and destroyed my mother, and then he had come here, hoping for what I'd given him without question. Hoping to be seen as something other than what he was. And then he'd sent me away instead, knowing that I would not find what I thought I was looking for, because all along it had been here with him. I wanted to hate him, but I found, to my dismay, that I could not. *There's always a mystery that other people don't have to reckon with. Was he a good man? An awful one? Would we have loved each other? What did he have to pass down to me, that I had lost?*

"Tell me a story," I said, and he flinched, but he did not look away.

"A long time ago," he said, "a king called Minos ruled a

dead country without stars. He had a daughter . . ." He paused and licked his thin lips. "He had a daughter," he continued, in a stronger voice, "called Ariadne—as sweet a child as any father could wish for, though he did not see it until it was far too late—and a wife, and they were both lovely and clever, gracious and kind, but he did not see the gifts in the world around him; he saw only what he lacked. He had a lover, too, who betrayed her father for him in the midst of a war, and so when he had defeated her father and watered the earth with the blood of her family he killed her for her treachery, because any woman who would betray her father was no kind of woman at all in his eyes. The certainty that his own life was one of emptiness made him leave emptiness everywhere he went. His wife bore him a son, and he saw instead a monster, and he imprisoned the child under the earth, where he grew into the shape his father believed him to be, and the king fed his son on blood and sorrow until there was nothing left in him that was human.

"And then one day a hero"—he said *hero* in a voice of such contempt that I breathed in deep—"landed on that distant shore, and spun a web of lies for the king's daughter, and went under the earth and killed the king's son, the monster, with his daughter's help; because she was so starved for kindness, for love, for attention, that she did not see the hero for what he was—a man whose every word was a lie dipped in honey. When the king's son was dead, the hero raped the king's daughter and put her on a ship and sailed away to a lonely island in the middle of the wide dark sea, and there he left her, laughing as she wept. The god Bacchus found her and sent her to live among the stars. The hero went on to do more great deeds, and his name numbers now among the great heroes of old. Hers is nearly forgotten, except to astronomers." He stopped and closed his eyes.

"What happened to the king?" I said.

"He died," he said, and his voice sucked all the air out of the room, slowed the beating of my own heart; I saw myself again in the cold apartment where Maddy had sent me, the dead starless sky, the black sea. "He died badly, as he deserved, and he went before the god of the dead, and the god of the dead made him into a judge and a collector, a harvester of souls, and that was what he became."

"And then you found my mother," I said, and he opened his eyes.

"Do you think your mother was anything to me?" he said. "Do you know what I have done, child? Do you know how old I am, and how many treasures like your mother, like your grandmother—do you know what I have gathered, what I have taken, on my long road? I knew once, a long time ago, what it was to love, and I threw it away, and since then my wake has been one of pain and sorrow. But your mother had a child, Atalanta, your mother had you—and I knew I could not begin to undo what I had done, but there you were, like a gift nonetheless. I had destroyed any love that had ever come to me, through all those long dark centuries, but you knew nothing of what I was—you believed in nothing but the order of the universe, the music of the heavens. You were blind to the possibility of real darkness, of the world I lived in and the world I had made. In your company I could mistake myself for a man again; I could give you books and teach you how the stars moved and watch you grow into something even I could not ruin."

"Did you think I would never find out?"

"I knew that you did not believe in what I was," he said. "And that as long as you did not believe, I would be only what you saw. But when you came to me, with that music, I knew I could not keep you any longer, and so I sent you to him, and I see that you found there more than what you bargained for. I did not mean to cause you pain."

"How can you—you're the one who taught me first about physics," I said. "About astronomy. If you're—if you're—" I could not quite bring myself to say it. "Why do you bother with science? If it's not even real where you're—from?"

"You know Georges Lemaître," he said, "the cosmologist—"

"Of course," I said, with a spark of my old irritation. "He was the first person to theorize the Big Bang model. Everyone knows that."

A ghost of a smile flickered across his face. "Indeed. I am sorry; I did not mean to insult you. But as you know, he was also a priest—he took great care to ensure that his careers as cosmologist and cleric never intertwined, but he was as much a man of faith as he was of science. Do you know what he said about living in both worlds all his life? 'There were two ways of arriving at the truth. I decided to follow them both.'"

"I saw her," I said. "My mother. I went to—that place."

"I would have spared you that," he said. "If I could."

"How else could I have seen her? *You* left her there," I said. "You brought her there, and then you left her, too."

To his credit, he did not look away. "Yes," he said. "I did. I hope you can forgive me."

I felt old and tired, and I did not want, anymore, to be strong; I wanted to be a kid again, the kid I'd been before he sent me away, the kid who knew everything about the world because she'd never before seen how big the world truly was. I thought I understood at last what Maddy had meant, about choosing to be a monster, because being anything else at all had to be easier than being human. There was no part of my life that had not been colored by her absence, no corner of my heart that was unmarked by the missing of her—my mother, Aurora, the girl he had ensured would never become a woman, the girl he had sent under the earth and away from me, the girl who would never have a chance to let me tell her about quasars, or make me clean my room, or give me advice about Shane, or sit with me and listen to my grandfather's music, or grow up into a person of her own. My mother. I had a family, and I loved them and was lucky in them; but because of him, I would never have her.

"I don't," I said, my voice clear in the still air. "I forgive everyone *but* you—I forgive my mother, and Jack, and Aunt Beast, and Raoul—they were all doing the best they could with what they had been given. Even my grandparents—but *you*—you knew what you were and what you were doing. They were only human. But you have no excuse." There was more I wanted to say, but I did not know how to say it, and trembled with the rage that had taken hold of me. *What would Maddy do,* I thought, and the answer was probably cut his throat, but I wasn't Maddy, and anyway I didn't have a knife. The tattoo she'd given me burned as hot as the night I had gone to hell and she had saved me. *You don't have to be a monster,* something said inside me, in her voice—slow blink of yellow eyes—*you, lovely, you alone among us are brave enough to be a girl.*

"That is true," he said, and I did not know if he was answering me, or if he had heard her, too, and I thought he would say something else, but he did not.

"What does it mean, for me?" I asked. "That I am—that I am not entirely—" I could not bring myself to say it; of all the impossible things I had come to believe in that summer, that thought was the most impossible yet.

He laughed, a dry rustling sound without a hint of happiness in it. "In a different time, child, it meant something, but now . . ." He tilted his head at the bookshelves behind him. "*Eritis sicut deus, scientes bonum et malum*," he said softly. "In the words of Doctor Faustus: 'You will be like God, knowing good and evil.' There are no secrets that can be kept from you."

"I thought Dr. Faustus was the devil," I said.

"There is always a catch," he said. "Atalanta, you do not need the magic of the old gods any longer. We do not make things; we can only transform what is already made into a shape that we like better, and orchestrate the lives of your kind to suit us, and collect those among you who bring us pleasure. But the race of men—"

"And women," I said sharply, and he smiled.

"Yes," he said. "And women. You grubby little animals with your tiny brains find questions in the heavens larger than those we have ever thought to ask. You have discovered the language of the universe and written out its laws. You built a machine under the earth seventeen miles in circumference and used it to shatter light into the smallest particles that exist. And even still you write symphonies, and paint pictures, and till the ground and make it fertile. It is not enough for you to have a single flower; you must breed a thousand kinds of rose. From our mountains, from under the earth, we can only covet what you have done with the short lives you have been given."

"We didn't discover the language of the universe," I said. "It was already there."

"But you have named it," he said. "You have used it to write a story that can be told and told again. Newton's equations hold true, at the greatest of distances and at the smallest scales, across the breadth of the universe; do you not think it is remarkable that your people are capable of such a marvel, Atalanta? All this rot and death surrounds you, and still you tilt your heads back to look at the stars, and say *how beautiful,* and teach yourselves to sail by their light, and even that is not enough; you must know what it is that makes them burn. Why do you ask these questions? Why do you make art? These labors have no bearing on your survival." He tilted his head at me quizzically and I saw that the question was not rhetorical; he meant for me to answer, to explain to him what it meant to live for joy.

"Because that's what makes us human," I said. I was suddenly very sick of him, sick unto death. I stood up. "Goodbye," I said; somewhere, some part of me waited for him to stop me, but he did not.

"Goodbye, Tally," he said. I took a page from Maddy's book, and I did not look back at him when I left.

My family and I took the train to Shane's show, all four of us. It was too hot to worry much about what I was going to wear, and so I didn't worry about it and wore the same clothes as always. Raoul had gone down and gotten the mail, earlier; there was a thick envelope covered in Jack's familiar, spiky hand, and I thought it must be for me, but when I picked it up I saw with surprise that it was addressed to Aunt Beast.

"Well," I said aloud. "Well, well, well." I put the letter back on the hall table with a smirk, and then the three of them came into the hallway and Aunt Beast gave me a dirty look.

"Aren't you going to open it?" I asked.

"Not around you."

"Don't you want to know what he *says*?"

"I've waited twenty years," she said. "I can wait another night. Come on." And with that she swept past me and I followed her out into the balmy night. We were quiet again on the train, but it was an easier quiet than the quiet home from the airport; something had lifted from us, the air around us easing. They were getting used to the person I was becoming and, I guess, so was I.

Brownies was on Avenue A, between 10th and 11th; I'd only been there once, years ago, when Shane had cajoled me into taking the train to Manhattan and sneaking in with him to see Peter Murphy play a show. Hearts pounding, we'd circled the block a few times; Shane was trying to play it cool, but I could tell he was as scared as I was, unused as we were to grift and intrigue. The guy working the door was a bored-looking metalhead in black and spikes who seemed like the sort of entity who would not think twice about thrashing the living shit out of two temerarious adolescents seeking ingress. We lurked down the street until the bouncer stepped away from the door, his back turned, to smoke a cigarette—"Come *on*," Shane hissed, dragging me by the hand, and we made a run for it, imagining ourselves fleet-footed hares outstripping a hungry wolf, and ducked inside the door just as the bouncer ground out his butt and resettled on his stool with a heavy sigh. I barely even remembered the show, though Shane had been ecstatic; all that came to mind now, as I told the surly black-clad entity guarding the door my name ("I'm in the band," I said breezily, hoping that Shane had remembered, that aping Maddy's cool arrogant confidence would suffice if he hadn't) and waited for him—The same bouncer? But smaller seeming now, less threatening; what had we been scared of?—to run his finger down a list of names and grunt assent. He made Henri and Aunt Beast and Raoul pay.

Inside was filthy—now that I thought about it, I remembered that much—and sweltering and dim, Christmas lights wound around up near the low ceiling lending a moderately flattering glow to what would otherwise have been a distinctly sordid scene. We were early, and the club was nearly empty; I spotted Shane immediately, standing on the low stage talking to a tall, beautiful girl with shaggy black hair and heavy eyeliner and the cool, radiant air of someone who was unmistakably on her way to being famous. And he looked different, too; calm, self-assured, unconcerned that the club was empty. They conveyed the impression of two people who knew exactly what they were doing and what they wanted. I called his name, and he turned and saw me and, to my great satisfaction, his entire face lit up with delight, and he leapt off the stage and ran headlong at me, sweeping me off my feet in an enormous hug and spinning me around as though we were in an old movie. "Jesus fucking Christ, don't ever leave me like that again," he said into my ear, and I nearly swooned.

"I'm going to college," I said idiotically, and he said, "You know what I mean," and I thought I did.

"I missed you," I said.

"I missed you, too." He held me at arm's length and examined me. "You look different," he said.

"I do?" My newfound maturity had lent me an air of grandeur, I thought, or all the sex I'd had over the summer had given me a ravishing and irresistible glow.

"Tan," he said. "You look tan. You got a tattoo."

"Oh," I said.

"Did you find out—I mean, is he?"

"No," I said. "It's complicated. I have a lot to tell you. I saw him play, though."

"Shut *up*."

I could not help feeling smug. "It was pretty incredible. The thing about the wolves, in California? I think that might have been true."

"You can tell me about it—god, I can't believe you saw him *play*, that's *unreal*. This is Karen," he added, indicating the singer, who'd gracefully hopped off the stage and come over to join us. I took her measure; up close, she was even more arresting, possessed of the near-alien beauty of the bevy of colt-limbed models who flooded the subways every year during Fashion Week. I considered whether they were sleeping together, and whether I cared if they were, and found, to my dismay, that I did. Apparently I had not learned quite so many life lessons as I thought.

"Hi," I said.

"Hi," she said. "I've heard so much about you, Shane hasn't stopped talking about you all summer."

"Oh," I said again, uncomfortably. *But what did he* say, *exactly,* I thought, and kept my mouth shut. And then Raoul and Aunt Beast and Henri, who'd respectfully let us greet each other in peace, had to come over and congratulate Shane, and I watched him preen under their attentions as though I were seeing him for the first time. We'd grown up together so closely that it seemed as though in recent years we'd forgotten to look at each other, how to see the people we were becoming instead of the children we had been, and whatever I'd felt for him before I left was something larger and more complicated now than I knew what to do with. But I didn't have to figure it all out, not now, because love wasn't quantifiable; it was as vast and full of mystery and beauty and math and particles as the whole universe, and all the science in the world hadn't taken the wonder out of that, either. I watched Shane hug Raoul with a big dopey grin on my face, and then caught Karen giving me a complicated, unreadable look of her own—*Oh well,* I thought, *we'll all figure it out, sooner or later*—and then they had to go backstage because more and more people were coming into the club and it was almost time to start.

They were good, of course. They were better than good. They were great. They had a drummer, too, a serious-faced black girl with her hair done up in dreadlocks, in a white undershirt that showed off her skin and her arms, solid with muscle—where had Shane *found* these girls?—who played intricate, complicated beats so fast and so hard that you didn't even notice there wasn't a bass player, just Shane whipping out sledghammery, looping licks and the singer's throaty banshee howl over all of it. The crowd was ecstatic, surging up against the stage with a giant roar by the middle of their second song, moving as one sweaty frenzy of bodies that turned the already-hot air almost unbearable. I shrank back against the wall with Raoul and Henri, shooting them worried looks, but they seemed perfectly happy, and Aunt Beast, to my total astonishment, gave a whoop of glee and threw herself headlong into the surging crowd, disappearing immediately in a melee of flailing limbs and hair.

And Shane, my Shane, beloved and best known, dark hair falling in his face—he played with that slouch-shouldered carelessness that belied how unbelievably good he was, a solid counterpoint to Karen, who spun across the stage like a dervish, whipping the crowd up into mania; he played like I had never heard him play before, polished and sure and brilliant. He looked so cool I could hardly stand it. *That's my best fucking friend,* I thought, with such pride I thought my adoration must be visible, leaking out of my pores like light. Here we were again, the both of us, our lives in front of us: the rest of the summer to figure out what we were, or weren't, and to get my job at the bookstore back, and finish the *Principia,* and think about whether or not I wanted to go see Jack again and make him teach me to sail by the light of the constellations we both knew, and whether Maddy would still be there if I went back—it didn't seem likely, but you never knew, with monsters, where they might turn out to live.

It was William Herschel—with the tireless assistance of his sister, Caroline, who was as fine an astronomer as he was, though her own horizons were curtailed by the time in which she had the misfortune to be born, and her name is always footnoted to his—who, in the eighteenth century, first realized that looking at starlight was the same thing as looking backward in time. While his contemporaries focused obsessively on establishing the distances between planets and fussing over orbital calculations, Herschel taught himself to build the finest telescopes of his era (Caroline, tirelessly heating pitch with which to polish telescope mirrors, feeding him sandwiches as he worked, assisting him during long, frigid nights of observations, and going on to discover eight comets on her own in her off time) and used them to look farther than anyone had before him at the edges of the known. When his early theory that all nebulae were clusters of stars was proven wrong by his own observations, he responded not with vexation, but with glee. "But what a field of novelty is here opened to our conceptions!" he wrote, overjoyed that the cosmos was even more marvelous than he had dared to first imagine: He could spend his whole life devoted to what he called "this magnificent collection of stars," and barely begin to understand even the right questions to ask. I had begun my summer certain I knew everything, and wound up in the same place I'd started, undone and remade and stitched together again with all the threads that made up the great stories: suffering, and love, and loss, and still—always—hope. I had found my mother and lost her again; discovered my father and given him up, too; I had traveled even further than Herschel into those great shoals of light, and somehow I was still the same girl in the same body, sweaty and confused, and loved, and brilliant, and here in the world with all the possible in front of me. And all around me the hot night waiting, spattered with bright stars and darkness, waiting for me to choose what happened next, now that I'd come home.

ACKNOWLEDGMENTS

I am hugely indebted to Mike Brotherton, Christian Ready, Andria Schwortz, and the Launchpad Astronomy Workshop; to the Amateur Astronomers Association of New York; and to the work of a number of writers, particularly Timothy Ferris, Dennis Overbye, Amanda Gefter, and Richard Panek. Any errors in *About a Girl* are most emphatically my own.

Thank you: Everyone at St. Martin's Press who's worked on *About a Girl*: Alicia Adkins, Marie

Estrada, Stephanie Davis, Jeanne-Marie Hudson, Bridget Hartzler, Elsie Lyons, Anna Gorovoy, and Lauren Hougen; my peerless editor, Sara Goodman, for trusting me with this story—and believing in it when I did not; my fantastic agent, Brianne Johnson; Sara Sams, for letting me steal the aunts; Hal Sedgwick, for the *Argonautika*; WORD Bookstore, Jenn Northington, and Molly Templeton; my dear friends and tireless support system—Melanie Sanders, Nathan Bransford, Mikki Halpin, Meg Clark, Kat Howard, Kat Broadway, Tahereh Mafi, Neesha Meminger, Meg Howrey, Bryan Reedy, Emily Barrows, Bojan Louis, Cynthia Barton, Clyde and Gigi and Carol, and Sarah Jaffe; my parents—I told you I knew what I was doing. Cristina, you already know, but I'll tell you again over whisky. Justin, you treasure; I love you more than language.

And for all the girls who are part monster: This book is yours.